ALSO BY LINDA GRANT

Fiction

The Cast Iron Shore

When I Lived in Modern Times

Still Here

The Clothes on Their Backs

We Had It So Good

Upstairs at the Party

The Dark Circle

A Stranger City

Non-fiction

Sexing the Millennium:
A Political History of the Sexual Revolution

Remind Me Who I Am, Again

The People on the Street: A Writer's View of Israel

The Thoughtful Dresser

The Story of the Forest

Linda Grant

virago

VIRAGO

First published in Great Britain in 2023 by Virago Press

1 3 5 7 9 10 8 6 4 2

A CIP catalogue record for this book
is available from the British Library.

Hardback ISBN 978-0-349-01410-4
Trade Paperback ISBN 978-0-349-01409-8

Typeset in Goudy by M Rules
Printed and bound in Great Britain by
Clays Ltd, Elcograf S.p.A.

Papers used by Virago are from well-managed forests
and other responsible sources.

Virago Press
An imprint of
Little, Brown Book Group
Carmelite House
50 Victoria Embankment
London EC4Y 0DZ

An Hachette UK Company
www.hachette.co.uk

www.virago.co.uk

To Talah Rose Ari,
whose history this is

'Don't worry about me. Write next about the stubborn beauty of life throughout all human idiocies.'

DEBORAH ORR 1962–2019

PART ONE

1

In the olden times, in the old country of Latvia, a girl walks out of the city into the forest to gather mushrooms in a basket, like a child in a fairy tale.

Her name is Mina Mendel, just turned fourteen years old.

She's on the brink of something but doesn't know it. Folk tales begin when a person sets out on a journey; *then* a story is in the making, with a beginning, a middle and a satisfactory conclusion ending in a marriage and the defeat of all your enemies. Peace reigns, fortunes are restored, wrongs are righted. Granted, these tales of myth and legend generally concern young men embarking on heroic deeds and quests, but on this occasion it's a curly-haired Jewish girl who picks up her basket, steps from the house and walks with purpose along the streets until the city runs out.

The rules of the forest are not those of the town. Primal creatures of pre-civilisation are supposed to live there – spirit animals, ancient beasts existing now only in folk-memory. At the very least, there are wolves. Weaving through the trees, spotting likely fungi, plucking the thick-capped stems from the damp earth shaded by the canopy of trees through which sunshine weakly glimmers, she hears in the distance the sound of voices singing. There is nothing eerie or other-worldly about the music, it is a harsh utterance from the human throat. It sounds to her like drinking songs, and the singers sound drunk.

Young girls are right to fear drunks, it can't end well. Young Mina is not so innocent as to be ignorant of this basic truth. It is the responsibility of her father to protect his family from the evil eye which lies not only in supernatural forms but also in rowdy taverns and on the streets and in the form of anti-Semites riding on tooled-leather saddles borne forwards on a quartet of clanging metal hooves. She has heard of inebriation which turns men into animals, addles reason and causes them to lunge, fall, vomit. Drunks are ridiculous and contemptible, low, unclean. You can detect the stench of liquor coming off their faces, their clothes. What a drunkard could do has no limits, it is where the moral centre gives out, collapses into bestiality. Drunks wearing crucifixes are the very worst. Worse than actual wolves, they are never sated in their hunger for blood. And Christians are the natural predators of the Jews with no known predators themselves.

Now Mina recognises the trembling sensation of danger, alone without protection, stumbling over tree roots. They could violate and kill her and her body would be eaten by wild animals, only a collar bone, a hip bone, a thigh bone scattered on the mossy earth. There is every reason to be afraid, she thinks, they'll have your guts. *Oh!* I will never see my mother and father again, and all for a basket of mushrooms. What was I even thinking? I could slap myself, I could turn my cheeks red with such a slap, and— But wait a minute, *what are they singing?*

There is a point at which you go forward or you turn back, you have to choose, you can't stay rooted to the spot. If you did, time would freeze, history would end. So Mina Mendel steps towards them. The story begins.

The singing stopped. The world stopped. She could hear the wind in the trees, the boughs bending, the branches live with birdsong now the raucous clamour of their voices had died down. She felt a great tension. The air vibrating, or her own body trembling?

Adolescent faces turned and stared at the young maiden advancing towards them with a steady uninterrupted step, they saw curves beginning in all the right places, clothed in a grey everyday woollen dress, a raspberry-coloured scarf tied around her hair. An ordinary girl of what they would call Semitic appearance – the lack of delicacy in her features, the lumpy nose, the crow-black hair and currant-coloured eyes.

The boys were all thinking different things as they watched her approaching. Some experienced a simple shaft of desire, others a more aesthetic appreciation for her healthy young features and flushed skin, the prelude to lust. For others it was simple curiosity, questions about who she was and what she was doing there and how one needed to keep up one's guard against spies and agents of the police. One was reminded of his cousin who had died of diphtheria, inducing sad memories, and he made up his mind that his rowdy friends would not lay a hand upon her.

Looking at each other for confirmation and with some whispering and finally general agreement, the boys started to stamp their boots, smiling, gesturing in a friendly way, and the one with the dead cousin came forward and gently (for him), relieved her of her mushroom basket, took her hand and brought her into the middle of the crowd, where they asked her name and introduced themselves, and some added their ages. The youngest was seventeen, the oldest was twenty-three. After these awkward formalities were complete, they asked what she was doing in the forest, where she had come from, was she alone, did her parents know she was wandering through the trees by herself, was she not frightened, did she need a chaperone home to her front door? When they had the measure of her, were reassured that she was not a spy, just a harmless young girl, then they were willing to let her in on their secret, why they met in the forest. Not, like her, to collect fungi but to take refuge in the beauty of nature from a hostile society and to avoid being seen and overheard.

'We are Bolsheviks!' they explained. 'We are agents of the coming revolution.'

What were they talking about? She hadn't a clue, had never heard of Bolsheviks. She was the daughter of a flour merchant, a middleman. She lived in a good house and her mother had maids to help her with the running of everything. Mina went to school and learned basic mathematics, history, geography, but she had never been taught about revolution. Was it to do with the rising and setting of the sun? She tried to look wise, she nodded and smiled, as though she was familiar with these matters and Bolsheviks were not something you ate fresh from the oven with butter and a smear of honey, accompanied by a glass of tea.

Her basket rested under a tree, the boys raised their voices in an unfamiliar song but with a half-remembered melody she had once heard. The notes flew about above them, it was rousing and exciting. Then once again their voices dropped and they started talking.

After a few droning minutes of lectures on political science and contemporary Latvian history, one of the boys asked her to dance. Mina thought that would be fine; she got the picture that their minds were on higher things, reminding her of her studious brother Jossel at home to whom she would return to get to the bottom of this situation, for if he didn't know from Bolsheviks, no one would. And dancing would shut them up with their labour and capital, and this and that she couldn't remember a minute later. So she accepted the extended arms of a young man who took her by the waist and started to stamp and roar and twirl her around. She began to sweat patches under her arms, and her thighs were slippery with heat. Her tongue licked the perspiration from under her nose.

The sight of the young men, their joy and humour though they were outcasts and oddballs, struck a chord – a bronze clapper beating against a dinner gong. She breathed a new kind of oxygen, the potent chemical mix of freedom. *Frei, frei!* thought the girl who was a good Jewish daughter, destined to become a good Jewish wife and a good Jewish mother. Exultant under the trees, she felt something dislodge in her, the mechanism that was winding her down like a cheap clock to early marriage and a replica of her mother's pale floury form. Because who wanted to be like her mother, that silent, sad, resentful lady who emitted no light of her own? Whatever weak radiance she had had was banked down long ago into some interiority that had no outward expression.

What animated Mina now was the sight of something so immensely different from rooms full of relatives breathing too hard, and the smell of fatty cooking, the fug of the shul – the sight of the men's heads bent, praying, seen from the separation of the ladies' gallery. Everything at home was enclosed, it was all inside. With her cloth-covered basket, her shawl, her headscarf, she might have resembled Little Red Riding Hood, and the boys wolves in sheep's clothing, but here under the trees with the handsome young men with their stamping boots and wild eyes there was nobody around to tell her what to do. Which meant anything could happen. That was really the point. All the doors of possibility were open to her at a time when there was no possibility at all but to live the way your mother lived and her mother before her and so on until back into the dawn of history. There were no female prophets in the Bible and the only women who did anything interesting were queens. Take Queen Esther, for example, who married into the Persian royal family and stopped the persecution of her people stone dead with her clever stunts. But mostly it was mother of mother of mother of mother of wife of wife of wife of . . .

She passed a couple of hours in the forest, dancing and singing and talking. Was she a bourgeois or a worker? they asked. Was she on the side of capital or labour? These questions required her to consider her father and his flour business and the extent to which he was an exploiter of others. Did her mother exploit the young maids? Should they be sent home to their villages and the children make their own beds? But then what was to become of those two meek, hardworking girls? Should they starve for want of work? These naïve questions were dealt with firmly but with good humour. The maids would be given labour more dignified than picking up the dirty linen of the bourgeoisie, they would be sent to work in factories to produce useful commodities for the benefit of all mankind. They would take part in the great electrification

of the country, no more filthy gas or tallow candles. This seemed
to Mina fair enough, the camaraderie of the factory floor, everyone
in it together, no bowing and scraping to your betters. Bread would
be made in vast industrialised plants, millions of loaves every day
feeding the people. What a nice dream, she thought. There had to
be something in it. Ideas, she would say to herself as she lay in bed
that night. I never knew.

The boys were trying as best they could to behave like young
gentlemen, to argue with reason not threats because they were
hoping she would come back a second time. Mina was not a great
beauty but at fourteen she was pleasantly attractive, with abundant
coarse black curly hair. She was sturdily built with a tight neat
waist and broad hips. She had an open, smiling, affectionate face
and even as a suckling baby her aunt had looked at her and said,
'That one is full of mischief!' Dancing under the trees, her forehead
gleaming with perspiration, a sweat moustache glowing above her
upper lip, she seemed slippery and sensual. They felt a great tug
inside their trousers. Their underwear, worn by those who could
afford such luxurious garments, was getting tight.

At last Mina pulled away from the dancers and ran home,
excited and out of breath and feeling guilty about what she had
done and wondering if she had had a lucky escape not to have been
mauled by their male hands or if they were genuinely welcoming
her to their secret fraternity. What she knew was that she had
had fun. She felt drawn to these muscular figures who seemed to
have access to a code, a cryptology which unlocked the door into
another life. She didn't understand much of what they said, but oy,
how they said it!

2

When she got back from the forest, having forgotten her basket, which lay upturned and abandoned under a tree, the very idea of mushrooms having been discarded during the first dance, she waited until her brother Jossel was available. Jossel was the intellectual of the family, the oldest of the five living brothers and sisters. It was with him that one discussed affairs that were of no concern to the diurnal round of floor-mopping and baking. The house was of a good size, but crowded with people – parents, brothers and sisters, servants. Particularly the devil Itzik who was sixteen and a menace. Who liked to overhear and who lifted bags of flour with his bare hands, up and down, up and down – what for? To build up his runtish strength. A sly, cagey boy, known in the family as trouble. Who Mina and Jossel were indifferent to, as if he were not flesh of their flesh, blood of their blood. 'He is not one of ours,' Jossel said. 'The bad spirits brought him to this house.'

There was a four-year gap between Jossel and Itzik. A missing place at the table, a boy whose name was never mentioned. A sudden high fever had come in the night, a stiff neck, a headache. The next day he lay like a marble statue in the bed he shared with his older brother. Jossel always felt there was absence from his right side, a buttress between himself and the wall. But he was too young to be able to remember his brother's name. They brought him another brother, Itzik, who squirmed red and screaming in his mother's arms, angry, Jossel would think, at having to be a replacement, angry for having to be born at all. His birth had been awkward, something had gone wrong, the doctor sent for. But he was saved, he had rat's eyes in a human face. He seemed to have difficulty blinking.

Next, Mina, then Rivka. The pretty one, the dainty girl, the feminine spirit. A dark braid of shining hair standing crying at the top of the high house because her dolly had fallen and was lying wrecked and smashed on the tiles below and Jossel saying, 'I'll go and get it, don't worry, she'll be fine.' But the doll's mouth and nose were caved in and Rivka let out a wail of anguish, and tears came into her eyes, so Jossel took her to buy a new one. She chose one with yellow hair and a blue ribbon, like the sun and sky. A perfect innocence.

Jossel never told anyone he loved Rivka the most. He would have called his own daughter after her but it was bad luck to name a child after a living relative. And Rivka was still living when his daughter Bernice was born. Rivka was a darling; if she'd gone into motion pictures she would have become the world's sweetheart. When her braid was unplaited her hair hung loose in shining curls unlike Mina's coarse wiry mop. The death of her dolly was the greatest tragedy of her childish life and the purchase of a new one proved that reincarnation was possible, the spirit of the old dolly had entered into the new. She told Jossel this crossing the street. 'You have a mystical nature,' he replied.

How could she be so unlike her terrible brother? She was the shining star of the Mendel family, the bright filament lighting the way into the future.

Last, of six live births and two miscarriages coming from the womb of Dora Mendel, was Solly, the baby, the little boy aged five, sturdy, boisterous, as boys should be, confronting the world with the repeated question *why*? Why is the moon in the sky? ('Moon, go away!') Why is flour white? Why does Poppa have hairs on his face and mine is smooth like Momma? Why do horses have four legs and people have just two? Why do cats and dogs have no hands? And, unanswerable, why are there corners?

Jossel and Mina were unamused by Solly and his incessant chatter; if they had lived then in the age of volume knobs they would have mimed switching him off. He got underfoot, they tripped over him, he came careering round corners at high speed making whoops. He had learned curses overheard in the street. Jossel, remembering them all in later life, said, 'Rivka was the beauty, Itzik was the beast, Solly was a happy-go-lucky kid with all the time in the world to grow up and be a prince among men, or if not a prince, a macher, a big shot. The kind of person who makes things happen. A smart arse. I don't know why, he was just born that way. It was always in his nature to get into trouble; he couldn't keep his mouth shut but he could make people laugh. Itzik, the little shit, was the opposite. He collected other people's words and stored them for future use. He harvested opinions, thoughts carelessly expressed, bad jokes, insensitive remarks, hidden feelings that found a way out into the atmosphere. I'm not doing him down, I'm not trying to be negative about a lost soul, he couldn't help himself, he never had a choice, stuck in that squat little body. I'd have wished him every chance of happiness except for what he did to us.'

To have a private conversation one must accept interruption. Jossel and Mina sat on the stairs and Itzik hung over the banisters and tried to overhear. Rivka plonked herself down on Mina's knee and was told to go and play with her dollies. Their father was somewhere else in the house, not in earshot, their mother was lying down, feeling unwell, pregnant again probably, Mina thought, with contempt in her heart, and no awe that with her body this person was able to make another human being out of her own flesh.

On the stairs Mina laid out the events of that afternoon in a rush of words, giggles and questions. Jossel said, never mind electrification of industry, did they lay a hand on you? She said, yes, but definitely not the way he was thinking, he shouldn't worry about that, it was just an arm round her waist, all they did was dance and sing. She would swear on their father's life that this was true.

He had not expected to hear about Bolsheviks. His sister reminded him of a kitten, one that sometimes found a patch of catnip and could go a bit wild for a short time.

'What was it that attracted you to them?' he said.

'It was just the singing and the dancing. But that kind of thing happens at a wedding, not out in the open air.'

'Were they good singers?'

'Meh. They were no chazans. Not all of them could hold a tune. Strong voices though. Very loud.'

'Manly?'

'That too.'

Mina thought of the reddish hair on the arms of one boy, and the rough white skin beneath it, and his fingers pressed into the small of her back. Another had white-blond hair like . . . She tried to think of a metaphor and only came up with a field of wheat under a noonday sun. (She was no poet, she did not have that originality of mind. Her soul arched towards the light but could not describe it.)

'Did you join in?'

'With the chorus of some of them, yes. The words weren't hard to remember, very repetitive.'

'What else happened?' Jossel continued to speak, slowly and clearly, controlling himself, with no current of feeling in his voice. One sentence followed the next like candlewax dripping onto a saucer. Best not to get overexcited too soon. There would be time to fly into a rage and threaten to run out into the forest with a gun and shoot them all dead. Not that he wished this on himself, but he'd feel like he had an obligation and that would land him in a predicament. He wasn't by nature a warrior, actual guns gave him the creeps. He was by definition a man who was no use with his fists: soft, white-skinned, a dreamer, all words, plenty of words.

'Well, you know, we talked a little, as well as the dancing and singing.'

'And what did you discuss?'

'The situation.'

'What situation? What do you mean?'

'Mankind is in chains?' she said with a questioning inflection.

'Oh yes. Of course we are. Let me explain something to you, Mina, my dear little sister.'

'Okay, I'm listening.' She smiled; Jossel really did know everything. He had read books his father said he had no business reading, for everything you needed to know had been written down already in the Torah and the Talmud. It was all there, the answer to every ethical question you had. You might not like the answer, but that was what the answer was. *Take it or leave it?* Jossel had said to him, smiling. *No, you take it. Whomsoever leaves it is damned.*

Now Jossel told his sister to imagine that he was holding in his hand a glass.

'Watch my hand, see what I'm doing? The glass is full of water or something – tea, coffee, it doesn't matter. Now I am turning it upside down, now this glass is empty. What do you see? Not in the glass, but where I emptied it. Here.' He pointed to his trousers.

'A mess. You're all wet.'

They laughed.

'I know! Maybe I peed myself. Embarrassing. But listen, some people like a mess, they don't care. They enjoy blowing things up – what happens when you start again with nothing? That's what interests them, disruptive people who are attracted to chaos. Like our father, as it happens, he just doesn't go about it in the same way. You might have heard him say he'd take a gun and shoot the tsar and who wouldn't want to clap your hands, and whoosh, he's gone in a puff of smoke, like a magic trick, him and the whole parasitic family? These boys in the forest you met – of course, they're more sophisticated, they have good intentions, they believe lofty, clever, complicated things, that it is possible to expel human unhappiness for ever, everything the same, no more injustice. For them reality is something you reorganise to suit your ends but these are not *ideas*.'

'So what are ideas?'

13

Like many inquisitive, open-minded young Jewish men, Jossel had been studying the philosopher Spinoza. He wanted to discuss with Mina defective reasoning, the inadequate conception of reality and the unity of all that exists. He was trying to penetrate the deep heart of what life means. What is God? How do we prove this 'being' is not just an extension of our thoughts? Where do ideas come from? Are they innate in the human mind or implanted by a divine force? Are human rights a human creation or do they exist in nature? These were his musings when he was handling his father's paperwork, for his role in the family flour business was to be in charge of the accounts, to keep the ledgers straight and to issue and pay bills. But how do you explain any of this to a fourteen-year-old girl who doesn't read at all and who is just a mass of feelings and sensations and an affectionate, optimistic nature, who is going to be moulded into a reproduction of her mother, a machine for propagating the human race? Which he did not question as an inevitable outcome, he was not that modern.

Jossel could have inducted his sister into his world that evening. He could have inspired in her a thirst for learning, but what would have been the point? Education was not for little girls. Instead his thoughts uncharacteristically turned to practicalities: that he needed to get her away from whoever she had met in the forest. Maybe she was right, and they were nice enough boys who meant no harm, but more likely they were trouble every other way you looked at it. He could not forbid her to go, he didn't have that authority over her. He could tell their father but he knew where that would wind up. The old man would panic, he would take matters into his own hands and make a rash decision to the benefit of nobody. He would be driven by shame and family honour, he would sacrifice a lively young girl to the shadchan, and his high-jinks sister would be married off in a month to some hastily selected old widower with hairs in his nostrils who would oppress and destroy her spirit. She would wither inside and become a discontented, bitter shadow of herself. He could feel *himself* withering at the idea of it, his senses alive to all the possibilities of being permanently thwarted in your spirit. Cautiously he tried to find out the lie of the land.

'And so are you going to go back and dance another day?'

Mina had already accepted without question her brother's critique of the Bolsheviks because it was the kind of thing he knew about and understood, these clouds of reason and unreason which were the preserve and privilege of men. The forest boys hated the tsar – a familiar impulse, everyone did – so what could be the harm in them? She had listened as they talked about the injustice of the exploitation of the industrial proletariat and peasantry. She had nodded. The words floated past her like smoke. If she returned to the forest she would not be drawn by the magnet of Leninist ideology but that didn't mean she wouldn't go. Because what was attractive to her about the boys was the simple impulse of excitement, of, as she thought of it, 'something different from flour'.

'I wouldn't tell anyone if I was,' she replied. He looked at her. So she was going to go back, he could see it in her face, that pert smile. She winked.

Before she went to sleep, she relived the afternoon in the forest, the light coming at angles through the branches of the trees, some of the young men handsome, others with faces like the pendular udders of cows, but all of them benign, more or less, some coarse jokes but nothing else. She felt that no harm would come to her if she returned: if she wanted to; if she had the opportunity; if it was not raining; if the trees would give shelter if it was; if there were still mushrooms to be picked; if she could get away without anyone noticing her, particularly Itzik, who would spill the beans if it was to his advantage; if her second-best dress was clean, not the old grey gown she had had on today.

In his own bed, Jossel was applying logic to the story his sister had told him. The girl was an adorable dope and there was no way this situation wouldn't end badly for any number of reasons. There was an outside chance that something would click inside her, she'd start to take an *interest*, they would win her over to their cause and she would be swept up in the revolutionary times, get arrested sooner or later, rot in gaol for the infantile notion that the world could be improved upon, that man's nature could be remoulded. At some point, dying on a filthy rat-infested straw pallet somewhere, she would realise she had been duped, that nothing was going to come of this nothing. Waste, all waste, and for what? But before it even got to that would be their betrayal of her. Having lured her into their company with politics they would take advantage of her, rape her, and not just one of them, but a pack of filthy beasts baying for her hymen's blood, each taking their turn on her still childish body. Corruption on corruption. The worst could happen, she would be pregnant, cast out into the world alone. The least bad scenario was the most likely, that sooner or later the little blabber-mouth would tell someone, and when she did, their father would hear of it and before any more harm could be done, her honour still un-besmirched, she would be married off. There was no shortage of nostril-hair widowers who would take on a nubile young girl from a good family.

Their mother had once let slip a thought. Her, a woman he believed had no thoughts.

'Men are the cause of all misery, Jossel. Men boast they love their mothers, a mother indulges her children, she gives them everything, she gives them life itself, no wonder they love her – but not so much boasting about how much they love their wives.'

He had been startled by this admission, made while she was supervising the pegging out of the washing on a windy day, as if she thought her words would be blown away into the harbour and borne out to sea. He had not forgotten them.

He recognised with a thump of disappointment that there was nothing in Spinoza that would help him here. It seemed to him that Mina was hemmed in by this single chance meeting in the forest, all routes out of there took her to a different undesirable fate.

He didn't even like mushrooms and she wasn't so keen on them either, she just enjoyed the act of foraging; she liked the mossy paths, the rustle of leaves, the birds and other manifestations of the natural world he had no personal interest in.

Take himself, born to slave in his father's grain business, to add up and deduct figures, make calculations, measure out his life in motes of flour dancing in sunbeams. Was there another way? A route out for him?

He found himself very troubled, and scratched his head and scratched his arse, and tried resorting to pornographic thoughts of bosoms possessed by demons to drive out his anxiety, and so he managed eventually to get off to sleep.

In his own bed, Itzik thought over all he had overheard while creeping behind the banisters. It was pure gold. He had never had better information since he learned of the pull of the moon on the strange internal workings of women's bodies when he had seen his mother wash out a bloody cloth in the basin. He had thought, at first, she was dying, that this silent woman would go where his absent brother had gone, to the other side of the sun, its shadowed darkness, but eventually he had found out the terrible truth. Under the influence of the moon it happened every month, stopped, started again. When Rivka's doll was smashed and large tears gathered in her eyes, he had said to her, 'Do you want to know a secret?'

Thinking it was something nice, a spoon of something sugary, she managed a smile. 'Yes!'

'And it will happen to you one day. But not to me. Boys aren't cursed that way.'

Now he knew something else. He had a treasure, riches, more than the tsar himself had.

The house grew quieter, then louder, as internal dialogue was replaced by snoring. The rafters shifted, creaked. The moon was on the city. In the harbour the ships and their crews and passengers lay waiting restlessly on the Baltic swell.

3

A few days later Mina returned to the forest. The reason she gave herself when she woke up that morning was that she needed to find and reclaim her mushroom basket. A basket is a basket, it costs money after all, it's not nothing, you don't leave it lying around under a tree for anyone to make away with and claim as their own. So off she sets, still looking like a fairy-tale child, outside time, the basket a motif in a story. But now she is conscious, as she had not been before, of the downtrodden lives of those who laboured among the hot ovens, the infernos of the bakery from which an innocent-looking loaf was produced by the alchemy of flour interacting with yeast and heat and water. Not to mention the ignored toiling maids on their knees washing the floor in her own house, crossing themselves in reverence to Jesus Christ who had done *nothing* for them except reinforce obedience and docility. These thoughts rushed through the mind of the girl as she entered the damp shade of the forest under clouds the colour of mushrooms.

She was following her ears, not her eyes, not listening out for birdsong but for the human voice, the singing from healthy young throats of lusty loud revolutionary songs. She followed a narrow track through the undergrowth of fallen leaves and rotting vege-tation until she saw pairs of eyes turning to her, holding out their arms, remembering her, welcoming her, and yes, they still had her basket, but now it was resting on the ground filled with bottles of vodka and loaves of bread and pork sausage, treyf in every respect.

'So, you're here again,' she said, feigning surprise. 'Still plotting to overthrow the tsar?' She laughed. It seemed funny that such kids should be the ones to get rid of the horrible tyrant; she didn't believe it, it was as pretend as the games she played with her sister. He was a terrible man, that Tsar Nicholas and his sick son and the pampered daughters and the weird wife, bad, very bad for the Jews, no question, but how do a bunch of boys do anything about it? Yet here they were, completely serious and apparently with a plan. She wanted to hear all about it.

'It's no laughing matter,' said one of the boys, frowning. His name was Janis. He was not the most intellectual of the Bolshevik boys, but he was the most ardent and naturally suspicious of those who entertained any doubts. Doubters were potential renegades. If it had been up to him he would have sent her packing back to her bourgeois home and her bourgeois Jewish family. He didn't like Jews. It was nothing personal, not motivated by suspicion of Christ-killing; he just couldn't see how they could be a revolutionary force, they were in the tight embrace of the capitalist bankers, for the Rothschilds ruled the world and they were all in it together.

'My brother says . . .' And Mina recounted the conversation, feeling proud that she was holding her own against these young men, albeit with the second-hand opinions of Jossel.

'Your brother is wrong,' Janis said, cutting her off. 'We don't destroy for destruction's sake. We have a plan. The world will be a very different and better place when we're finished. It starts with the tsar but it doesn't end there. It never ends, that's the point.'

Mina paid attention at first, she absorbed the difference between labour and capital, between the proletariat, the bourgeoisie, the petit bourgeoisie and the lumpen proletariat, who were hopeless, an inactive anti-force incapable of rising up in their own class interests. The place she saw herself fitting in was right smack bang in the middle of the bourgeoisie. But then, she learned, there was the Jewish Question.

'Now Marx said Jews are practical and self-interested. He said that the worldly religion of the Jew is huckstering and his god is money, which degrades all the gods of man and turns them into commodities. Of course, Marx was a Jew himself so he knew, he understood these matters better than anyone else.'

'But without money what have you got?' she said. 'You starve. It's crazy to say money doesn't matter.'

'Spoken like the bourgeois you are, *saturated* in false consciousness. Don't you yearn to throw off the shackles of your class and be free?'

Sentences like these seemed solid pillars, different from the casual words of ordinary people who didn't think before they opened their mouths, because why would you need to most of the time? They were educated words, you would have a tough time knocking them over. A little girl like me would not know where to start, she thought. And he was a boy, and boys had more rights than girls, their world was bigger and they ranged around it looking for things to discover. Apparently their quest took them to Marx and what they called the lumpen proletariat and what her father called the dreck.

'Free from what?' she said, the only counterpoint she could think of. Because she genuinely could not see what was supposed to be oppressing her; she had everything she wanted in life: a good family, plenty to eat, a warm house.

'The relentlessness of capital, of supply and demand, of bourgeois morality, of the need to oppress and be master.'

She sighed. 'I'm just a girl, what has that to do with me?'

'Ask yourself, when you see the torment of the workers, *how do you benefit?*'

But she had absorbed as much as her brain could take. How he went on and none of it made interesting like a story. If there are to be black coals in your mouth, why not sweeten them with golden honey? She had taken in the basic lessons (and she was not going to turn into a frustrated intellectual, would never get much further than this) and now she wanted to know when the dancing would start again. She longed for the hot exhilaration, the damp armpits of her dress, the blood rushing through her limbs, the sense that there were no right steps, just the audacity of being flung around from one hand to the other, stamping, cheering, singing, laughing, and being the only girl so the centre of everyone's attention. All the boys courting her, wanting her, trying to attract her, and her scarf discarded and her basket missing again, because who cared about a mouldy old mushroom basket when you could throw yourself about and collapse on the mossy earth, panting, shaking, laughing, then briefly resting and up again for another round until you were cherry red in the face and your hair was sticking to your face in damp streaks.

They were sitting on the ground, lounging, talking, thinking, arguing with each other, now ignoring her as if she had not even turned up, for it seemed that this day their spirits and good humour were suppressed. The unopened bottles in the appropriated basket had not yet loosened them up. Maybe if she stayed long enough it would come to that, but the sun was starting to lower above the treeline in that way that foretells the coming of the end of the year, a smell of woodsmoke in the air, and a sombre blurriness in the sky.

A boy called Andrievs saw she was bored. He moved next to her. She pulled back her skirts to make room for him. He was not the best-looking boy in the forest but in the future what she would recall about him was the colour of his eyes. 'So blue, like sapphires, you know, the jewel, full of light like the sky itself is in them.'

She thought she could hear his calm breath rising and falling in his chest. His right leg was extended easily in front of him, the left bent under, his upper body supported by his left hand, and he seemed to her such a specimen of masculinity with his long heavy thighs and his shirt open at the neck, so she could see a few chest hairs poking out to catch the light of day, that she began, without the effort of dancing, to feel quite hot. He turned and smiled. One of his teeth was missing.

'I know what you're looking at,' he said. 'My father, he did it. Another tyrant.' Mina had no idea men did this to their sons. Her father was an authoritarian but not like that. Not with fists. 'Then he should be overthrown too.'

21

'Oh, he will be, I'll make certain of that. Do you care to come for a walk, stretch our legs? We can talk. I want to know all about you.'

They stood and walked a little way off. The other boys looked up and watched them go.

'Don't get lost,' they cried sarcastically. 'We'll come looking for you.'

Boy and girl walked away until they were out of sight of the others but could still hear their voices rising and falling in the distance.

'Why did you come here today?' he said. 'I don't think you're so interested in our politics. Are you discontented at home?'

'No, I am very happy. I came, if you want to know the truth, because I enjoyed the dancing. I hoped you'd be singing, and singing would get you on your feet.'

Actually she was waiting to be kissed. It was the only conclusion she could see to their temporary isolation from the others. The sound from the group had not changed. They were still talking, no signs of any rising into song. Her tongue moved in her mouth, she gathered up her saliva and wet her lips in preparation.

'There are those who say the revolution will be the orgasm of history, do you know this expression?'

'I don't even know that word. I will ask my brother to explain it to me.'

'No, don't do that; brothers have a habit of taking things at face value. Brothers should be left out of it altogether. You know, I think it is always best if you let the trees do the explaining.'

'What are you talking about it? I don't understand you at all.'

'I like trees, I like the forest. The trees know exactly what to do, they have all their wisdom in their wood.'

'Did Karl Marx say this?'

'No, just me. Marx didn't know everything. I know I have a mystical disposition the others would like to cut out with a knife; they say I talk in riddles but I am true to the cause, you mustn't doubt me. My sixth sense tells me you would like to be kissed and it will be your first kiss. Am I right?'

'Is it so obvious?'

'We wondered if you would come back. I said, "She will, mark my words. She enjoys something about us, and I don't think it's ideology.'"

'Well, kiss me then, I'm waiting. Hurry up.'

'You really want this?'

'Why not?'

His hand was trembling, he was a virgin kisser himself; at the brothel there were no kisses, it was over too quickly. He knew the difference between a respectable girl and a tart, you had to do things differently. The kiss was on her lips, chaste, dry, then he let his wet tongue lick his own mouth, then hers. His hand had a life of its own, robotic. It strayed up to the bodice of her dress and lay trembling on her breast. Mina was in a state of physical confusion, parts of her body which had had no connection with each other suddenly tied together by a moving flame. 'Oh!' she cried. 'I like it, I didn't know if I would, but I do.'

'That makes me very happy. It's my first time too.'

A tree stump stirred behind them. A bird instantly ascended from a branch into the sky. The forest was awakening. It had eyes and ears. The stump took the form of a boy, a stunted manikin.

This is gold and diamonds, Itzik thought. There'll never be anything better than this. The information was so great he could hardy begin to think to what use he could put it. But he had the rest of his life to work that out.

The pair got up and walked back hand in hand to the others. He examined the trampled earth to see if they had dropped anything, a basket, a scarf, a ring, a notebook. But they had left behind no evidence. As they reached the others their hands parted.

From her chair in the old-age home Mina would say, 'I let him kiss me; the Bolshevik boy kissed me on the mouth, so what do you think? Was I a bold wild girl? Was I pretty once? My brother here can tell you all about that. Jossel, wasn't I kissed in the forest by a genuine Bolshevik?'

'How should I know? I wasn't there. I didn't see.'

'But *somebody* saw, the wretch.'

4

After Jossel found out about Mina's second excursion to the mushroom forest, and the kiss under the trees ('What do you think of *that*? Your little sister had her first kiss'), he told his mother and father that he wanted to have a conversation about the family's future when the younger children were in bed.

He had a sense of unease. It might have been his imagination but something in the atmosphere on the house was off. Solly cried more, sudden wails; Rivka had not yet fully bonded with her new doll; Itzik was starting to resemble the tsar himself, bloated with power. What did he know? And how did this knowledge infect everything else? Jossel stared down the path of doom, his sister lost for ever in the primeval forest where people like them did not belong. All his life he would fear and distrust the density of trees and woods and copses, the antithesis of the modern world, the old places as he thought of them. There were other lands where the horizon was flat and it was possible to imagine the curvature of the earth, the ceaseless rotation through the days and nights and seasons, the impermanence of time.

'Uh-oh,' Mowscha Mendel said, 'what's this about? Has he come up with some ideas about the business? A young man's head is filled with wild horses.'

'Or there's a young lady,' said his wife. 'He wants to get married.'

'It won't be a girl, Jossel isn't the type. He's a dreamer.'

'Of dreamers, a certain kind of girl can take advantage.'

The house at night had a breath of peace. The clock ticked in its walnut case, the table linen had been folded and put away. The day was over, the day was something else now, another realm. Father home from business, Father was supreme. His beard was still black, only his face was lined in vertical runnels by his mouth.

His mother tended to the coffee pot. A few months ago Jossel had brought it home from the market and presented it to his mother as a gift, proud of himself that he had chosen such a lovely delicate thing, decorated with hand-painted roses and entwined leaves. It was the kind of thing a woman likes, daintiness, fragility, prettiness, and not entirely useful, for the spout was not what his future wife would say of successive items in their own home, 'a good pourer'. Getting out the coffee pot was a sign that something was up, that his mother knew there would be a need to tamp down emotions. Dora knew her husband would not dare slam his fist on the table while the coffee pot rested there. He was an impulsive man, but he knew better than to upset his wife. He did not understand her, never had. She never explained herself. It was her own kind of power. The boy had bought her the coffee pot, sooner or later it would be smashed, as everything was in the end, but Mowscha Mendel did not want the responsibility and the silent blame. He kept his hands clenched, under the table.

Looking across at him Jossel thought, No one in the future, whatever comes about, can say I didn't make my case like a man. And is his authority really so strong? He must have his weaknesses, you have been too much in awe of him. He's just a person, after all, a middling flour merchant with a high opinion of himself, not poor, not wealthy, just an average character. And regard him touching his nose like that, tapping the nostril. He looks like a mechanical toy made of tin. No, there is nothing to be afraid of.

Jossel set out his proposition. A plan for the uprooting of the

25

family and its wholesale transport to America. A new start, a new life. His proposal took in everything as if it were a bulletin:

The hostile atmosphere in the city.

The future turn the country might take.

The possibility of revolutionary upheaval and who knew where that would lead, what discomforts and dangers.

The opportunities open to an energetic man of business in the vast grain states of the Midwest.

The chance to provide for the children a brand-new life.

The accounts he had heard from those who had already departed and established themselves amid abundance.

And on and on he went, seeing his father leaning forward in his chair. Mowscha Mendel had heard nothing like it before, not even in shul, had no idea the boy had such eloquence in him, it was worthy, he thought, of a prophet, of Amos and Ezekiel. His wife had not moved, barely blinked, placid and unperturbed, as if she had no say in the matter, was not part of the conversation. Her wig was slightly adrift on her head, she pushed it back into place. How hot it must be here by the fire, Jossel thought.

'Don't tell me you've never thought about it,' he concluded. 'Don't tell me you've never once dreamed of another life.'

The old man pulled himself together, said what he had to say briefly and in the firmest manner.

'What nonsense, are you out of your mind?'

'And what do have you against it?'

It scarcely seemed worth the breath to reply, the answer was obvious, the answer was as constant as the sun and moon and stars, day and night. His son had got himself up as Moses, thought he was leading his people out of bondage to the Promised Land, when he was just some light-headed luftmensch with clouds instead of brains. Jossel, a man of action! Tears of laughter should come to his eyes.

Light winked off the coffee pot's garish floral designs. The coffee pot remained unbroken. There was no need for rage.

His wife pulled his sleeve. Gave him a look.

26

'What?'

'If you have something to say, tell him. He is worthy of an answer.'

But before he could reply they were interrupted. It was Solly, the little one, down from his bed, crying from a bad dream. He dreamed his brother Itzik pushed him down the stairs like his sister's doll. And here was that nasty boy flattened against the wall outside the kitchen, for purposes Solly could not understand. Itzik put out his foot and tripped him over. Solly yowled. Itzik ran round the corner. Dora took her youngest child in her arms, he sat there on her knee for the remainder of the conversation, silent witnesses to family history, five-year-old Solly, and a cheap coffee pot that didn't pour well.

Itzik thought he had been seen by his mother, he thought he had heard his name hissed like a snake. From his mother's lips, a hiss. Now the dialogue was lower when he returned to his place. He did not catch all of it. But he got the general gist.

'What do I have against it?' his father was saying. 'Everything. Who knows me in America? Who remembers that once I was a respected person? Others can take their chance, I'm staying put. That's it. You have my opinion.'

'Men have legs, we're designed for travel,' Jossel said. 'Trees have roots, they stand in one spot but Jews dwell in time, not space. We were slaves in the land of Egypt, then we were free. A sea parted for us, we returned to a land flowing with milk and honey, then lost that. We have, and are, a *story*, not a plot of territory.'

'That's not what the Zionists say.'

'They're irrelevant. I'm not talking here about sand and malaria swamps.'

'Anyway, those were different times, a completely different situation, why are you bringing that up? It's the wrong time of year to talk of such things. Save it for Pesach.'

'But the opportunities! Here you have a living but *only* a living, there you could become a wealthy man beyond your wildest dreams. Use your imagination.'

The mushrooms in the forest were nothing to what was sprouting up in Jossel's mind. A change of gear had been engaged deep in his brain. What began as a stunt to rescue his sister had turned into an ambitious scheme for his own redemption, a pragmatic assault on the passive acceptance of one's fate. Once they were in America anything was possible; for example, he might no longer be tied to his father's business but seek out new opportunities, whatever they were. There were great cities, New York, Boston, Chicago, San Francisco. He had seen photographs of these metropolises, had mentally begun to walk their streets. The future for him in Riga was narrowing like a tunnel: an existence of adding up columns of figures, stunted by numbers, the foetid prison of the counting house. And in America he had no doubt Mina would flourish. She would not meet any young Bolsheviks, how could there be communists in America? The land with no tsars would be inoculated against such plagues.

His disdain for his father's timidity and narrow horizons now led to a growing exasperation in his daily dealings with him, short temper, irritation. His father's small red mouth yapping in the middle of that glowering bearded face drove him mad.

Jossel described the state of Kansas, which was all grain as far as the eye could see. Undulating plains of ripening maize.

'Maize I don't know anything about. I know rye,' his father said. 'What has maize got to do with me?'

Rye made a dense chewy loaf, they ate it every day with slices of brine-preserved herring. Mowscha Mendel felt diminished, shrunken in his size and his soul by his son's description of the Great Plains of the American Midwest. As a landscape it made him feel lonely and insignificant. The whole place sounded far too big, daunting, the scale was all wrong. Too much, too unknown. He did not grow a thing himself, he was a broker; he went out to the flour mills and came back to the bakers' yards. The transactions were based on having a wide circle of acquaintances, knowing who to trust and who was a gonif. And that was just the business side of things. He had sons and daughters, the daughters would require husbands from good families, how could you know who was who and what was what when you were a stranger?

Jossel was not discouraged. He had expected his old man to dig his heels in, be unreceptive at first. He ignored the maize question, it was a technicality.

'Mother, what is your opinion?'

'You want to know what I think?'

'Of course. The family is nothing without you.'

Diagrammatically, his mother was the radius out to every other member of the household; she had borne the children who originated in her coupling with her husband, who had little to do each day with the younger ones, had been known to mix up their names. Apart from Itzik, the devil child, *his* name he remembered.

Mowscha was a pillar, Dora was the earth it stood on.

'A kitchen is a kitchen,' she finally said, 'wherever it is.'

But she would not be drawn any further on this enigmatic thought, whatever it meant, and Jossel declared the conference over until his father had had more time to think about it and come to see that this was the correct course of action.

5

But Mowscha Mendel did not come round and his passive wife had nothing more to say about the situation – or not to him.

One day she roused herself from her torpor and went to her son and said, 'If you want to go, you should go.'

'What, *I* should go?'

'Why not?'

'But I'd never leave you.'

She looked at him as if there was a fly up his nose. She was not a woman of tenderness.

'Don't you think you can do better than this life?'

'I *know* I can.'

'So, this is your situation. He is stubborn, he is a fool. Don't take after him. But take Mina with you, she's getting out of hand.'

His grey mother was striking words out like a clock, what had got into her?

'Have you heard something? What do they say in the town? It's all lies, nothing is wrong with Mina.' Already her reputation was ruined, and all for some mushrooms.

'I heard nothing, I can see what's in her eyes. A person knows without the mouths of gossips. If you wait, he'll get her married off.

And why? To save himself trouble. He'll take anyone who can give him an advantage, and then who will pay the price?'

'She's too young.'

'Is she? I was younger.'

He thought, You cannot say these things to me, you can't talk like this. I don't want to hear. He stopped himself from holding his hands to his ears. But she saw his face, she saw him withdrawing. She thought, They are all the same. None of them had an ounce of feeling. But who was worse? Mowscha or Jossel? Jossel would have to do.

'You will look after her; it's like she'll have a father by her side. That's my opinion.'

He saw that she was serious, that she was asking him to rise to the occasion, to become a man and take off on this adventure, to uncouple himself and his sister from the great possession of their father's love. Spinoza was no help here.

'But how will we go? I have no money.'

'About that side of side of things I don't know, it's up to you. You have to decide what kind of bed you want to sleep in in this life. If it's a feather bed all your days, then you must stay comfortable.'

'What do you mean?'

'Mean mean mean, too many questions.'

'That's it?'

'Yes, that is all I have to say.'

'Sometimes you should say more.'

'Your father has most of the words; the few he leaves to me I use as I can. Talkers are talkers, you are a talker, you take after him.'

For the rest of his life he would remember how he came out of Latvia, through the agency of his mother who wore a wig, and eased off her shoes to relieve her corns, and had a low opinion of the human race, thinking men were beasts and women took advantage of them. She would remain an enigma to him. He wished he could reach back through time to that conversation and ask her a thousand questions. In his lowest moments he

31

would raise his fist to heaven and cry out, 'Mother, Mother, where are you?'

But she could not answer.

'I forbid this,' cried their father. 'It's not happening.'

It happened. There was a ship, they went to the dockside. Their father stayed at home. Their mother, brothers and sister waved goodbye from the shore of the old land.

Rebellion had been incited in the minds of those who were open to new ideas. The following year Itzik would run away and disappear into the black maw of the twentieth century, the earth burrowed from underground and thrown up in mounds and mountains of history temporarily obscuring his movements. To his father he was already dead and he turned the mirrors to the wall and rent his garments and then said, Good riddance. Be happy in hell.

Rivka and Solly stayed in Riga. For the time being. That was to be their fate, not to board that ship.

Dora's face was a white disc in the sunlight. She was drained of any recognisable emotion. Solly didn't know what was happening. He did not know from a ship. He did not understand. The day was a game, his brother and sister were high up on the deck, waving. Mina was shouting something, the wind carried the words away. Rivka said, 'When are they coming back?'

Itzik said, 'Maybe there will be a storm and the ship will sink and they will be shipwrecked. That would be an excitement.'

On deck, as they pulled away from the land, Mina burst into tears. The tears wet her face, the wind dried them. For the first time she understood what she was doing, what she was about to lose, her mother's face frozen in a photograph, never to speak to her again, a heavy hank of false hair weighing down her sorrowful head. The smell of her, her hands that could be rough, but gentle with her children, her mysterious maladies, her emphatic silences, her wrists sore, rubbing them, and little Mina darting forward to wipe a kiss on the bone. She felt her father must change his mind;

how was it possible that they would never see each other again? It could not be, she did not believe it. And baby Solly toddling round the kitchen in his little shoes, falling over on his backside, everyone laughing, picking himself up and looking round with a wronged expression. These recent memories were full like an overflowing well. Only yesterday. The world of yesterday.

She cried until they pulled away from the coastline. In the sky she saw seabirds, patterned white against occasional patches of blue. Her cheeks were rosy in the wind, she looked really pretty. Her sorrow was distracted. Boys her own age glanced at her and tried to become friendly. America, they were all going to America, and what would it be like and who would they become?

The actual voyage wasn't as exciting as they had expected. No storm blew up, the lifeboats were not launched, no spies or international criminals were on board, it was the usual mix of passengers. Jossel had plenty of time to walk about the deck and admire the majesty of the sea. The air grew colder, they passed the coastline of Scandinavia and he thought of Hamlet, for even Jewish boys in Riga had heard of Shakespeare. Hamlet seemed to him now like a bit of a sap, unable to take matters into his own hands.

A young woman saw him gazing out at the salt spume. Her name was Lia. She was twenty-four, older than Jossel, a young widow travelling with her father; her husband had been kicked in the head by a runaway horse as he was crossing the street and had lingered painfully for a few weeks before dying. They had only been married for three months when the accident happened, and she had already forgotten what he looked like, though she had a picture of him. He would be found in a box of photographs in a hundred years and nobody would be able to work out who he was. 'Just some random,' Mina's great-granddaughter Zoë Fletcher would say. A sepia young man in a too-large bowler hat and a mark, as if from spilled tea, across the lower half of his face.

Lia had married later than was the custom because her mother was ill with consumption and the wedding had been postponed until after she died. Her father had been satisfied with her waiting if it meant a delay in handing over the dowry. Her husband was not really interested in women, and would not live long enough to understand or express his true desires, so he didn't mind either. The whole marriage was one of various forms of convenience, but not for her.

'I have no luck,' she complained to her friends. 'An unlucky woman is on her own.'

Now Lia approached Jossel on the deck of the ship. He could almost hear her breathing behind him, her leather shoes tapping towards him on the wooden planks. He turned and saw a good-looking young woman aiming for him like an arrow. Like an arrow she was going to pluck his heart. Lia knew how to make something of herself, she knew about the latest fashions, she cut a nice appearance and had a new hat in the latest style, for Riga. These were advanced arts that were unfamiliar to Jossel. His mother was what they called a haimishe woman, she looked like she belonged indoors sweating over the stove. Lia would be a natural at strolling through a park on a summer's afternoon under the shade of a parasol.

They fell into conversation. It turned out their families shared some acquaintance in the city, the trade of baking and of flour milling allowed a wide circle of connection. She was also educated. She had not read Spinoza but she had consumed some chapters of *David Copperfield*, in translation. She had a smattering of polite phrases in the English language and was assiduous with her dictionary in acquiring more.

The only contact Jossel had had with a young woman had taken place at family functions where the matchmakers hovered like flies, and these stilted chats were truncated by the fear in his eyes. But on board ship, in the general atmosphere of optimism and of being fellow-travellers reaching out towards a new reality without the need for parental authorisation, they spoke easily and naturally, exchanging information about the cities of America and where one might find the most hospitable welcome if you were an energetic, modern young person willing to do your very best. He told her about Hamlet. 'I can be too much of a dreamer myself,' he said, 'but maybe it gets you nowhere.'

'Poor young man. Seeing ghosts. The dead are dead. My mother is dead, my husband is dead, I don't see them, they don't speak to me. You've got to think of the future.'

'You're right.'

All her life Lia would be known as the decisive one. Decisions came down like a sharpened chopper decapitating a Friday-night chicken. There were no U-turns and her mind operated at high speed. Jossel was a pleasant young man. He was unencumbered with relatives. No interfering mother-in-law or overbearing father-in-law, just the sister, who seemed to her to be impressionable. They could make an effective team if she got to know the girl and got her on her side. Without the presence of a shadchan, Lia was her own shadchan. All the covert enquiries she made added up to a good match. She unfolded from her trunk her best dress, she smoothed the straw-coloured silk with her hands. On the deck the sunlight formed a halo round her frizzy light brown hair. A crowd of young admirers followed her round the ship. Jossel grew inflamed with jealousy as she had intended.

As if, Mina would later say, he spent all his money in the first shop he walked into, Jossel boarded the ship in Riga a free man and disembarked in Hull engaged to be married. When he tried to account for his impulsiveness, he concluded that there was a bundle of reasons – defying his father, leaving home, travelling halfway across the world, and becoming a man in the sense that a man has a wife and will have children. It was all flowing into each other, this sequence of events. He would justify his marriage by telling himself that it was in Mina's interest to have an older sister to protect her. 'I did it for you,' he would say.

But Mina replied, 'No you didn't. You did it because of sex. She versext you.'

Ashore in England, they went straight to a rabbi and were wed. As short as her brief first marriage had been, and as unenthusiastic

35

as her late husband had proved to be in bed, Lia still had more sexual experience than Jossel (a single evening in a Riga brothel, a place so phantasmagorical to a student of Spinoza that once he was relieved of his misapprehension that the belly button was somehow involved in reproduction he never went back).

6

They disembarked at Hull and crossed the Pennines by horse-drawn power. The horse took them to Liverpool. 'Magnificent city!' cried Jossel, deeply impressed with what was obviously a forerunner to New York but already surpassing his imagination. The Three Graces stood guarding the waterfront, the Irish Sea lapped their shores, gave way to the Atlantic, a vast turbulent waterway leading to the promise of freedom and riches. A life of salty commerce and unending possibility. Wasn't it fine? Wasn't it grand? It made Riga look like a small town.

They found temporary lodgings on Brownlow Hill, a three-storey red-brick house in a neighbourhood dense with other Jewish émigrés, to await the next ship. To Mina they might as well be in New York already but this, Lia said, was *nothing* on where they were going. Mina looked up at the white birds circling and squawking in the grey cold sky and felt nostalgic for her old home. She thought about her mother and father, brothers and sister left behind. Moving was disrupting, upsetting, exciting.

A few days later Jossel asked her to join him for a few minutes in the backyard by the outside privy with its torn-up pages of the *Liverpool Echo* to wipe your backside with. He had a confession, he tried to make it sound not too much of a catastrophe, he laid it out: faltering, ashamed, '. . . not enough money to get us all the way to America.' That is, he *had* the fare, yes, but only the fare for steerage, and he did not dare tell his new wife.

'Mina, darling, what am I going to do? Our father would give us nothing. How do you think I got us this far?'

'You told me you sold your books. The books that made you a learned man.'

'Not so much sold, as cooked.'

'What do you mean?' She imagined leather-bound volumes stirred in a pot by her mother.

'I embezzled a little from Father's business. Only so much as I dared. Nothing too drastic, a bissel here, a bissel there. Whatever you do, don't tell Lia, it's our secret.'

'You turned yourself into a criminal and still it wasn't enough?'

'Not to sail the way she wants to sail. She will be with her father in second class, we'll be with the common, rough people in the bad part of the ship.'

'Who cares? We'll meet them on the other side, and I'll have you to myself for a week. Brother and sister once again.'

Stinks drifted over from the wooden lean-to. Jossel held his breath and tried to talk at the same time.

'Lia will definitely care. You don't know what goes on with these steerage types, the fighting and the sex, the beastliness of them.'

'I'm open-minded, I've seen a little of life by now, not like what I'm going to see in America, but don't forget, I've been kissed by a goyishe Bolshevik, so I'm not so green.'

'Lia won't stand for it. I'm finished, I don't know what to do.'

'Let's get out of here. We'll find a cup of tea.'

They went to a cheap café. 'Kelly's' was painted over the door. Jossel jingled a few coins in his pocket to calm himself. Maybe he had been a fool to marry so quickly, had forgotten his own situation. The waitress spoke to them with an accent they didn't understand. Everything was foreign but not the right kind of foreign. Not American, irradiated with the glow of optimism.

'When are you going to break the news to her?'

'Tonight, it has to be tonight, or I'll lose my nerve. What am I going to say?'

'Let me do it, I'll talk to her and bring her round.'

Next morning Lia and Mina walked up and down Brownlow Hill as Lia heard her sister-in-law out.

'What is it, five days? Not even a whole week. You already have your ticket with your father, it's just me and Jossel who will have to make do below deck. It will pass in no time and then we'll be there and it will all be forgotten, or maybe a funny story for your grandchildren.'

Lia, with the security of a wedding ring on her finger and the promise of arrival in the New World as a married woman not a widow, had not anticipated that anything would now stand in the way of a new life. She took the news with her characteristic determination not to be thwarted. God had sent her Jossel. Her father had funny ways, he was overly religious, for a start. Jossel was a gentleman, or a Jewish version of one, which would have to do for her.

'And when they say to me, where is your husband, what am I supposed to reply? In the hold with the muck? I'm not having it. We sail together, we disembark together, we are at Ellis Island together.'

'What's the difference?' Mina cried to the salty sky. 'You don't have to be so fancy-schmancy, just because you have a parasol.'

'You're a child, you don't know what you're talking about. I'm glad my Jossel wants to protect you from the sordid realities of life.'

'Oh, I know all about them.'

'No, you don't. I have a husband; in fact, I have had two, come to think about it. I know all about men and the ways of the world.'

'I was kissed by a Bolshevik,' Mina said stubbornly.

'Please keep that quiet. I don't want us arriving in America with this old story hanging round our necks.'

A horse slid on a heap of dung in the road. It was a baker's dray. The familiar sight of sacks of flour falling from the cart set up a commotion in the street. They hurried on and reached the Adelphi Hotel, where languid-looking women mounted the steps enrobed in furs.

'Now *that's* the type we're sailing to America with,' Lia said, energised by their upper-class manners.

Mina looked at them. They seemed to her like pipe cleaners without the wire inside them, with a tendency to fall over. If Yiddish-speaking Lia from Riga with a few sentences of governess English thought she'd be hobnobbing with them on the ship, she was a fool.

That night, in bed, Lia said to her husband that she had a plan. She had worked it out while mending a broken spoke of her parasol.

They would stay in Liverpool for a few months and earn enough money to go in the best class they could afford, with the best type of passenger.

'How will I make the money? I have nothing to sell, it's hopeless.'

'Don't worry, I have it all figured out. This place we're staying, what's all around us? Jewish businesses. Every house is also a shop. Now you have a finance brain, you know numbers and money. Go down every street, knock on every door, offer to do the books. The people who keep chickens and bake bread haven't got the time to do their own bookkeeping, their money is bound to be a mess. My father can go on ahead, he can establish himself in America and make a home for us when we arrive.'

Jossel told Mina the next day.

'You have to hand it to her, she's got it all worked out. She wants the best that money can buy, it's what she's used to.'

'Is she? What did that first husband ever give her? Be careful, Jossel, she will wring you dry if you let her.'

'She's what your friends from the forest call a bourgeois, that's just the way it is.'

'God forbid that should be my fate,' said Mina, who was mildly disappointed not to be travelling steerage and seeing how the other half lived.

But God laughed at the Mendels; Mina thought he must have tears running down his face when he heard the dreams of this funny little family.

He sent a man with a gun to a city in Bosnia who shot the Archduke riding in his carriage and this riled up all kinds of feelings and created what Jossel called 'a situation' and next minute there was a war. The Atlantic was menaced by enemy submarines, uncrossable. This they had never thought about, never considered in all their plans. And whose side were they supposed to be on and why should they care? What did it have to do with them? They were not fighting people.

For a few months they received letters from their mother, very short, not much information, she was not a person for words, whether with a pen or with her lips. There was news about Rivka and Solly, growing up fast, missing their brother and sister, asking when are they coming home? But Itzik had run away. Itzik, the one who Jossel always said had the soul of a murderer, in his element, already gone to the war with his rifle on his back. He never thought, *Why are they shooting at me? Run!* like any sane person. No, he, he thought it was a big opportunity. His life had finally begun.

Jossel said, 'The good thing is we never have to see him again. How long can he survive?'

'But he's our own flesh and blood, whatever he's done. Have pity on him.'

'He's a louse.'

'That's not a nice thing to say.'

'You never had to share a bed with him, and know the things he got up to.'

'Like what?'

'Never mind, forget about Itzik, he won't bother us any more. He must have broken Momma's heart and for that he deserves whatever is coming to him. How can a runty like him survive a war?'

'I don't know.'

'You never had any affection for him before, why start now?'

'I never really believed when we left home we wouldn't see everyone again.'

'We will, we will, just not Itzik. Take my word for it, a louse is a louse.'

For he remembered how Itzik would crudely imitate the sound of his older brother pleasuring himself in the night back when they shared a bed. For that there was no forgiveness.

7

Brownlow Hill. Red- and yellow-brick houses, each with a shop opening up to the street selling something or offering a service. People living there who had failed to get to America. Some had been sold a fake ticket back home in Poland or Romania and found themselves duped and dumped, unable to get any further. Some lost heart at the sight of the vast cold turbulence of the ocean and would not move another inch. Some were swindled out of their savings. Some saw a lucrative opportunity to set up in business selling supplies for the journey and for landfall in the New World. Some had got all the way to Ellis Island and been turned back for having tuberculosis or smallpox, never even setting foot on real American soil.

Brownlow Hill had once been part of King John's hunting ground in the township of Toxteth, but what these Hetties and Moishes had to do with English history was anybody's guess. The teeming life of the Hill was a microcosm of whole societies left behind at various homes on the planet, intermingling with the bedrock of who was there already, because as well as the Jews there were the Welsh and the Irish and the Scots and the Germans, all living cheek by jowl, hugger-mugger, doing each other favours and the little ones scrapping in the streets.

Lia had rightly assessed that there were enough small businesses in the neighbourhood to temporarily support a young man with brains assisted by an ambitious wife. She tramped the streets of Brownlow Hill, up and down, up and down she trod on her broad feet, taking down names and addresses in a fancy notebook she had once thought she would use for love letters. He should start at the top, with Dr Arthur Hurd's surgery, one of the few educated Jews from a generation of earlier arrivals, whose popularity, she learned, was based on always making sure you got your money's worth, coming away with a bottle of coloured water whatever was the matter with you – your head or your heart or your gizzards or your knees. At the other extreme was the notorious shtarker Osher Blackstone, famous for hitting you first and asking questions later; she did not add him to her list. But what about Tower's Scientific Apparatus next to Narefsky's sweet shop, which was next to Kantarovitz's, the Hebrew bookseller, which was next to Tessie O'Gorman's, who made the best home-made ice cream, then Owen Jones' pawnshop, where you took your suits and your jewellery?

And Selig Dover and his dairy cows and Blackledge's grocery. Sam Gordon, the all-rounder who mended your boots, repaired your watch and made you a pair of trousers. Kesselman's chip shop. Silver's the grocers, where you went for black bread, bagels, smoked salmon and sprats. Aronovitch's Vorschte Company. The Tailors' Union headquarters, a big filthy room full of tobacco smoke and men playing cards, the cutters and pressers from the workshops all bent over the tables.

Eighteen Brownlow Hill, the place you went for *puch*; the feathers they plucked from the hens ended up here, you took a pillowcase and filled it and got a good night's sleep. Kron's olive oil shop, which supplied rubbing oil to the football teams. Pearson's cap shop, Ginsberg's bakery, and on Back Great Newton Street the main business of Friday night was managed, the place where the chickens were slaughtered and plucked and with the doors closed the scene resembled a snowstorm.

Lia sent her husband out every morning with his collar spotless and the crease in his trousers sharp. As he approached another door

43

he stiffened himself, he braced for refusal, then relaxed his face into a fake smile. Expecting to be turned away, but often invited in for a glass of tea and a negotiation that ended with a handshake. Lia was right, it was possible to build up a regular living through ledgers. They just had to wait out the war; when the war was over it would all be different. Lia, cut off from her father, who was settled in the Bronx, accepted this temporary condition but only as a stepping stone to a respectable profession with an office and a secretary, for as far as she was concerned a professional man had a girl with a clean white collar and white cuffs to do the filing and bring in her boss a cup of coffee mid-morning.

In the yard at the back of the rooms they rented, the landlady kept hens. Every Jewish family, every Friday night, ate a hen in assorted ways, boiling the bird and eating the flesh, removing its livers and turning them into a nutritious pâté, the carcass rendered into soup; every part of the chicken ruthlessly exploited. On Friday mornings the women of the street would assemble in the yard and select their hen, which would be taken to be slaughtered. Small children would adopt and love a favourite fowl not realising that in a few weeks it would be served up with carrots and celery and lokshen pudding. These were the people Mina and Lia were mixing with now. If they'd gone ahead on the ship like they'd planned, it would have been a week in their company, now they seemed to be serving a life sentence.

Lia said, 'How long can this war go on for?'

Jossel replied, 'Sooner or later they'll get fed up with killing each other, and we can make our move.'

'If we must wait, then we must prepare. We will go to night school, we will learn the best English; when we get to New York they won't believe their ears how beautiful we talk.'

'Call me Lily, I'll call you Joe,' Lia said to her husband after the first lesson. 'Mina, you're Millie now. We should all get used to it.'

But behind closed doors Mina and Jossel went on calling each other by the old names that they had brought with them from the old lands.

8

By 1916 they have been cooling their heels for two years already, the war is still the same murderous enterprise and it will take anyone it can get, even a Yiddish-speaking itinerant bookkeeper. Jossel was filed into the East Lancashire Regiment, part of General Allenby's forces in the Battle of Gaza, and was discharged back to Liverpool in early 1919 with no medals or war wounds or tales of bravery, but with a complete re-engineering of his personality so he had half-forgotten the name of Spinoza, couldn't remember how to spell it and certainly had no recollection of anything he'd read. He knew what death was now, and that there was no God. Nowhere was that large, domineering personality with his commandments and promises and threats to be seen on the battlefield. Boys had wept and called out for their mothers. They also cried for Jesus but he didn't turn up either. There was an absence of miracles. It wasn't even worth debating Spinoza's questions, his disciple's mind had been washed clean of that fog.

In later life, accompanied by his usual paraphernalia when he could afford it – a cigar, a glass of his beloved Haig & Haig whisky – and easing off his shoes, Jossel would embark on his war story. It reverberated down the generations, it became the Mendel gold standard for storytelling, a challenger even to Mina's story of the forest.

During his period of active service in the Holy Land, as everyone called it (but to Jossel was the setting for what he regarded as family history), he had palled up with another Jewish soldier, Private Polack, whose mother and father at the close of the nineteenth century had come from Poland before he was born, no recollection of the ship, the masts, the rigging, the rushing water. The family had got no further than Leeds, where his father set himself up in the chamois leather business and prospered. Now, in hot Palestine, the two conscripted young men (one of whom didn't even yet know the tune of 'God Save the King') vowed to look out for each other. The heat, the dust, the noise of the guns, the constant barking of their sergeants and the distant figures of the officers, beautifully attired, on horseback, got on their nerves. For what exactly were they fighting?

The two of them moaned in Yiddish about the war when nobody could overhear them, fearing they would be mistaken for speaking German and shot. Everything was, in Private Polack's expressive phrase, verkrapped. What war does, Jossel agreed, is to *makhn ash un blote* of a man. It grinds him to dust.

One humid afternoon Louis Polack came under enemy fire. Not dead yet, but worse than a flesh wound. He looked done in, his face as white as a blank page in a book, his breathing shallow. He's a goner, Jossel thought. The captain ordered the stretcher bearers to take him back out of the line to the field hospital. As he was waiting, lying on the ground, Jossel looked down at him, at the life ebbing away, and a cunning thought entered his head. Years later he said he couldn't account for having even dreamed up such a stunt, the devil must have got in him. But it was the war that had entered his brain, the war and all its scams and wheeses. War was rebuilding him. He had seen so much, he had endured boredom and fear and tension and weariness and inexplicable orders and movements under cover of darkness so that he felt reduced to the small core of his own survival. His father would not have found any trace left of the airy luftmensch.

He seemed now to one observer to walk *at* an obstacle, a rifle left unattended on the ground. Walked straight into its path and fell over it. Came down heavily on his knee. An hour later the joint was swollen, he started to hobble. Then he presented himself to the captain. In his best night-school English he outlined the situation.

'Private Polack is seriously wounded,' he said. 'Look at him, he's on his way out. Me, I'm no use with my knee, it's nothing, it will go down in a day or two. But why don't you let me accompany my friend here back to the field hospital, gee him up, stop him from losing hope and pegging out? He gets treated, my knee gets a rest, you get two soldiers back instead of maybe only one.'

Captain Bostock was beyond caring. He had been an auctioneer in a provincial sales room before the war, an expert in old furniture. The two lads were nothing to him, let them go. Anything to stop the man yapping in his ear in an accent. It could have gone the other way, but that's the way it happened to go that day.

Behind the lines the doctor examined Private Polack. He had lost a lot of blood. 'Well, it's touch and go,' he said. 'If he falls asleep he'll lose consciousness, then he's a goner. Can you keep him awake?'

'How do I do that?'

'Just keep talking; talk to him, don't stop.'

Jossel pulled himself up to his full height (he was only five feet seven) and said, 'Sir, in the whole of the British army you could not have found a better man.'

When the sun was setting over Gaza, Jossel began his monologue, mustering all the resources he found he possessed when he had set out his plan to his parents to emigrate to America. He spoke of the conduct of the war, of the idiocy of the officers, those pale strips of piss with brows full of pimples under the shadow of the peaks of their hats, of the hot strange land they were in, the sound of the muezzin, the Oriental Jews who were their cousins and the Arabs who were even more distant cousins – the descendants of Ishmael. Of moving pictures he had seen starring Mary Pickford, of his father and mother back in Riga from whom there had been no word for a long time, no letters at all. The inner secrets of

47

bookkeeping, the streets of Liverpool with the grand buildings of the waterfront, the Liver Building topped by its winged chained bird, what a sight! The temples to commerce and insurance, and how he had not abandoned his dream of sailing to America where his wife's father had already gone and made a new life in the Bronx and had a new wife, too, and everything there was waiting for them.

The night passed like a ghost emitting a strange chill. The usual chorus of groans added its voice. Jossel's knee was throbbing. The face on the pillow held eyes that were still open. Jossel began to tell old folk tales he had heard as a child. On and on he talked.

Finally he began to run out of things to say. He had been talking for seven hours in one of the great acts of oratory and filibustering of the era, though it had only a single witness. Jossel felt he had found a voice worthy of a world-famous rabbi; if he were still devout he should start writing sermons. He felt in his pockets to see if there was anything of interest there, letters from home, photographs, and he came across a picture of his little sister Mina, now working in a munitions factory. The photograph had been taken in 1915 in a photographer's studio. She was demure beneath a fan of ostrich feathers which partly concealed her chin. A rope of artificial pearls, another photographer's prop, was round her neck and she was standing in front of a painted balustrade by a painted potted palm. The impression was that of a young girl who had never in her life so much as heard of Bolsheviks let alone set foot in such a savage place as a forest. The photograph had been hand-tinted and her eyes had been covered with a watercolour wash of bright Arian blue.

'This,' he announced, 'is my little sister Mina. We call her Millie now, it's more modern. Is she not pretty? Don't you like the look of her? Back in the old country she fell in with the Bolsheviks in the great forest, can you imagine? Only fourteen and knew about Marx and all them troublemakers. But I got her away.'

He waved the photo in front of Private Polack, whose eyes were looking like those of a dying fish, filmy. His concentration returned for a few seconds, the eyelids flickered, he made a slight nod of his head and then fell back, exhausted by even this tiny effort.

'Well,' Jossel said, his throat extremely hoarse, still wanting to impart hope in a probably unattainable future, 'when this war is over maybe you will come to our house and meet her and ask her to marry you.'

The Mendels and the Polacks imparted to their descendants the following advice.

Never take after the English with their reputation for being taciturn and prone to meaningful silences. For where would Louis Polack be without Jossel's incessant chatter? Definitely dead.

'Never let anyone say you talk too much,' Mina told her daughter. 'And they will; believe me, they definitely will.'

9

Not the shells of the seashore, not the scallop and the conch, but canisters constructed to blow up the Hun. Built by young girls in rubber shoes, caps and masks, boiler suits that showed off, in a star-tlingly modern way, their slim figures. The men were at the Front, ninety per cent of factory workers were women. They clocked on in the morning, changed into their masculine clothes and poured molten explosives into the cans, capping them using a wheel to clear the screw threads, adding the detonator. Then sent them over to France to blow a German soldier to smithereens, take his head off, pulverise his heart, smash the soft tissue of his genitals, leave nothing but a few scorched scraps of flesh. That was who would be in the tomb of the unknown warrior, fragments of a man, sent to this state of atomisation by the hands of a Liverpool girl released from the domestic servitude of carrying trays up and down stairs, cleaning out grates, sponging spots from a dress, tending her lady's hair, arse-licking the Lancashire gentry.

Mina did not work on the factory floor. She was a foreigner, her English was still ropey, she had a brother serving King George but could you trust the immigrants with deadly armaments? She was assigned to the canteen, where the girls broke for what they called their dinner at twelve o'clock, and got a hot meal inside them.

She walked up Brownlow Hill to Edge Hill before the sun was up. Walked home when it was setting. On the Hill there were now cars, there were dresses that stopped short above the ankle, the waist had disappeared, fashion had aligned with the times to make the female body more comfortable in its clothes. She saw poor amputees begging, saw piteous widows with their orphaned children. Everything was suffering and torment and waiting for letters, and she was waiting for letters from Jossel in Gaza, from her parents in Riga. But nothing at all came from the old world. War had suspended communication. The supply lines of language had been cut off. Behind the heavy curtain of silence anything could be happening to her mother, her father, to little Rivka and littler Solly. Safe in their house? Who knew? But Itzik, who had run away to the war, roaming the land with a gun in his hand, up to trouble, would be in his element. Whose side was he fighting for? There was only one side, Itzik's own.

Mina as Millie clocked on wearing a government overall. She did not cook, she would have had no idea how to make the pies and stews and steamed puddings the factory workers shoved down their necks at midday. Her job was to be there by half past six in the morning, then spend long hours dicing and slicing – carrots, swedes, turnips, onions, Bramleys – and stagger across the linoleum floor bearing in her arms the flayed sides of a cow, a pig, a sheep from the cold storage.

Now I am a worker, she thought. The Bolshevik boys would be proud of me. Andrievs who kissed me, what would he say if he could see me now? He'd want another kiss! Now history was on their side and it had recruited her to theirs. Here was the camaraderie of the great social enterprise. She was part of it at last. If only she could tell Andrievs, whom she had never seen again after that one forest kiss. It had all happened so quickly, the flight to the New World and Jossel with his eye on her every minute until they boarded the ship. Sometimes the forest was a dream, but if it was, where had she learned about labour and capital?

The cooks were bulky women with large manly hands, strong

51

from kneading dough. They had beefy red faces and sweat moustaches. Mina was in awe of them, they had completely discarded their femininity, or never had it in the first place. In the munitions factory she existed to be bossed around by them, to be shouted at, made to run and fetch, chastised for not chopping fast enough, made to go down on her hands and knees with a bucket of soapy water and a scrubbing brush and mop up spills, and she adored and hated it, the work, the day, their company. I am the daughter of a grain merchant, she wanted to tell them, my sister-in-law had a governess, we're going to America when all this is over, we will join my brother's father-in-law in the Bronx and have a fine life. But she never said a word; they'd tear her to pieces if she opened her trap.

When the great rush of dinner was over, when the last munitionettes had returned to their dangerous labours, the plates wiped clean of gravy, the surfaces restored to cleanliness, the canteen women would sit down to their own meal. Lia had offered to make her a packed lunch to bring with her, but even if she had been allowed to bring in alien foodstuffs, Mina wanted the shared experience, and the excitement of consuming a treyf lamb's kidney and the ultimate transgression: a slice of boiled ham, meaty, salty, tasty.

The women of the canteen spoke of their miscarriages, their stillbirths, their curdled insides, their kids with rickets, their husbands with tubercular chests, their brothers who before the war had worked on the docks, or at sea, or at Tate & Lyle and were now away in uniform with a rifle and a gas mask. They ignored Mina. They were deep in a huddle of shared suffering, borne with the help of cigarettes, beer, gossip, Mass. They grumbled about short pay and money docked and why one job got a bonus and another didn't. The few men working in the factory were their lords and masters. They got the lion's share of what was going. The women of the canteen weren't even allowed to take home scraps from the kitchen, everything was inspected, they all had to wash in communal sinks at the end of every shift.

Mina piped up one day, thinking of the lessons of the Bolshevik boys, and said, 'Why aren't you in a union?'

The women laughed. Tears poured down their happy faces. For once, an actual joke.

'What's so funny?'

'Now your union, if that's anything it's a men's arrangement,' said Martha O'Keefe, mopping her eyes.

'Why?'

Martha O'Keefe reached across and flicked her around the face with a wet dishcloth. The tea towel smelled of lard and malt vinegar.

'Oh, don't do that, Martha; she doesn't know any better.'

'Is it kindness she's wanting? Here's kindness. Have a gasper, time you learned to smoke.' She passed the cigarette from her own lips and pushed it between Mina's fingers. 'Go on, stick it in your gob.'

'What am I supposed to do with it?'

'Take a drag.'

Mina took the thing into her lips, stray damp strands of tobacco stuck to them. A cloud of smoke entered the cavern of her mouth. A moment later she thought she'd be sick.

'Do you really need to get a rise out of her? Leave her alone, she's only a youngster.'

'Our rent collector is a Yid. He's a right skinflint. Goes home every night to count his gold, doesn't he? They say he's got an inside lavvy *made* of gold.'

'What, him in that old moth-eaten coat?'

'That's what he wants you to think. Our walls are dripping, all the kids have got bronchitis, what can you do? I've buried four.'

'And me three.'

'My Charlie.'

'My Betty.'

'My Mabel and my Hubert.'

'The house isn't fit for a pig.'

'Is it true your people don't eat pigs at all, not any part of them?'

'No, it's in the Bible.'

'I never read that part.'

'You *can't* read, Mary, let's face it.'

'Well, the priest said nothing about not eating pigs and he likes a few rashers himself, so you've got that wrong. The priest would know all about it.'

So it went on, the years in the canteen in the munitions factory, when the little socialist learned about how real women lived and what it was like to be down there among them, and what their particular sorrows were, which nobody in the forest had thought to mention.

10

When Louis Polack turned up in Liverpool in 1919 to ask for the hand of Mina Mendel in marriage, he did so primarily out of a sense of obligation and in the strong hope that the situation would have resolved itself by now, and that she was already married or at least engaged, or possibly even dead of the Spanish flu. He had taken literally Jossel's suggestion in the field hospital, consulted with his father, who talked to the rabbi, and the consensus was that he was bound by the iron shackles of indebtedness, that he must be a mensch and at least make the offer. Jossel remembered Louis but had completely forgotten what he had said during that long night when he was running out of words. It had been nothing more than a foolish postscript, but the speech had been enough to get Louis to cross the Pennines to make an offer and Jossel thought that Mina should at least hear him out. She could make her own choice, though the Jewish boys of Brownlow Hill offered slim pickings during the war and some were dead, and others in a bad way in their minds, and others without an arm or a leg or both or all four, so when a serious proposition turns up on your doorstep you don't send him away without giving him an opportunity to make his presentation.

Louis could not have been more nervous. The photograph of

Mina, as far as he could remember it, had been acceptable to him at the time, but wasn't he then on the brink of death? Wouldn't any old sow have looked pretty enough? Even if she had seemed okay, that picture was out of date. She could have changed, coarsened. And what kind of girl was she? One who had been employed in a munitions factory with the roughest types. He also had stood shoulder to shoulder with the common man, but men are crude by nature and must do what they can to elevate themselves, whereas women are naturally flowery and can become debased. He knew about the visits to the forest, which told him she had a certain amount of spirit, zest that could go bad, become rancid. Of Bolsheviks he knew next to nothing. Of political theory he was completely innocent. His father had made something of himself in Leeds. The business was thriving. He had a future. There were plenty of young girls who would gladly marry him, even if imposed by the shadchan. He could do very well, he believed, but he had to go find this girl and set out his stall. God forbid he should not do his duty.

He had not rushed straight to the house when he arrived in Liverpool; he had carried with him his courting clothes, getting changed in the lavatory of a tea room, and presented himself, carnation in his buttonhole, at the front door of the address scribbled on a piece of scrap paper, folded in his wallet. Looking like a suitor, wanting to be taken for one, but not too disappointed to receive a refusal and go straight home to Leeds, fully discharged of his responsibility. His whole idea of himself was that of an honest person, somewhat in the shadow of his older brothers, somewhat overlooked, laughed at and mimicked because he took care of his appearance and dressed the best one could. His brother Mottie thought the wound on the battlefield had left him a little soft in the head, a disposition already easy-going, susceptible to being taken advantage of, and the debt to this unknown girl was no exception. There were always ways to get out of a situation. But there he is knocking at the door in a navy serge suit, a bowler hat, carnation in his lapel, and a prepared speech he has rehearsed on the way in his head so he's word perfect.

56

A knock on the door. Lia opens it. (He thinks, This isn't the girl, is it? She's a bit of a heifer.) She hears him out, says, 'I know you, my husband wrote me letters from the Front. He never said nothing about you marrying Millie, but here you are so you should take your chance.' Shouts, 'Millie. There's a fellow here says he wants to ask you something.'

Mina comes into the hall. Sees a respectable-looking young gentleman with a fair complexion and a flower in his buttonhole. Listens to him recount the story of his salvation from certain death on the battlefield. They go into the parlour to wait till Jossel gets home. She's not, like Louis, wearing courting clothes, her hair is a mess. She is conscious that she is not making the best of herself.

Lia picks this up and whispers to her to go and get changed, she will entertain the stranger herself.

Mina runs to her bedroom and combs her hair and puts on a dress that has been waiting for such an occasion. The bedroom has a suffocating flowery wallpaper, blooms she does not know the name of – she has the word for violet and for rose but not these viney monstrosities with their fleshy leaves. The dress is folded into a wooden chest carved with Oriental faces. The sharp tang of mothballs stifles her throat. In the marital bedroom Lia has a small vial of scent Jossel bought her when he came back from the war, claiming it was from Paris (but he had been nowhere near France). Mina, on her mettle, goes in there and finds it where she knows it's hidden in the second drawer of the tallboy and presses a few drops against her neck and hopes for the best. It is the first time she has worn perfume. She feels herself no longer to be a girl but a woman teetering on the edge of womanly maturity, and all it takes is the essence of a few flowers. From a kiss under the trees to city courtship by a war hero.

Down in the parlour Lia is interrogating Louis. He answers all her questions in a satisfactory manner. Jossel arrives home, is astonished to see Private Polack in the parlour with his wife, remembers him, they cry out and embrace, begin to reminisce about the army when Mina comes back downstairs and the speech Louis has so laboriously prepared goes out of his head completely. Impulsively he cries, 'I'm Private Polack, your brother saved my life on the battlefield and I've come from Leeds to ask you to marry me.'

Have you now? We'll see about that, she thinks.

The boy looks okay to her but she knows nothing about him. She's not going to throw herself away just because someone has come all the way from Leeds, and probably wants to take her *back* to Leeds, which as far as she knows is a city that has something to do with wool and sheep. Where it isn't is America, which she has not yet given up hope of getting to one of these days, though it is a long time since anyone discussed arrangements for the next stage of their lives.

'What a mensch,' says Jossel to Mina, genuinely surprised. How is she going to do better than this? Louis has done everything by the book so far and further questioning reveals he works in an expanding family business.

Yes, Louis is agreed to be a mensch, you can't fault him on that count, now it's just a matter of leaving the two young people alone together to see if Mina likes him. There will be a courtship, but if she doesn't, no dice. There will be no arranged marriages in this modern post-war world. Jossel has got her away from the Riga shadchan, he'll let her make her own choice, but on the other hand why shouldn't she choose Louis?

Why not? Mina has not been kissed again. Before all the boys were called up there hadn't been time to find a sweetheart. She has never given much thought to whom she will marry, she doesn't think there's any rush. The war is over, she's liberated from the canteen and back home doing some sewing – mending and alterations. She's not bad at it; it's a life on hold, though. That is how it feels, the impetuous side of her wants something to happen; she wants to try her luck in the world.

On the other hand, from the moment she laid eyes on Louis and heard his story, she is pretty certain she'll have him, pending further acquaintance. Because, as Louis wants to do his duty, what Mina wants is to get away from Lia. To no longer be the third point in the awkward triangle of her brother's marriage and be bossed about and expected to take her share in the management of what is going to be sooner or later a whole brood of children.

A month of courtship followed, in which Louis took her to the moving pictures and for a promenade along the central boulevard of Princes Road on a Sunday with the strolling gentry.

'I owe your brother everything,' he said. 'I owe him life itself. I'll always be good to you, I'll make you a wonderful husband.'

As Louis suspected, she had been exposed to the coarseness and vitality of the working-class women of the city, their familiarity with sex, with ribald jokes, with hunger and hardship. Down among the women on the factory floor Mina had felt not so much solidarity as sorry for them, for their bad feet and bad backs and bad husbands who beat them and their children who got sick and died and all the woes and ailments of being women. God forbid this should be her own fate. And it turns out Louis is the type who always wants the best, the finer things in life. As he would later say, when they entered the lobby of a splendid hotel while actually staying at a lesser establishment, 'We can at least have a cup of tea; nothing is too good for my family. Walk in like you own the place. Why shouldn't everyone have a silver teapot and an Irish linen napkin?'

So, no argument, Louis was better than she could have hoped for. Away from the horrors of the battleground he was soft-spoken, beautifully dressed. His health would never be as good as it had been when he marched off to the war: he was bronchial, wheezing, coughing phlegm into his handkerchief but doing so discreetly, his back turned to her. Taller than Jossel, broader in the chest, better proportioned, with a soft chin and prominent ears and sensual lips, he was a good-looking boy. He would surprise his young wife by coming home with a box hidden behind his back and inside it was a beautiful pair of white kid gloves. She tried them on at night when everyone had gone to bed, they were a wasteful extravagance, but Louis said, 'Never mind, *I* know you have them,' as he would pay extra to have his initials handblocked in gold into the sweat band of his hat. 'I will know.' And Mina could see it in the way he walked, that yes, he knew.

59

She accepted him by the boating lake in Sefton Park. He accepted her acceptance. Neither of them was in love, love did not come into it, that kind of love had barely been invented. Louis had fulfilled his side of a bargain with the Almighty, who had sent Jossel to save him on the battlefield in exchange for a wife. And Mina would have her own household. She would be on equal terms with her sister-in-law. There was nothing wrong with Louis. Exciting, he wasn't. Her heart didn't jump when she saw him. It was more like choosing quality goods. Maybe, she thought, I've had enough excitement to last a lifetime. (But the idea itself was discouraging, it sank like a sour weight on her stomach and rose back like acid in her throat.)

They got married in shul. A posse of Polacks came over from Leeds to see Louis wed to the girl by whom he had done the right thing. 'We'll never want for family,' said Jossel, looking round at the men in good suits, smiling, straining their necks to see the bride as she walked down the aisle on her brother's arm. 'You've landed the best boy in the world, one of a kind our Louis,' the brothers said. 'Mazel tov, mazel tov, let's dance and be happy.'

That night Louis waited in his nightshirt on the edge of the bed for his bride to come in scented, adorned in her best nightdress, ready, knowing what was to happen. Her sister-in-law would have told her everything. He knew what he had to do and how it was to be done but he didn't want to give her a fright. She opened the door of the bedroom, her hair was loose, black, unpinned. His hands were trembling, he did not dare bare her body. Was there a prayer a man could say so God could guide him through this holy act, the deed of increasing, like stars in the firmament, the numbers of the Jewish people? Minutes later he pushed himself inside her. She gave a small sigh, of pain or pleasure he did not know.

So this is the big deal everyone talks about, she thought after it was over and something wet was seeping out of her onto the sheet. Fuss and nothing. Better I should have run off with the boys in the forest and died young and beautiful and the outlaws would have sung songs about me.

*

Mina wrote a letter to her mother and father and sent it to the last known address they had, which was the old house in Riga. She told them all was well, still in Liverpool, but soon, sure enough, they would be on their way to the golden land, America. She omitted any details of the factory: her father would not be happy about his child labouring with her hands among the common folk. She extolled the virtues of her young husband and affirmed she was happy and content. She did not know how long it would take to receive a reply, it could be weeks or months. War had made a mess of everything. It was a long time since she had heard from them but letters got lost, people moved around, plans were altered as theirs had been. She wondered about the fate of Itzik. Jossel said, 'Dead on the battlefield is my guess.' 'You hope, you mean.' Her little sister Rivka would be not so little any more, would have grown out of dollies. Solly, the baby, she could not imagine as anything but a little kid.

Mina was set along a course now, a transformation as great as her brother's. She was in the process of being and becoming, fulfilling her destiny: a housewife and mother. She reminded herself that she should not forget, never lose the recollection, the sliver of her true self she wants to hang on to. Here in Liverpool there is no forest, just some woods out beyond the limits of the city where the wealthy people live. If you owned a motor car you could drive north to the land of the lakes where there was nothing, just hills and fields, and here, she thought, you could build houses for the workers. That is what the Bolshevik boys would say, she told Louis, and weren't they right? 'No factories,' Louis pointed out. 'Where are people supposed to work? Leave it at that, land good for nothing.' (One of their great-grandsons would in the next century own a farm near Keswick which his wife ran while he commuted to London during the week doing digital consultancy for environmental organisations. But that was a long time after Mina and Louis had been resting together in their adjacent plots in Rice Lane cemetery.)

So they stayed in Liverpool, America forgotten. The young couple got the hang of sex, got the hang of each other, made love with gusto once a fortnight. Mina sat in the warm kitchen with her children, Harry, Benny and Paula, crowded onto her lap or hugging her knees. Above her on the clothes airer raised up and down by a pulley the shirts steamed in the heat of the coal fire. Little Paula, the youngest, looked up and saw her toy rabbit hanging by pegs from its ears, floating in the airy draughts from a poorly sealed window. The kitchen smelled of chicken, everything smelled of chicken. Her mother was a dark round woman with a faint moustache. What was she thinking about? Words so worn and faded in her mind they resembled much-thumbed coins whose raised imprints have started to smooth away. She might go to the library and take out a book on the subject, a refresher course, but she could not command the language necessary, hers was still simple, everyday English with bad grammar and a small vocabulary, for who had time to apply yourself to night school with three children? And her husband, the almost native-born speaker, could resolve any matters beyond her own power of speech.

So big ideas grew like mushrooms in the dark inside her, stunted, needing more light, never emerging into speech.

11

After Louis and Mina got married the two brothers-in-law went into partnership, opening the north-western headquarters of the Polack family business from premises on Mount Pleasant, round the corner from the Adelphi Hotel, which felt like a prestigious address when you could stroll past and see the gentry arriving in their motor cars, ladies ascending the steps in furs and silk stockings.

Starting out in 1904 as a two-bob operation in Leeds, the company was now supplying cleaning leathers to the motor trade. From garages and car showrooms in Liverpool, the clientele started to expand down into Cheshire and Wales, across almost to Manchester, where it was brought up short by larger competitors, then up to the cotton towns of Lancashire. According to their promotional literature, no garage mechanic or car salesman was complete without his supply of Elite Cloths, offering a Superlative Finish To All Chromes and Silvers. Jossel handled the finances, Louis was in charge of sales, advertising and public relations, placing ads in local newspapers – first classifieds, then a quarter page in the *Echo* with a specially commissioned hand-drawn illustration of a man in a white coat buffing the bonnet of a Wolseley Silent Six.

The new operation needed staff. They took on two employees: Bob Wilson, the commercial traveller out on the road, and

Margaret McGlone, always known by Jossel and Louis as 'the girl', who arrived as a teenager from Scotland Road with a reference from the priest at St Anthony's who said she was a good girl from a good family who got good marks in her schoolwork and would be a good employee in any enterprise but was best suited to a position where you went to work every day in clean white collar and cuffs and didn't get your hands dirty. He had known her since she was a snotty-nosed tyke and seen her better and better herself, and she deserved to be given a chance. She could start at rock-bottom wages until she proved herself. The priest was proud of this letter. Jossel laughed when he read it. 'You couldn't get a girl cheaper if you tried.'

Her duties were to answer the telephone, pack up the orders and organise the filing. After a probationary period they sent her on a shorthand and typing course one evening a week, where she picked up secretarial skills and got herself a certificate that was framed and put up in the parlour at home. With her new responsibilities Margaret acquired the title of Administrator, which her mother said had given her all kinds of ideas and now no boy was good enough for her, did she want to marry a priest? Well, she couldn't and that was the end of that, so she should think twice before labouring all the hours God sends for the Yids, what had they ever done for her?

Bob Wilson remained aloof and separate from the life of the business, going out in the van with the merchandise and return-ing home to his wife every couple of days with new orders. He was ashy blond and pale with pimples. He played the cornet and was a member of Toxteth Orange Lodge. He and Margaret managed a détente through the neutral status of their employers, who weren't one of either of them. This was the advantage of working for the Hebrews, he said, they don't take sides.

Mina rarely saw Bob, he was a name, 'the traveller'. She imagined him in a painted gypsy caravan roaming the dusty roads of Lancashire and North Wales, a corncob pipe stuck in his mouth. She'd seen a picture of a man like this in one of the children's storybooks. Margaret McGlone, on the other hand, was

64

always there when she popped into the business, bright, charming, friendly. Everyone liked her. Mina wondered if she should be jealous of little Miss Sunshine, if her Louis might canoodle with her in the backyard, you have only one life, why shouldn't the girl take her chances while she can? But when she said to him, 'Margaret is a pretty young thing, happy as the day is long,' he replied, 'She whistles, gets on my nerves.'

News began to reach the immigrants that way out of the city on the number 86 tram route going past Penny Lane, where there had until recently been the blankness of fields, pasture, farms, the white mansion houses of Victorian shipping and commercial magnates, now there were *houses* racing down ribbon roads. Rows of semi-detacheds, stuck together like conjoined twins, radiated south, then dived off forming avenues, drives, closes and cul-de-sacs. Traffic lights and tram lines cross-hatched the carriageway. Fine coloured pebbles were dashed at the wet cement walls. Ornamental stained-glass panels were fitted to front doors. Gardens were laid out with roses and laburnum bushes and crazy-paving paths. A category of investment Jossel knew of as 'bricks and mortar', non-liquid assets, of which he was suspicious. With cash and jewels, easily carried, you knew where you were.

In the shops on Allerton Road you could buy a hat, a coat, a dress, a pound of apples, a car, a joke-shop prank, a shin of beef, a piece of cod, bread of all kinds, cakes, biscuits, chocolates, newspapers, magazines, Epsom salts, medicines. The women walked with their string bags and wicker baskets, their hats were of the latest style. They were all slim, in skirts of the fashionable length, and appeared to be without anxiety of any kind. What was there to be worried about?

Lia rode the 86 on her own, down Upper Parliament Street and along Smithdown Road, went out there like an explorer to take a look, to see what all the fuss was about. She came back, walking into the house with her hat in her hands, the overcrowded, rented house of two expanding families, full of cooking smells and dirty street shoes, moth-eaten curtains and furniture that didn't even belong to them, a house that had never been good enough for her, and a husband who came home smelling of leathery goods washed in a yard. Along the street chickens clucked out the back, strips of newspaper hung on a nail in the outside lavvy. More smells, and cats and rats and damp and the tally man coming to the door for the rent. All being suddenly completely wrong, and even alien to her true nature, and inimical to the carrying of a parasol.

'You should have seen it, Millie, you should have seen how they carry on out there, how they're dressed and how they walk around. We schlump with our shoulders round our knees, waiting for the next piece of bad fortune. There they haven't a care in the world. That's what it's like to be a real English person, what we could be.'

She went again a few days later, a second secret visit. She had not planned to waste her money on a new hairdo but when she saw what was going on on Allerton Road she knew there was no alternative. For Shmuel (Sammy) Brassey – 'the Brassey boy', as he was universally known – had set up a hairdressing salon by the junction with Menlove Avenue doing perms using a machineless reagent, which when Lia went in to make enquiries turned out to mean you didn't have burning wires attached to your head like an electrified octopus. She came out of the salon hours later resembling all the other suburban matrons popping into Boots lending library to borrow an Agatha Christie. She studied her reflection in a shop window. She couldn't believe it. The Brassey boy was a magician. For if you resemble what you aspire to be, she asked herself, why shouldn't you be taken for it, and ultimately *be* that Englishwoman with the refined speaking voice, the bicycle, the wicker basket full of mince and Bovril, the brown lace-up brogue shoes for day and the midnight-blue suede for evening? The pearls, always pearls, and cameo brooches. No longer to aim for the crème de la crème of the Yiddenfolk but to be accepted among the true English.

When she got home her children screamed. What had been done to their mother? The boys cried out, 'A man, a man, like a man!' The daughter, little Bernice, wept. Jossel was terrified, Louis calmed him down. 'It's the future, Joe, we've all got to adapt.' Jossel feared what new demands his wife would make next. She had a look in her eye, she had that expression he had not noticed when she walked towards him on the deck of the ship, spying quarry. The perm didn't suit her. She had a double chin, and the shorn neck emphasised her fattening throat. He found her undesirable.

Lia had scurried along the Allerton pavements, snooping, trying to see what was inside the front windows of the new houses. She had penetrated beyond the privet hedge, through the glass and observed, craning her neck, displayed along a shelf, a row of ugly little men in old-fashioned dress with handles where their arms should be and a hollow in their hats. She had detected an ivory Chinaman with a fishing rod, and a porcelain ballerina. She had witnessed with her own eyes big mats in swirling floral patterns which went from one side of the room to the other, covering all the floorboards. Now, her head full of decorative wonders, she said to her husband, 'The Brassey boy did it to me, but that's not all there is to it. Wait till I tell you what I saw.'

Mina put the kettle on. They all sat at the table and drank tea in glasses with sugar lumps and slices of lemon. There was about to be a new disruption. She could feel it coming. She had heard about Allerton Road and the Brassey boy's salon and thought it had nothing to do with her. Who had time to sit in a chair while chemicals burned your scalp? Her hair was still long, held up with pins and clips. It was starting to come in a little white in places. Her appearance embarrassed her, she was not the live-wire girl she had once been. For the first time she envied her sister-in-law. What was a red scarf tied round your neck to the latest permanent wave? A scarlet rag, a piece of cloth you take on and off; a new hairstyle was a transformation in a different league. But was it a door to freedom *frei, frei* or to something else?

'Well,' Jossel was saying, 'I suppose we better go out there and take a look.'

The two families went out to the new suburb one Saturday

afternoon. They saw everything, the gardens, birdbaths, plaster gnomes, miniature ponds. It seemed to Mina, looking round the crowded sunny streets, the shop doors open to the bright air, that the passers-by did seem to walk more lightly on the pavement, they almost skipped. Their frames were narrower, their feet longer, the women wore their hats more rakishly. What cares *could* they have? What could possibly harm them with shop windows full of silver-plated cigarette lighters, cut-glass fruit bowls and other middle-class paraphernalia?

'A different world,' she said to Louis. 'And I never knew.'

And there was the Brassey boy standing in his shop doorway in his short white jacket, his moustache hiding the scar of his hare lip, and behind him rows of women, heads drooping under metal helmets like stricken soldiers. The salon was pungent with touchy chemicals, the hot roar of the hairdryers was pain and metal rollers dug into their scalps. It was suffering, but with the ordeal came a cup of tea, a biscuit and a side of gossip without which it was not possible to make sense of life.

The Mendels and Polacks walked south in wonder, taking in everything, until they reached a wide avenue. Houses were already being erected along the opening hundred yards. The bucolic emptiness beyond seemed newly provisional. Nature was being suppressed in the form in which it had always known itself.

A van drew up at the pavement and workmen carried out a pair of saplings with bands of bronze around their trunks.

'Little trees,' Louis said. 'I wonder what kind they grow into.'

'They're flowering cherries,' said one of the labourers. 'They're pink or white in the spring. Like a wedding.'

'What are you doing with them?'

'This is an avenue, you see. Mather, it's called, and avenues are lined with trees. It's going to be all cherries along here, a sight for sore eyes in the spring, wait and see. Come back in May, then you'll know.'

May seemed not too distant a time. Louis ardently wanted to see the cherry trees of Mather Avenue in blossom.

'I don't think they have these in the Bronx,' Lia said. 'No, it's all streets there, no trees.'

Thus was America screwed up like a piece of paper and finally discarded for good.

Lia began to assemble a scrapbook of photographs cut out of magazines of stylish interiors – armchairs, sofas, lace-trimmed anti-macassars, footstools, ornaments, coffee tables, pictures of Scottish sunsets, a canteen of silver-plated cutlery and the dream now of her life: a walnut sideboard, the kind of rig in which you kept family heirlooms (they had none but she could make a start).

Once, Mina had left home to make a journey like a hero in a folk tale. The journey had failed to arrive at its intended destination. Was she supposed to be content? Twice a month she took in her mending and alterations to Ettie Beilinson's parlour where every-one was talking about the suburbs, but not all were lighting out there. They couldn't afford it, or they didn't have the mentality of pioneers. The Mendels and the Polacks were the advance guard, the expeditionary force. Some of the women wouldn't so much as step onto the tram to get there and take a peek, despite the Brassey boy's salon being a flag planted in the New World. Others just liked it where they were, the old ways were enough. They had shops and businesses which relied on local custom. Who would want to buy a herring or a pickle or a bagel way out on Penny Lane? It was all right for the chamois leather crowd, that was a neutral piece of merchandise, they were in another league.

When the news broke that the foreigners were moving in, the neighbours got up a petition. Mr Godfrey Hughes, the dentist who lived in green-rooved 'Hatherley', went from door to door soliciting signatures. You buy a house in good faith in a nice neighbourhood, he argued emolliently and persuasively, where you can expect the professional classes to be residing, where you will see them at the golf links on Saturday afternoon and church on Sunday morning and where your lady wife will be making chutney and jam and Victoria sponge for the WI bring-and-buy, and before you can say Jack Robinson, the *aliens* are arriving with their *accents* and their tight-fisted intention to make a profit come what may so they can splash out on domestic vulgarities. Not, he said, that he was prejudiced, not at all, a Jew may well turn out to be as good as the next fellow, but you had to draw a line; yes, the line needed to be drawn and it was ruled at the point where Menlove Avenue ran into Allerton Road.

But capitalism is capitalism. The foreigners came with money and the builders took it off them. The neighbours watched as the first invasion, the beginning of the hordes, implanted themselves in suburbia. Fund-raising began to build a synagogue out in Childwall where they could all cram in on Saturday mornings and probably carry out stunts against Jesus.

12

Mina received a letter which she thought at first was a reply to her own of years earlier, announcing her marriage. But it was obvious that that had never been received. The letter was from Rivka, trusting that they were either still at the same address she had last heard from or, more likely, settled in America and the landlord might forward it. Mina read the letter in disbelief. Jossel was harrowed. Any doubts that he had done the right thing bringing his sister out of that place were chillingly confirmed, but what if he had been more patient and more resourceful, argued with his father until the old fellow cracked, and the whole family had left together? For years had passed and while everything was happening to them, everything was happening to the rest of the family.

Rivka did not know how to explain the nature of the events that cracked about their heads. She saw everything at street level: when the soldiers came and drove them out, deported the Latvian Jews into mainland Russia. What were they supposed to have done wrong to be kicked out of their houses, their businesses? Now they say we are spies, shouted her father, spies for Germany. What has Germany got to do with us? A soldier got sick of the racket and thought he'd shut him up. Mowscha Mendel was shot through the head and his beard ran with blood as he lay face down on the pavement.

The address from which Rivka was writing was an unfamiliar town in the Soviet Union. Rivka, Solly and their mother Dora were now Soviet citizens. They belonged to the USSR. They had become Bolsheviks without ever having to venture into the forest. Itzik's whereabouts remained a mystery, he was last heard of as a deserter rumoured to be living with a gang of outlaws, not revolutionaries – scavengers and criminals, Rivka wrote.

'Didn't I tell you, Mina?' Jossel said. 'He always had a taste for blood.'

'A terrible person,' Lia said, who had never met him but wanted to disavow the connection.

'A louse through and through.'

'You were right about him,' Mina said. 'He's come to a bad end.'

Rivka wrote that their mother was clinging on in a shadow world, a wounded widow not right in the head who was apt to say the wrong thing when outside the protective confines of her family and attract attention to herself, bringing down the gaze of The Authorities. Jossel knew that it was a fact of life for every Jewish family that you always told The Authorities what they wanted to hear, for the noble authentic truth was rarely of any help in such circumstances when someone in a uniform was examining your papers to see if they were in order. You assembled a story, a narrative that fitted the current requirements. Authority and bad times were like cockroaches, unavoidable.

Solly, now a young man, was doing fine. He looked after their mother with tenderness, he had found work in a bakery, he was strong and barrel chested, looked just like their father. His beard was coming in thickly. Rivka was bringing in money dressmaking. The Soviet Union was wonderful. The People looked after everything, and the people in charge of the People made sure they got it done.

Mina and Jossel came to the end of their sister's letter. At least now they had a fixed address, Jossel said. They could write again with all their news. Jossel remembered the fate of Rivka's doll, fallen down the stairs; the Bolsheviks would throw everything out in a fit of destruction.

But Mina wanted to believe that somewhere in the Soviet Union her Andrievs, the young dancer in the forest, was in a position of authority and was working for the good of the Common Man. In reality he lay buried in the frozen earth, a body murdered by White Russians during the civil war then thrown out like a gnawed chicken bone. Wolves tore him apart.

It was all leading to death, but here in Allerton they were near a park and the park was beautiful. In the park was a boating lake, and there were ducks, swans even, big white clacking creatures with huge beating wings – who had ever seen such a thing? Only in a picture book.

'Did you know,' said Jossel to his family, 'I read about this, the King owns all the swans, *personally*. You try to kill or steal a swan, they put you in the Tower of London. What a punishment, what a tsar, what a country we are living in.'

They laughed at the harmlessness of their overlords.

There was a thousand-year-old oak tree. There were standing stones which went back to the Druids. None of this history had any meaning for them, but they lapped it up anyway, it was their *right* to walk in the park, nobody stopped you. There was a white stucco mansion house with an open-air theatre and in the summer they would go to see the singers and dancers perform their hearts out, singing and clowning, red spots of greasepaint on their cheeks, crazy costumes under the blue suburban skies, high kicking, making jokes the immigrants didn't understand but laughed at anyway. They had the *right* to laughter.

Louis took out an account for Mina at Bon Marché. She bought silk stockings to wear at simchas and a butterfly brooch with glass eyes. She learned about fitted carpets, carpet sweepers, Madeira tablecloths, hostess trolleys, coffee pots with matching cups, soda siphons, whisky decanters, coal-effect electric fires. Lia's house was a great maw into which she emptied objects Mina didn't need, and didn't even want, but a home, Louis insisted, must be furnished, made nice to come home to, nice for visitors, and for the voices that thronged the parlour streaming through the mesh of the wireless who should find themselves in polite company.

A load of hooey, Mina thought.

So much of life was hooey. But you must put up with it.

She forgot to dust, to clean, she was not much of a cook, but she was a wonderful mother to her three children, willing to get down on her hands and knees and make her back a horse for them to ride on. Here was her hearth and she rose in the cold dawn to sweep out the ashes and build the fire before the family came thundering downstairs and Louis eventually appeared, smelling cleanly of soap and toothpaste, his chest proudly bearing his new gold-plated tiepin glinting in the weak sun of an English winter morning filtered through leaded windowpanes.

The garden was not as it should be. The neighbours had had a word. 'I'll get a man in,' Louis said, 'or a boy. There are people who can do these things. What do I know from flowers?'

Around the house, he couldn't even fit a cup hook. 'I don't have the tools. You must have the right equipment for the job.'

Mina waited so long she finally banged them in with the heel of her shoe. Was everything around the house this easy? In the ironmongers she enquired the price of a hammer, a saw, bags of nails. Louis said it wasn't ladylike, these were ideas she got from the factory during the war, there was a certain coarseness in her that made him queasy. 'But what do you want,' she said, 'a living doll?' And then he felt ashamed. Perhaps he could help her, she said, perhaps he could kneel on the floor and straighten the seams of her nylons? 'Kneel?' he cried. 'And get dust on my trousers?"

She sat in the garden with the children and smelled the summer. What more could you want? *What?* she asked the birds and the trees and the roses.

On Wednesday half-day closing, in the middle of the afternoon, she went to the pictures by herself with all the other Allerton matrons with time on their hands. She liked the knockabout American comedies, she didn't have to understand every Marx Brothers joke to understand who they were – a bunch of anarchists!

They were crazy people, Jews who had escaped the fate of history and lived in the present tense, gone wild. Another time she took a solo voyage on the Mersey ferry and back again, gazing down at the rushing water with the inclination to push herself off from the side of the boat and plunge into the dirty river and be swept out to sea. Why am I doing this? she asked herself. Why would I leave three orphan children and a grieving husband and a stain on the family?

Only for the momentary exhilaration, then you'd have a mouthful of muddy water and your lungs would fill and you would die screaming for fresh air and your body would be swept out to the Irish Sea, though maybe this way you would finally reach the shores of America.

13

One late afternoon in drab midwinter in the back room of Sammy Brassey's salon, Mina succumbed to him fondling the nape of her neck. The salon was like a private club, a place of secrets unknown outside its four mirrored walls. Who had got a taxi with a dear friend to Rodney Street and returned empty and white-faced, a head supported by a fur shoulder. For these days, three children was enough, you had another one and you might put your head in the gas oven, so don't say a word about it but you had the name and address on a slip of paper in your purse, folded up tight. The Brassey boy gave out the details. Everything a woman needed to know to navigate beyond Allerton Road came from him.

There were women who loved it in the neck. It had a profound effect on them, it was always surprising to Sammy to find out who. Some were numb in this place, others had nerve endings which led 'straight downstairs'. If you could get your hands on these women, they turned into putty, they couldn't stop themselves, you had them for as long as you wanted. He knew which one Millie Polack was, he had known for a long time, from an expression on her face of boredom, a sunken look around the eyes some women got after twenty years of marriage. Something gone awry that needed to be fixed and the husband no idea how to do it, looking at her afraid, bewildered, and her not able to say what was wrong because she didn't know. The wives of vicars and of rabbis, their days filled with good works, and the ones who had nothing to do, who went to the pictures on their own pursuing something that did not exist, he could only scratch the surface of what it was they were after, he didn't know what they thought they wanted, he only knew what they didn't yet know they were missing.

Now Millie Polack, who was supposed to be a communist, or a socialist, he didn't know the difference, and what was all that about but deep discontent? She came in with her Red newspaper and spread it on her lap while she was under the dryer. 'How is factory production this week in the Soviet Union?' he would ask her. 'On the ups?'

'Everything is good in Russia.'

'Everything?'

'Better than you can believe.' (Or that she believed herself, for wasn't this news, too, a load of hooey?)

'I heard a few bad things coming from over there.'

'Propaganda.'

'Listen, when we've finished, I've got something to show you.'

She was his last appointment of the day. 'That's the only time I've got this week, any good, Mrs Polack?' he had said when she rang. Oh, the dirty dog, she thought, I know what you're up to, I've heard the rumours, for there was supposed to be a secret book with the names of all of his clients with a special mark next to those he'd invited for an unspecified extra treatment – was it a massage, a new formula, a look at the latest shade charts? The hell as like, said Ettie Beilinson, the dressmaker; we all know what goes on.

He led her to the back room. 'It's in here.'

'What's happening?'

'This.'

His fingers moved to her throat and trickled down the front of her three-guinea navy polka dot with puff sleeves and a ruched neckline. Her hat was resting on the shelf next to the bottles of Broll cold wave. Her musquash coat was round her ankles. The

77

fingers pushed into the silk of her brassiere and tweaked her nipples. Surrounded by cards of hair clips and hairnets, she thought, Well, anything is possible now. I should have seen this coming but what can you do?

Her underwear was on the floor, he was caressing the spot where her stockings, taut, met the dimpled flesh of her upper thigh. He gently twanged the suspender. 'Are you all right, darling? Are you happy with your . . .'

His fingers crawled around. He was doing something to her and even in the blackout she thought she was going to black out even more.

Was she going to die? Was he going to kill her with sex, with just his hand?

'Make as much noise as you like, Mrs Polack my dear. Don't worry, nobody's going to hear you, you're safe and sound.'

His wet fingers unsnapped the nylons from their clips. They trailed down her legs, lay in a mess by her feet.

'Now we get to the grand finale, are you ready? It's a surprise.'

She was far beyond ready, ready was a line in the past, a starting point that had long ago befallen her.

'Just lean against the wall, here, if you don't mind. I don't want you to fall over. How good are you at standing on one leg?'

He picked up one foot, she felt nothing but a tickle. After a few minutes he picked up the other foot, she was in limbo.

'Now we're finished. You had the whole treatment, do you like it?'

Her face was blotched, a red rash had appeared on her cheeks.

'What the hell did you do to me?'

'A special treat for one of my special ladies, that's all. Look down.'

Past her knees, past her calves, past her ankles, her two broad feet had erupted in vermillion nail varnish.

'The shade is called Flamingo Nights. Very popular. We go through bottles of it every week. No extra charge, of course, it's on me.'

'And what do you get out of it, Sammy? I never even touched you.'

'Good question. Nobody ever asked me this. All my ladies run home without a word, only Millie Polack wants to know. It's a mystery, leave it at that.'

He winked. He was still wearing his white jacket, he smelled of chemicals and cigars. He was balder than when she had first come to him seven years ago, his moustache was going grey and his wolfish, sallow face had sunk, was jowly. A devourer of women who would never be satisfied. And did he not have a wife called Wendy tucked away somewhere in a house over the water while he slept in the flat above the salon?

Some of them cried afterwards, some thanked him, some left and never came back, one went home and put her head in the gas oven. One moved away to Wallasey where no Jews were. One told her husband who kicked her out. No one was ever invited into the back room a second time. There were always more depressed wives to start afresh with. He could never get enough of their feet; he thought of them walking home to their husbands, clattering along the avenue in their high heels, their toes blaring out a secret signal to each other. He had marked them, until they got the remover out, but still they remembered.

'Millie, Millie! I adore you, you're an attractive woman, I wish you'd make the best of yourself. You're a plump little minx. I got through to you, what's the harm in that? The citadel is intact, I made no invasion, it still belongs to your husband. Think of this as a beautiful dream you had, just a lovely dream. You'll go to bed tonight with him beside you and you'll wake up tomorrow and poof. Nothing happened, it was just a dream, a dream come true.'

Men are such swine, she thought as he helped her into her musquash.

Penny Lane was shut up for the night. The façades of the shops were dark, cups and saucers and other pretty little things had their heads down in the unlit windows. If she never went back to the salon then everyone in the know would guess why. The pig had got her, she could not tell a living soul.

She passed a man in a mackintosh with a satchel over his shoulder. He looked back at her as she walked on, leaving the shops behind, treading along past the never-ending ribbon of houses each flying a small flag of individuality in the form of a bay window or an olive-green front door and brass knocker. Gardens full of shadowy rose bushes and glittering alpine rockeries had eaten up the farmland.

As she walked, leaving behind the man trailing fumes of breath, she returned to the darkness of the back room and experienced again the sharp pang of pleasure she was not able to suppress. You have fallen off the edge of the world, she thought. How can you go back now, back to that grey life?

She was too close to home. She could not open the front door in this state. Louis would be there, the boys would be racing around, Paula would be listening to her programme on the wireless – she was such a fan of the concerts and plays and high-minded talks, though Mina thought she didn't understand a word of what she was listening to, just taking it all in like she was being breastfed words. They would all look up, they would detect something wrong, she might pat her hair and pretend that she had taken up a new style, she had nothing to explain, it was the last appointment of the day, 'I know I'm late but it was the only time he could fit me in.'

Footsteps approaching, the man with his white breath, his leather satchel. 'Good evening, are you quite all right? You look done in. Do you need any help?'

A tall bony Englishman. A long face under a soft felt hat. A belted fawn mackintosh flapping round his knees.

'I'm ... I'm ... '

'Look, I'm a doctor, you may know my surgery, I'm on Smithdown Road near the hospital. If there's anything I can do, you seem—'

'I come over with feelings, terrible feelings.'

'Oh dear, what sort of feelings? Is it pain?'

'Not pain.'

'Nerves, then?'

'Yes, maybe it's my nerves.'

'Do you live far? I can escort you home if you like.'

'I'm only round the corner, but I don't need no help.'

'I'm going your way, you know. I have some leaflets to deliver.

I wander the streets on my little route.' He smiled. 'You might be shocked at what I have in my satchel.'

'I'm beyond shocking tonight. What have you got?'

He withdrew a bundle. 'Do you see? Are you sympathetic?'

She laughed. 'You don't know what you're asking me. Oh, it's funny.'

'You find the Party humorous?'

'No, but I keep running into you people. I don't know if it's a blessing or a curse.'

She had left her paper in the salon, too flustered to pick it up when she left. And had thought, Someone else will maybe read it. Now here was a man, a good-looking Englishman, a professional type, with Communist Party leaflets on a suburban street. The leaflets were all about the coming war. In this battle the Soviet Union must do everything in its power to save itself, the price of not doing so was too high, for saving itself it would save the world. One made alliances that were not necessarily savoury, but then the imperialist Churchill ... and so on. Russia should not become involved in a bourgeois war, it should pit the capitalists against the fascists and stand back and watch them destroy each other. Stalin was always right.

'Once upon a time,' she said, smiling, for it was funny to her that that long-ago meeting in the forest should come to this, a suburban road in Liverpool and a respectable Englishman spouting the same material as her boys. She began to tell him about the forest.

'Is this a fairy tale you read somewhere?'

'No, it happened to me when I was a young girl, almost a child but not quite.'

But his face was stern and unsympathetic. 'At that time,' he said, 'there were enthusiasts for the coming revolution who were not properly aligned with the common purpose of the Party. Some of them were just romantics, or anarchist hotheads. We had to purge them from the Party so they would cease to spread like a toxic stain. Today, we ...' And on his words coursed, like a dam that floods a valley and with it a village, until her memories were nearly all drowned.

She felt the colour return to her face. He noticed it under the street light, and said, 'You look a little better. Might you be well enough to come to a meeting? We have an excellent speaker next week.'

Was there *anything* between a meeting and Sammy Brassey's back room? It was funny that Sammy Brassey and Stalin had the same moustache. But she did not know if she would like to go to a meeting. She did not know either how she would explain such an excursion to her husband. It would be a form of disobedience. He voted Conservative. He put up with her meshugenah ideas. But a meeting? No, she thought not.

The man, who now introduced himself as Christopher Tinline, seemed to her to oscillate between his roles as GP and local Party functionary. 'Well, do ring me in the morning if you're still unwell, I'm in the book.'

'I think the feelings are all gone by then.'

'Perhaps, but you know where I am. Please don't hesitate to—'

She broke away and walked quickly home where Louis was sitting in his armchair, drinking a glass of whisky.

'Don't you look nice,' he said, remembering where she had been. For the men of Allerton, who did not take their alterations in to Ettie Beilinson's, had no idea what went on.

She locked herself in the bathroom and took the varnish off her toes.

To hell with it, she said the next morning emptying the ashes from the grate. To hell with men and everything.

A few weeks days later Molotov and von Ribbentrop signed their non-aggression pact. Coincidentally, on the same day Sammy Brassey, possibly drunk, fell under the wheels of a tram on Mather Avenue and died in Sefton General before they could amputate his legs. 'He'd be nothing without his legs,' they said at Ettie Beilinson's. 'Or his hands,' several added. Or his tongue, thought a couple who had experienced something experimental. The back-room women did not attend the funeral, so everyone knew who they were. A week later the war started and the previous life was put away.

Rivka, Solly and Dora fell into a ravine of silence.

14

Mina and Louis' sons, Benny and Harry, were rowdy. They had started their education back at the Jewish school in Hope Place, shadowed by the never-ending construction of the Protestant cathedral, a sandstone colossus which formed a pinkish hulk above the city. When the two families moved out to the suburbs the boys went to a new school with all the Robins and Peters and Jimmys and Brendans and Owens. They raised their hands to answer a question. A Jewy sound came out of their mouths. In the playground the other kids got up to their usual tricks of punching, kicking, biting, humiliating. From the Catholics, in particular, the perpetual cry of *You murdered our Lord!* When they came home and told their father this he thought about it for a day or two then assembled the family in the lounge and announced that he had a comeback.

'Tell them this: tell them if we hadn't killed Jesus, he wouldn't have died for your sins like he said he did, and you wouldn't be saved, you'd be in hell. So don't you think you Christians owe us a vote of thanks?'

Benny said he couldn't remember all that. Of the two brothers he was the least interested in the life of the intellect, preferring to square off like a prizefighter against all comers, though often getting beaten due to his lack of tactics. Harry took it all in. He went back to school the next day and tried it out on 'Flinty' McPherson.

Flinty said, 'So you admit it then? So we was right all along? Come here and take your medicine, Christ killer. Kneel down so I can gob on your head.'

'But,' Harry replied, 'you haven't understood.' The words were still passing through his windpipe when Flinty decked him with his leather satchel and spat on his hair.

One time they bunked off school to go to the Aintree races. Benny pinched a pair of binoculars from the camera shop on Bold Street, planning to give them back at the end of the day. 'I'm no thief,' he shouted when he was collared. 'It was just an honest loan. I swear to God. I swear on my mother's life, I was never going to keep them, what for, it was just the one time we wanted to see the gee-gees!' Louis had to go in with the bins dangling from his wrist and make amends, smooth things over. 'They're just lively boys,' he said, 'they didn't mean no harm,' and the owner agreed they'd say no more because the people from the chamois business had a good reputation in the city for being honest and above board in their dealings. That was the last criminal act.

Harry was called up in 1940 and served in the tanks. He went off in a scratchy khaki uniform and returned on leave with a collection of coarse expressions which he passed on to his brother. Louis winced when he opened his mouth. Such a son that had sprung from his pale loins, a son who might be a mamzer in another life. Benny followed his brother into the army and after he was demobbed in 1945 refused the offer to go into the family business, the purpose for which sons were born, and behind everyone's back got himself taken on at a men's outfitters. He wore zoot suits and jazzy ties. He had a pen with a clear barrel, which if you upended it revealed the form of a scantily dressed blonde. Benny was into everything that was all the rage. He had some kind of mental radar, an alert system for what was coming next. Those watchful brown eyes, those ears out on stalks overhearing conversations on the street. He was absorbent for useful information.

In this family the Infant Prodigy had no confidante.

'The trouble with my sister,' Harry said, 'is she's *complicated*.'

Teenage Paula thought it was anyone's fault but her own if she was complicated. She barely remembered life before the semi-detached house and the back garden, her mother's grinning row of toby jugs, the patterned carpet, the sound of her father's car purring down the road home from business. Paula was a walking talking doll that could be dressed up in outfits, clothes that Mina didn't have the figure for herself, couldn't carry off the style. But the slim neck and the fox-fur tippet were nothing compared to her great asset, The Voice. She had learned to speak listening to the wireless and talked as if she herself was being broadcast from the BBC at Alexandra Palace. 'My daughter could go anywhere, be received anywhere,' Mina said. 'She could curtsey to the Lord Mayor and he'd never know she was born in the front bedroom off Brownlow Hill like Harry and Benny, and nobody would mistake them for native-born Englishmen even if they are.' Her sister-in-law was jealous of Paula's accomplishments; her daughter Bernice couldn't keep up with her younger cousin. 'But, big but,' Lia said, 'me and Bernice are,' she entwined two fingers together, '*like that*.' Could a mother and daughter be closer? Whereas Paula had her own private agenda and she did not tell Mina what it was.

Mina was unwittingly preparing Paula for flight, for disassociation and alienation, for the yearning for better things. In Ettie Beilinson's parlour, Mina would hoist her infant daughter onto a stool and tell her to recite a poem. If she became sulky, scowled, shook her head, shrugged her shoulders, Mina would cajole: 'Just say something, Paula, anything, tell us what you had for lunch.' And eventually she would obediently reply, '*Brid and butter, with sliced aig*', inducing torrents of laughter and applause among the parlour full of immigrant ladies with their Brassey boy machineless-reagent perms and polyp-riddled ovaries. So Paula was learning to appreciate an audience; she felt the benefit of it in chocolates and biscuits and lime soda.

At weddings and bar mitzvahs matters escalated. She would

be called on to do her party trick of speaking like the Princesses Elizabeth and Margaret, once again standing on a chair but this time at the top table with the hosts and guests of honour. Her audiences grew and grew, just for opening her mouth, before she even started singing. There were many of these occasions, the family on her father's side was huge, an extravagance of Polack relatives in Leeds and Manchester and as far afield as London and Glasgow, for his parents had come from Poland with five brothers and sisters. Weddings, engagement parties, bar mitzvahs were massive events, full of men slipping off their shoes, drinking whisky, inhaling cigars, women in feathered hats and diamanté brooches and mink stoles.

The Polacks were like the stars in the firmament, there were too many of them to count. One was a furrier, one ran a gown shop, one bought and sold gold and silver, one was in the wholesale bakery business, one was a rabbi (the naches!) who wore a full beard and a black hat, one was a teacher, one was in printing, one was a glove manufacturer, one had gone to the devil and nobody talked about him. And the women: one who ran her own gown shop, one who was an agent for Spirella corsets and one who played the piano in a Leeds branch of Lyons tea rooms. And on and on it went and there was no point, Paula thought, in trying to remember them all. Just perform her songs and recitations in the King's English and submit to having her curls tousled, her cheek pinched, her dimples pressed, smothered against a suffocating bosom scented with lavender water or, worse, a musty suit with a stinky miasma of nicotine.

One time a relative from America turned up, that other shadow family, the ones who had made it safely to the other side. Hearing of Paula's reputation, he taught her the words to the American Depression-era song 'Brother, Can You Spare a Dime?', chronicling the fate of the doughboys – 'Once in khaki suits, gee we looked swell ... ' The words coming out of the mouth of a six-year-old with a cut-glass accent brought the house down, but nothing induced laughter like the time she innocently crooned the words and melody to 'Away in a Manger'. 'The little lord Jesus lay down his sweet head.'

'Where the hell did she pick that up?' Jossel said.

'The wireless, they play all sorts, but what can you do? This is the country we're living in.'

Aged seventeen, she was vain, shallow, quick-witted. She had a sulky, sexy beauty, film-star cheekbones and her mother's raven hair, as if, Mina stated, 'Margaret Lockwood was waiting for the number 86 on Penny Lane'. She saved up her coupons for a Horrockses dress. She liked wide patent-leather belts that showed off her waist, and experimented with eyeshadow. To her hard-working older brothers she was a daddy's girl, a spoilt brat. She got away with murder and everyone let her because when she opened her mouth she sounded like the goyem, full of plums. 'Oh Mother, why do you have to . . .'

Benny and Harry played practical jokes on her. Harry bought a joke-shop turd and put it in her bed. The boys were irredeemable. She felt she was on her own, an orchid rising from a dung heap.

But she was not on her own, she did have an ally. Her father. He had a secret life, not what you'd think – not women or gambling, or boys. Sometimes if he had half an hour he would go into the Walker Art Gallery and commune for a while with the pictures. He had an aesthetic sensibility, underdeveloped, autodidactic, and shared with not a single pal, so he was never able to tell a soul how much he hated the smell of chamois leathers, deplored their existence, wished they could have stayed on the goats and sheep they came from. A chamois buffed everything to a high sheen, you cleaned windows and motor cars with them, but he adored gauzy nymphs and modest blue-robed virgins and society figures dressed in satin, ruffs, lace. At first he had no idea of the meanings, sym-bolic or otherwise, in these works; he didn't know 'school of' and 'after' and 'provenance' and 'brushstrokes'. He just derived a deep sensual satisfaction from the surface of the canvas, the richness of the costumes and the strangeness of the landscape. His heart was full. It was all going on in that beating region of his chest, roman-tically, emotionally.

Paintings moved him close to tears, and he couldn't say why so he said nothing to nobody. He would have been mad even to try. He stayed mute with his secret escape to the wind-strewn plateau by St George's Hall, where the art gallery beckoned him in for half an hour with the Pre-Raphaelites, the hyper-colouration, their lushness, their strange deathliness. He did not want more than to be left alone for a few minutes before a Burne-Jones and come out thinking himself a fortunate man until he walked back to Mount Pleasant, where the smell of chamois leathers entered his pores again. His daughter was the only member of his family with whom he could share his secret tendencies towards the visual aesthetic. He wanted to see if Paula could feel what he felt when he stood in front of a painting, he wanted a life-companion such as he had never expected to find in marriage; it had not entered his head to look for a wife with whom he had something in common.

On Saturdays he went to shul in the morning in a suit and tie and came home and changed into slacks, a fawn-coloured cashmere cardigan with wooden buttons over a pale blue shirt. He had bought himself a pair of leather driving gloves. They would motor into town after lunch. The car smelled to Paula of masculine fragrances, of his aftershave and cigars.

In the glove compartment he kept his book. It was the *Beginner's Guide to Great Art*, he had made a study of it. At the Walker Art Gallery he would position his daughter in front of a picture and try to sound knowledgeable. 'Can you see that, Paula? What he did there with just a spot of colour, it changed everything, the whole thing would be different without that little brushstroke.' He knew now what was meant by 'perspective' and 'schools' and the way each creative movement was a reaction against what had preceded it. He was self-taught with great gaps in his knowledge, but strolling arm in arm, the two of them seemed, he hoped, to others as worldly and engaged, that they had the *right* to be there, to discuss, to admire, to stand in silent contemplation, to point a finger, to study the card and memorise the name and dates of the artist.

Paula returned from these excursions energised. She saw young women walk about hatless and gloveless. They smoked cigarettes.

They leaned their elbows against a wall and expressed trenchant opinions. These views were often at variance with her father's timid art appreciation. What moved his breathing soul was condemned by them as sentimental. Beauty, it seemed, wasn't the point. She aspired to their casual insolence.

After the war, when the light had risen once more on the world, Louis would take Mina to Paris. They strolled arm in arm along the Champs-Élysées and he said to her, 'I hear they have a terrific museum here, full of the very best pictures.' She replied, 'What would you want with pictures? You never look at the ones on the wall at home. The little girl playing with the kitten and the ball of wool. It's awfully cute.' He suppressed the desire to say, 'You call that art? It hurts my eyes.'

15

Jossel's daughter Bernice, a year older than her cousin Paula, had a serene expression and a mass of fair wavy hair. Since she was fifteen she had been going out with Lionel Clumpus, a very nice boy. His father Morrie Clumpus was in towelling supplies to restaurants and hotels and they lived on Queens Drive in a double-fronted house with a pair of bay windows curtained in silver brocade which Lia admired beyond anything. Like Paula, both had been evacuated in early 1940 to North Wales and felt nothing but horror and loneliness in the wet hills, the sodden fields, the bulky figures of menacing cows in the distance. It was possible to be flattened by a cow and die in agony with its huge weight crushing your heart; this was supposed to have happened to a boy from Devon Street. Lionel, sequestered on a farm in the middle of nowhere, missing his mother and father very much and trying to do his best to be a little man as he had promised on the station platform, had had his shorts taken down by the farmer's wife to check if he had a tail. Then the Blitz eased up and he returned home resolving to never again set foot in Wales or on a farm or have anything to do with livestock, drawing the line even at a domestic pet like a kitten or budgerigar. 'No tortoise,' he would say to his daughters. 'Keep your distance from animals, you never know what might happen.'

A deep sense of shame afflicted Lionel, that they thought he was a beast or an emissary of the devil. Bernice tried to comfort him. After he had confided in her she kissed him lightly but tenderly on his cheek (the first non-parental lips that had ever touched his skin, he deeply shuddered with the wet surprise of it) and promised she would never tell a living soul and certainly not their parents, who had worries enough. The farmers of North Wales and their wives, far from being kindly apple-cheeked types from a picture book, were just primitive peasant people who didn't know any better, she said, to comfort him. Her own experience had been less traumatic but deeply boring. Away from the alarm of the bomb-ravaged skies there was nothing to do but listen to the sound of animals mating and her hosts quarrelling in a language with too many vowels. Now they were bilingual in English, Yiddish and with a rudimentary knowledge of Welsh.

In the post-war world there was plenty of fun. Bernice and Lionel played table tennis at Harold House, hammering each other with their ping-pong paddles. Bernice darted about the table in slacks and a polo-neck sweater. Lionel gazed at her in admiration – how accomplished was she, how pretty, what brio. They took long walks together round Calderstones Park deep in conversation, rested beneath the shade of the thousand-year-old oak tree and kissed for the first time on the lips. He stood hurriedly, suggested a stroll over to the mansion house hemmed in by a shallow ditch he knowledgeably told her was called a ha-ha. They watched amateur talent contests on the open-air stage. There was something pleasantly frivolous about all the singing and dancing and the summer frocks, and Bernice's hand on his arm as light as a butterfly. She was fragrant with Yardley lavender water. She was obviously what life had intended him for, a girl like her. What else could be the plan?

When he told his mother Ida that he was walking out with Bernice Mendel, she sat up straight and paid attention. 'Did you know that back in the old country her mother had a *governess*? Anyone can see that Lily Mendel is a lady and Jossel is a learned man, or used to be before he had to earn a living. Bernice will do very well for you.'

Lionel was short, plump, no matinee idol. The nice boy felt, in some way he couldn't put his finger on, that he was being strongly encouraged, even *rushed*, into popping the question. His future father-in-law was a benign if verbose individual who looked at him as if he were a steak on a butcher's slab. He had been earmarked for something. Why me? he asked himself. He didn't know why. Sometimes, at work in the family business packing towels for dispatch, he had a sensation of being driven *towards* something, like cattle being guided into a stockade. A hand had settled into the small of his back and was pushing him, away from what he enjoyed: the murky underground little jazz clubs of Liverpool where coloured seamen from America sold race records for hard cash and Cunard Yanks in surprising suits and hats brought home stories of Harlem and San Francisco. But everything was tending strongly, like gravity itself, towards towelling and chamois leather and Bernice, not yet eighteen, looking down at her left hand as if surprised to find nothing gold encircling her ring finger yet.

As in a Jane Austen novel, the twin enterprises of towels and chamois leathers were landed estates with the potential to increase in magnitude by amalgamation. His father and her father had cooked up a plot, and they were the young lives who must fulfil the business plan. Between chamois and towelling there were mutual interests. Lionel tentatively explained this to her. Did she really want to be a *merger*? But she just looked at him with large liquid eyes, her light hair fashionably waved, her cheeks a high, natural colour. A Jewish porcelain doll. 'What do you mean?' she asked him anxiously. 'Don't you love me?' It was obvious that she was expecting the question to be popped any minute. At home in front of her dressing-table mirror she practised various expressions she might assume as she accepted him. Gracious acknowledgement of her future devotion was her favourite, definitely no shrieks like Beverly Bloomberg, waking the dead when Cecil Carr proposed, and no simpering maidenly blushes like Sandra Copolov. She expected him to go down on one knee because she had never seen at the cinema a proposal that didn't involve this mandatory half-crouch. Then he would take her hand

and with the other offer a ring. She would try not to make too careful an appraisal of it and she hoped not to be disappointed: not with him but with the setting and size of the stones.

His reputation for being a good boy from a nice family, founders of Clumpus Towelling (Trade Only) Ltd, hung round his neck like a bright garland. His plumpness ruled him out as a rake, you only had to look at him to trust him. He had a dimple in his left-hand cheek when he smiled. He was going to make her a wonderful husband. He was not exciting but who wanted excitement? What she wanted was (eventually) a four-bedroom house in which each of their future three children would have their own room with an ottoman for toys and on the walls a painted frieze of ducks and lambs – a house right round the corner from her mother, popping in for morning coffee, dropping off the children to be babysat while she walked down to Allerton Road to have her twice-weekly shampoo and set. What better life could a girl hope for? It was *golden*.

Lionel waited until the day of her birthday before proposing. He was nineteen and a half. His father had got the ring wholesale from Monty Karshinsky. The choice of setting had been taken out of his hands. He looked at it and thought it seemed okay, but what would Bernice think?

Bernice screamed, nearly fainted. She genuinely couldn't be happier. Monty Karshinsky had come up with the goods: a three-stone, platinum-set sparkler which obliged by flashing in the sunshine streaming through the bay window of the lounge when she put it on. 'No good in Wales, sun's never out,' she said, smiling as he rose up from the carpet. They kissed, gently on the lips, he felt the lurking presence of her moist tongue behind her teeth and he jumped away.

Now he was on the way down the helter-skelter, he was plummeting towards married life by the time he was twenty. His future father-in-law was all bonhomie and cigars, his mother-in-law-to-be confiscated his fiancée and holed up with her in the bedroom making wedding plans. Only the best was good enough; Liverpool should remember such a wedding to the end of its days, even the goyem would take note. First of all, the service at Princes Road shul with the choir moaning out the prayers and the organ swelling. Then the reception at the Adelphi Hotel; you could not do better for quality and opulence. Lionel's mother Ida Clumpus embraced the wedding as if Princess Elizabeth and Prince Philip themselves were walking together towards married life.

They would not honeymoon abroad. 'What for?' said Morrie Clumpus. 'Abroad? That's where you're born or where they send you to get shot at.'

They would spend a week at a kosher hotel down south in Bournemouth, a resort with golden sands and an excellent reputation for table tennis facilities. Lia had acquired in a plain brown wrapper a guide to married life for her daughter. In childhood, her father had told her she had arrived in their family having been purchased in a shop, squalling babies lying on a shelf in their bassinettes, waiting to be chosen. 'And we chose *you*. We saw lots of other babies but you were the one we liked the best.' Bernice had hardly given reproduction a further thought since. She didn't mention the book to Lionel. She supposed his father must have given him something similar. After a few pages she gave up reading her copy; he would know what to do, he would take care of it. How bad could it be? What could a nice boy do to you that you wouldn't like?

It seemed to Lionel that something was bound to come along and prevent this relentless course of events, an iceberg would shortly be glimpsed from the bridge of the ship and the whole affair would be smashed up, sunk. Nothing so grandiose could possibly come about without major mishap. Yet here he was, standing in front of the bimah in Princes Road shul, wearing a tail coat and a top hat, waiting for Bernice to be powered up the aisle by her father's inexorable step. The atmosphere was charged, there had not been such a simcha since before the war, nothing so all-out as this, the uniting of two business interests and two respected families.

The air raid siren will go off, Lionel thought. It's got to. Then we'll run for the shelters and have a think later about what to do. They had both returned to Liverpool from Wales to see much of the

94

place flattened. The big church at the bottom of Leece Street was a shell, a roofless exoskeleton with saplings growing inside. The dock road was a shocker. If a bombing raid could not stop this wedding what could? Bernice changing her mind? Falling ill in the car on the way? Someone rising to their feet to object? But the siren only sounded now for testing, and the bridesmaids were already outside, his best man, Colin Grabman, was turning to smile enigmatically at him, patting his breast pocket for the ring. Upstairs in the ladies' gallery the women were rising to a pitch of excitement at the prospect of the first sight of The Dress, this capitalised wonder. The Clumpuses were out in full force, Bernice's uncle's family had come over from Leeds, the Polack boys commanded a bank of seats to make up the numbers on the Mendel side. The light from the stained-glass window was in his eyes, the lamps were bearing down on him, the organ swelled and there she was, or someone was, behind the netting veil, and Jossel advancing towards him with his daughter on his arm like a pilot boat on the river guiding a cargo ship into the safety of port.

Sitting at the top table a few hours later, Lionel looked out at a scene both familiar and phantasmagorical. There was his father, his arm round Jossel, cracking a slightly off-colour joke. There was Jossel's brother-in-law, Louis, a well-dressed man, whose suit sat suavely on his shoulders and whose tie was not yet spotted with grease stains and probably would not be. His wife, Bernice's Aunt Millie, a motherly looking woman but according to Bernice with a wild side. He had been subjected to a story about how she came to be married to Louis when he first came to call for his girlfriend at the house and sat uncomfortably in the lounge on the fake-French chairs upholstered in pale blue velvet. Next to Aunt Millie, her daughter, Bernice's cousin Paula, the oldest of the four bridesmaids, looking sulky. She had argued about the dress, the shoes, the way Bernice had demanded she wear her hair. 'Any girl,' Bernice had said, 'would give her eye teeth to be a bridesmaid and all she does is complain. Doesn't she get it? It's my day and my choices. She can take a back seat for a change, it will do her good not to be the centre of attention.'

95

And his mother-in-law, probably saying right now, 'I had a governess, you know.'

Out beyond the ranks of immediate relatives was the world of towelling, his father's most favoured clients and contacts. The hotel manager was present, the Clumpuses were suppliers of tea towels and dishcloths to the kitchens and hoping to get the big order for the hand and bath towels and washcloths upstairs in the guest rooms and suites. Next to Lionel, his new wife, looking, as they say, radiant, lit from within with a hectic, almost tubercular glow of accomplishment. The glassy chandeliers, the overpowering heat and cigarette smoke, the crowds of well-wishers, the first dance, his leather-shod foot tripping over her train and slightly ripping it – and was he happy? He supposed he was. He must be, for wasn't this what it was all about, what everything was tending to, the increase of the human race, mastery of the natural world? The band in white dinner jackets played the kind of tunes modern crooners sang. It all seemed syrupy to him, toned down, fake. But it was what Bernice had wanted and weddings were women's territory. The groom just had to turn up on time and go through the expected motions. The real test would come tonight up on the third floor where her negligee was laid out, and next to it his brand-new pyjamas bought from Jack Ralph's schmatte shop (everything wholesale, what fool paid retail prices?)

What should he make of these old people who came from foreign lands, who spoke in Jewy voices, who sentimentalised the world of Brownlow Hill? Should he admire their tremendous immigrant vitality, their imaginative leap to a new world? Or mark them down for not having made the trans-Atlantic hop? But these are not the thoughts of a nice boy. A nice boy is a future pillar of the community. A nice boy is not so modern as to deny where he came from – from these very people.

I am Lionel Clumpus, he thought, and this is my wife Bernice Clumpus, who says she does not want to be called Bernie, even affectionately, who tonight I shall carefully, tenderly ravish according to the secrets imparted to me by my father, including some

96

surprising information I had never considered, but which is guaranteed to deliver pleasure to my wife such as she has never dreamed of. This is called foreplay.

'But what will she be expecting?' he asked his father.

'She'll have a book that will explain everything.'

He felt sick.

So this is it, Paula thought. This is the end, this is how it comes towards you like the finishing line in a race, and all you can do is swerve to get away from it. You have to swerve or this is what you'll end up with – some 'nice boy' who looks like a doll and if you took his trousers down there'd be nothing there. Though she barely knew what was *supposed* to be there, a year younger than her cousin and her mother had told her nothing. For what, Mina had asked her husband, does she even *need* to know? 'I didn't know a thing and everything worked out for us, didn't it?'

Paula watched the proceedings with critical attention in her terrible dress, baby pink, a length of flounce and frilling, huge puff sleeves, satin shoes with a Louis heel, a garland of artificial flowers pinned to her hair. One of the Polack cousins had asked her to foxtrot; she had told him to shove off. He had backed away as if shot. Eventually she had been persuaded to dance with Sidney Schwartz, Lionel's cousin, Brylcreemed and full-chested in his dinner jacket. He had been in Berlin after the war with the Allied Control Commission doing what he called de-Nazification. It involved interviewing Germans who wanted to get back into public life – teachers, judges, policemen, newspaper owners – and being satisfied that they had all been part of the Resistance.

'A huge organisation dwarfing the Nazi Party. Everyone was part of it; I don't know how Hitler found the men to fight the war. A mystery.' It had made him view human nature with a droll disbelief.

Everyone called him Ringo because he had the gift of the gab. 'My Sidney can run rings round anyone, even the Nazis,' his father Mottie said, full of pride, 'and he's a university man, you know? He doesn't have any letters after his name because the war came along and invited him to a higher calling, but he *could* have. That's another thing I'll always have against the Krauts, that my boy never got to graduate in cap and gown.'

'I was Ringo *before* Ringo,' Sidney would be forced to say in later years. 'I was Ringo when little Ritchie Starkey was in short trousers. I'm not saying he got the name from me but word gets around, it gets around.'

Over his shoulder Paula saw poor Lionel Clumpus like a pigeon frantically beating heavy wings against the confines of a cage.

'No good can come of this,' she said to Ringo precociously. 'You would be just as married in a smart navy suit and this season's hat. You would look more ...' She groped for the word. 'Chick.'

Ringo was impressed. The girl had class and pep. She was a bit young for him, but he liked what he saw. He needed additional clarification. He asked her if she wanted to go outside for a smoke. He had a packet of Gauloises in his pocket.

'They're French, be careful,' he said, 'they're strong. They might go straight to your head.'

They looked out from the grandeur of the steps into the post-war world.

'You're right about the dress,' he said. And he began to speak knowledgeably of peplums and hemlines.

'What line are you in?'

'What do you think? I came back from Germany and went straight into the family schmatte business.'

Paula tried to take him in. He had a *presence*, she thought, he was a good-looking boy, he could give Clark Gable a run for his money when it came to a moustache, but he also had an accent, a Liverpool accent. What had it all been for, learning to speak like the princesses and studying art with her father at the Walker? He had travelled, but who hadn't? Even her brothers had tramped across Europe, seeing ruined towns and liberating farmhouses. Then had come home and settled. She would not settle.

'Oh, Ringo,' she said. But whatever she was about to tell him was quelled by a rising tide of nicotine nausea and she ran into the hotel, too late not to be sick on her dress.

16

Paula claimed she always knew something was wrong, just from looking at poor Lionel standing there *drowned* by his top hat. She could have told them not to go through with it, but who would have listened to her? She was just the younger cousin, the tormented bridesmaid; they'd have thought she was jealous. Lying on the floor of the hotel toilet after being sick, she was certain that something was off about the whole business. She did not know what was at the bottom of it all, but still she was sure that the marriage was doomed. It was something about her uncle in his dinner jacket and dicky bow, his hair slicked back with pomade, smiling with the air of a man who has just won big on the football pools and is mentally counting his winnings. There was more going on there than the satisfaction of a proud daddy. And Lionel out in the lobby with his best man's arm around his shoulder giving him a little squeeze as if to gee him up for what lay ahead upstairs and the rest of the night. But the next day Paula forgot all about it. She returned to her secretarial school and wrote lines and lines of Pitman shorthand, preparing her for the life to come as a helpmeet to management.

The happy couple, and she supposed they probably were happy for a few days, got back from Bournemouth like innocent babies after a week of playing ping-pong and crazy golf, to find the family home in uproar, Jossel gone, Lia alternately screaming or sniffing smelling salts. That was what Paula was told; she didn't go there herself, the house was completely off-limits. She had to overhear to find out what had happened and why Mina was on the phone all the time and Louis was so distracted he left the house one morning with no hat and no tiepin.

The boys, Bernice's brothers, one in the chamois business, one already qualified as a dentist and doing fillings at the Fiveways, one in business with his wife's father, put up a wall of solidarity and outrage round their mother who two weeks after it happened was still understandably hysterical and was not taking events with any kind of calm equanimity. *What he has done to me!* she screamed. And later, more tiresomely, and repetitively, *I'm the only one . . .* Paula assumed she meant she'd been left all alone, but it wasn't that, she was terrified. She had a status now which at that time she shared with no one else she knew: the abandoned wife and, to come, the divorcee.

Jossel had left her, and not just for one of the other wives of the community but for a shiksa, for the person the family always called 'the girl'. Margaret McGlone the office manager. She was pretty, lively, willing, had proved very willing because Jossel had been carrying on with her since 1934, had promised her he would leave Lia the minute he got his daughter married off. Men say these things, they're always saying it, but in his own mind he was as good as his word. He pushed Bernice into marriage as soon as she was eighteen years old so he could say he'd done right by her, made her a wedding that would be the talk of Liverpool, which was true in more senses than one because even the Catholics on Scottie Road knew all about the aftermath. There hadn't been such a scandal since the abdication and Jossel also talked about 'the woman I love' as if he was giving up a throne, which it turned out he was if you counted being pushed out of the business. But he wanted to be happy. 'What can you do?' Mina said. 'If you ask me, he knew he'd made a mistake marrying Lia by the time we got to Liverpool. If it hadn't been for her we'd have gone steerage to America and been living another life by now.' And her brother would not have been called up, and he would not have met Louis on the battlefield and who knows who her husband might have been?

And while the fallout lasted the rest of Jossel's life, what everyone agreed, even if it was between gritted teeth, was that Margaret made him a wonderful wife. They took up ballroom dancing together, they had *fun*, which nobody had ever had with Lia who wouldn't do anything just for the pleasure of it but only if there was some social advantage. But when Louis felt he had to completely cut Jossel out of the company he had to go back to doing what he started out with when they came over from Riga, which was itinerant bookkeeping. Nobody would speak to them. He was left with Margaret's family who were awestruck at what had fallen into their laps. He would come round with black market cigarettes and they talked about the war, he had been in the Home Guard protecting the docks so he expressed great sympathy for what they had had to go though on Scotland Road, the Blitz hurt them worse than anyone. He remembered digging out a young child, a little girl, and there was just her head left of her, her torso was yards away, torn apart by the blast. He wept at the memory. In the end they were prepared to forgive him for being a Christ-killer old enough to be Margaret's father.

The merger of the two companies never went ahead. The Clumpuses didn't want the association, even with the pariah pushed out. The only person who stood by Jossel was Mina. She would meet him in town for morning coffee at the Lyceum on Bold Street and occasionally she would entertain the pair of them for afternoon tea at the house, with the Madeira tablecloth on the table and the best china and napkins, making a point that they were welcome. Louis would always make sure he was out. It was one thing to have had his life saved on the battlefield and a great story to go with it, but everyone in the chamois business in Liverpool and Leeds agreed that Jossel could only be a liability.

Before those visits Mina told Paula she must be on her best behaviour and make sure she made them both feel welcome, particularly Margaret, because she would be out of her depth and it wouldn't hurt to act graciously. For Margaret might have expected when she finally got her man that she'd be wearing the latest styles from Cripps and George Henry Lee and Henderson's, but they were at first badly off while Jossel was scraping together a living out of odds and ends. It turned out the bulk of his income would come from the little flyblown shops and pubs and chippies on Scottie Road, because there was a belief that a Jewish bookkeeper had all kinds of tricks up his sleeve and you'd only have to declare tuppence-halfpenny to the taxman.

The doorbell would ring and there they were, not even on the step inside the porch, but out on the path by the rockery as if they might be shooed away like pedlars. Jossel would be holding his hat in his hands, a supplicant, smiling that heavy-lipped smile, but his trouser cuffs had been darned. Margaret had a hat with glass cherries pinned to it, and immediately Paula noticed it was quite out of style. Then they came in, he shuffled slightly, and she was holding his arm in the crook of hers. And Paula knew then that whatever was going to happen to her in her life, it wouldn't be *this*, this air of knowing that they might not be welcome, could be rejected, turned away. The community had destroyed this couple, humiliated them and made them feel unwanted, and to Paula it wasn't fair, they didn't deserve it. Sitting with a cup and saucer balanced on her knee over a linen napkin, she experienced the first stab of longing to get out of there, to get away. That the whole place, the Jewish community of Brownlow Hill that was decanting itself into suburban Allerton and Childwall, was claustrophobic, smothering. It would kill her if she let it.

And yet, it was so obviously a very happy marriage. They did love each other deeply and intimately. Margaret was a breath of fresh air, and she always kept her figure. Even if they were cheap, clothes looked good on her as they did not on Mina or Lia. She even tried to keep a kosher home, which wasn't easy when the Jewish shops didn't want to serve her and out of respect she used to wait, and go when they were just closing and all the best was already gone.

Mina said, 'How can I give him up? Blood is strong, blood is the strongest! He did a terrible thing to Lia, nobody can say otherwise, but I will entertain him like I always have, and the girl too.'

So they came to the house and Margaret did her best, and commented on the line of toby jugs in the hall and where did Mina get them, and how lovely her home was, she'd always wanted to live out here in the south of the city, where there were tree-lined streets such as you never saw in town.

Jossel said, 'Well, you know soon everyone will live out this way, the corporation is building brand-new estates and factories so no one has to work on the docks any more by that oily brown river.'

'Where?' Margaret said.

'Halewood; it's going to be quite something.'

Margaret said she'd go and powder her nose, to give brother and sister a few minutes together alone. Mina started talking quickly in Yiddish and Jossel just sat there, taking it like a round of bullets, and he nodded, and said, 'I know, I know.'

But then she said in English, 'Lia was always a pain in the neck,' and turning to her daughter, 'Paula, you never heard that.'

17

A letter arrived at the house. Mina had great hopes of letters in those days. There was always the possibility that something would come from the Red Cross containing information about the family back there, on the other side. Nothing had been heard of Rivka and Solly since before the war. Louis said they could be anywhere, still in the Soviet Union, or a DP camp in Europe, waiting to be processed to go to America or Palestine. She should not lose hope of eventually hearing something.

So a stamp and an envelope was a cause for excitement when it dropped on the sisal doormat with the afternoon delivery and lay face down beneath the toby jugs, where Mina picked it up and propped it up by the morning-room mantelpiece clock.

It was addressed to Louis. When he got home, he opened it with his silver-plated letter opener, a birthday present from the boys.

'Anything nice?' Mina said.

'Read it yourself.'

Polack

As your name infers you are a Jew. We don't want any more parasites in this Country.

Get Out!!!

Otherwise your address will be entered in our list for destroying.

We, the Anti-Jewish Organisation, have, and still are compiling, a list of the Jewish property to be destroyed.

Take Warning!!!

Signed 'Anti-Jew'

'Well, the handwriting is nice,' Mina said. 'Very fine, what do they call it? Penmanship. Must be a person who works in an office.'

Louis stayed on his feet, taking care not to lean his elbow against the mantelpiece. Sitting down to take in the contents of such a letter was not the way of a man. A soldier stays upright when confronted with the enemy, he draws his gun. The contents didn't surprise him, but the question was: who lay behind it? Was it one little pisser or was there an actual organisation? It was hard to tell.

'I fought a war for those people,' he said. 'I nearly died on the battlefield and this is the thanks I get for it. Disgraceful.'

It did not occur to either of them to go to the police. The police were as bad, maybe worse. They had truncheons instead of fountain pens. Neither of them felt like eating but Mina laid the table and put out a bowl of cholent, which sent savoury messages to Louis' brain. He had thought of a million schemes to get his own back, but the anonymity of the letter precluded all of them. He thought he might write his own letter, to the *Liverpool Echo*, saying did decent people know what their neighbours had to put up with? But then he would have to sign it and that would only attract more trouble. Masticating a slice of strudel, he had a brainwave.

'They don't want us here, they don't want us to be Englishmen. So to hell with them, let's be double English. For Paula's sake, if nothing else. Why should she go out into the world with a *name* hanging round her neck, dragging her down?'

'She'll get married, she'll change her name soon enough.'

'No I won't,' Paula said, coming down the stairs from her bedroom, where she had been practising eyeliner flicks. 'I'm never getting married; well, not for ages. It might be as late as thirty.'

'Someone will grab you long before that,' Louis said, 'but in the meantime, we're finished with Polack. Let's find something new. What's a nice name? What's a name that doesn't get us into trouble? Smith? Jones?'

'Churchill,' Mina said sarcastically. 'Can't go far wrong there.'

'Not Attlee,' said Louis, who didn't like the bald fellow with his rules and regulations.

'Phillips,' said Paula, 'like the prince.'

'Perfect!' Mina and Louis cried together.

Louis knew no one could mistake him and his wife for anything but Jews, the same with the boys, but their daughter was another matter. She could pass. He wanted her to pass. She was an experiment: how far could a Brownlow Hill-born Jewish girl go with the right clothes, hair, accent and name? She had learned to talk from the wireless, from the BBC, listening in those days was an elocution class from start to finish. She could do anything, go anywhere. And that's what he wanted for her, she could marry a knight of the realm as far as he was concerned, didn't even have to *be* Jewish, which was a big hurdle for him to be able to leap but he had leapt it in his mind because Paula was his treasure, his princess. She became Paula Phillips, they all became Phillips, but no one used that name in Liverpool, it was just for forms and what happened when she went to London.

PART TWO

18

London. A bed linen company with its headquarters on Kingsway, which was not quite Bloomsbury or Fitzrovia. A nondescript commercial highway leading down to Aldwych and the Strand then to the great dirty pointless Thames. There was nothing Paula thought of as nice there. She had position and poise. She was personal assistant to the managing director. His name was Arthur Topping, like an exclamation from a character in a girls' school story. But it was all sheets, pillowcases, bolster covers; a mountain of sleep-inducing cotton. Mr Topping had taken her out to lunch on her first day and congratulated her on the excellent reference from the secretarial college, 'who have sent us so many wonderful girls over the years. But a friendly warning, if you don't mind me saying so, please try not to fraternise with the typing pool. They are all very jealous, hoping for a promotion. Silly fillies. I never promote from that gaggle, they don't have the polish. *You* have polish. Despite being, ha ha, a LiverPUDlian. A puddle, do you get it?'

She ate her sandwich at her desk alone and aloof. Colleagues moved across the office floors in segregated groupings. She was probably best organised as an addendum to accounts, but accounts found her too new to fit in, too recently varnished. Loneliness is never interesting, it is an absence and a failure. It's a cancer that invades the other cells. Stay lonely long enough and you forget to brush your hair or apply your warpaint. Even taking a bath becomes besides the point. After a few weeks Paula was afraid that if she did not meet anyone soon she would start talking to herself.

If she went and sat in a café she might strike up a conversation and meet someone nice but at other tables people were engaged in social interaction of different kinds, they had matters to discuss. Old friends meeting up, couples having a row, business associates talking trade. There life was. But never anyone nice by themselves, just sex pests and, today, a fusty middle-aged woman at the next table who gave off an odour of mothballs. Who was also wishing she had a friend to chat to, but her friends had gone missing in various ways: moved abroad, been killed in the war, married, taken permanent refuge in county towns and had not come back – because why would you when London was as dreary as this, and it was cold and coal was in short supply and the dampness of the city drove you mad. The girl at the next table was drinking a cup of coffee. She was smoking a cigarette and looking around, in hope, no doubt, of finding a young man to talk to. But there were no young men. She didn't realise that it was the wrong place, the wrong neighbourhood for the types she was on the lookout for. Poor green young thing. From the provinces, presumably. There was a web of isolation in the city and they had both got caught in it. One had to steel oneself not to come out of one's flat until after the lunchtime crowd had left. One only wanted a cup of coffee and company. Eating lunch was too much of a preoccupation, one could not strike up a conversation over chops and rissoles.

She leaned across her handbag. 'Isn't London *terrible*? Doesn't it make your heart sink, looking round to see everything so worn down and everyone so worn out, also? I came back to town from the country – my people have a house in Devon – and it was such a shock. Nothing like the old days.'

'I don't remember the old days. We came once before the war when I was a child and stayed at the Regent's Palace Hotel, I had an ice-cream sundae. It came in a glass and I had to kneel up on my chair to reach to get the spoon in. That's what I remember of London. It seemed very glamorous.'

'You'd be lucky to find an ice-cream sundae now. How old are you, dear?'

'I'm twenty.'

'Marvellous. I wish I were twenty again. Such a carefree age. You must be out at parties every single night, I know I was.' For she did not want the girl to think she had always been like this, sitting over a cup of coffee and a currant bun in a fur coat that had survived the Blitz, lost and forgotten in a London wardrobe, a cloud of wings as she shook it from the hanger.

But she doubted that Paula went to any parties, or she would not be alone in a café on Southampton Row in the middle of a Saturday afternoon, looking rather too carefully dressed, as if she had quite deliberately and with art put an outfit together to attract attention, to be noticed by someone. There was a hunger in her face, not for seed cake or chops, but for company. One could kill for it, one knew that oneself.

Lost girl. She would invite her home and make a friend of her, they might have outings together to the department stores and a concert at the Wigmore Hall. They might advise each other on little feminine things. She would introduce her to her nephews in Torbay. To have a young protégée might be a tonic.

She rattled on. Wasn't the clothes ration *mean* and thank heavens for the beautiful jackets and stoles and evening gowns and day dresses she had from before the war, all in the very best materials, no rayon, real silk, 'Because there used to be a marvellous little woman in St John's Wood who kept a shop, a strong accent from somewhere. Austria, perhaps? Well, I never asked. She was a very brisk lady, neat as a pin, standing on high heels all day, running around the floor gathering things up for you, quick-witted too, knew the value of everything but she had the most wonderful eye for what suited her customers and how to put an outfit together, the gloves, the hat, shoes, all of a piece, very clever and sharp and one couldn't help oneself, when one was standing in front of the mirror and it all looked just so. "See if you take a fancy to this," she'd say, and one was weak and couldn't help oneself, she'd just wrap it all up and off I'd go with another lovely thing to wear. Because, you see, I went to many parties back in those days, before I was exiled to bloody Devon. Would you like to come home with me and take a look at my treasures? It's not far, hardly ten minutes' walk.'

Paula had nothing else to do. They walked down into Fitzrovia. The stairs had an eighteenth-century air about them of maids hurtling up and down with tea trays then retiring to the attic to sleep. The woman's place was an indeterminate stage between a flat and a bedsit: a sitting room, a bedroom, a bathroom along the hall and a hotplate next to the dressing table. The curtains were of a once-good claret-coloured brocade, the tassels moulted silk hairs. The air was stale and the ashtrays unemptied. The general atmosphere seemed to suggest mouldiness. She had hoped to enter the woman's social set, be invited to the parties of the people who used to give them and must now be doing so again, but looking round she thought it unlikely that any cards were dispatched to this shabby address. There were none on the mantelpiece, a place where, she had learned at the secretarial college, formal invitations, 'stiffies', were displayed. There was nothing stiff here. Only limp lifelessness and dust and motes of long-settled talcum powder and cigarette ash and a badly made bed, the eiderdown awry. It was Paula's first introduction to failure and middle age. She hated it. I will never be like this, she thought, even if I have to go home to Liverpool and live like cousin Bernice round the corner from my mother. For she was young and beautiful and she was certain she would stay that way for ever.

The woman pulled out a trunk from beneath the bed and removed one by one her precious children, with a commentary on their provenance and when she had worn it and who she had danced with and who had said, 'Oh how lovely, now where exactly is that mysterious little woman you keep up your sleeve? Do tell.' So many Maudes and Hugos and Daphnes. The costumes were stained beneath the arms, they stank of heavy Parisian perfumes long gone rancid.

'Now why don't you try something on? You have a perfect figure, anything that doesn't quite fit can be taken in. Just tell me how much you think they're worth and we can come to a nice agreement, I'm sure. You'll be quite ready for all your parties. Oh, what a lovely time you are going to have, I quite envy you.' And she stood far too close to Paula, pale eyes, their colour washed out almost to nothing, parchment skin in creases and folds and a dab of badly placed rouge on each cheek. 'Oh, I have been so unhappy in Devon, you've no idea. I ran away even though there was nothing to come back *for*, d'you see? They made my life such a misery, but that's what happens when you're just a cousin and not one of the daughters of the house. Still, we soldier on, don't we? All we good little soldiers.'

Paula gave her two guineas for a set of diamanté clips and ran down the stairs and left while her back was turned. That was one café she could never go back to.

The following week, under orders, she went for Friday-night dinner in Finsbury Park with the uncle on her father's side who was not in chamois leathers. He was something in brochures and leaflets, printing tickets.

'The competition is cut-throat,' he said, drawing a finger across his jelly-neck. He was nothing like her father, there was a coarseness there which had bypassed Louis.

His wife Ida had invited friends over to drink the soup and eat the brisket and ease into the plum kuchen and 'to hear our niece talk like she's on the wireless'. One of them was a taxi driver. He said, 'I've had Ivor Novello in the back of my cab; he talked just like you, but he's a pansy.'

These Jews, she thought. Why should I mix with them? What do they have to offer? I, who speak like Princess Elizabeth, should pretend to enjoy their jokes and sympathise with their hardships?

Post-war London. Vast, filthy, exhausted, anonymous, indifferent. She had made a mistake from which the only recovery was defeat.

19

A week later, a different encounter. Standing in a queue waiting to enter the Conway Hall to attend an academic lecture on Propp's *Morphology of the Folktale*, Paula saw a small drab man staring at her as if (quite understandable a misapprehension) she was waiting in the wrong line, with diamanté clips on the lapels of her coat: chic, frivolous, uninterested in Soviet studies or the principles of formalism. Now he was approaching her, was introducing himself, a brief wolfish smile, his hand outstretched, and her own hand reaching abruptly up to her face, surprised, shocked, taken off guard, touching her mouth, then tentatively offering the hand to him in return, as though she thought she might not get it back. They stepped away and left the queue altogether and walked over to the edge of the square and began a discussion.

'Yes, it was many years ago but I remember your uncle like it was yesterday,' he was saying, 'the type of Jew with autumn in his heart and spectacles on his nose. Your mother was nothing like that, she was – what do you call it in this age of electricity? – a live wire.'

'Autumn in his . . . ?'

'An expression. Not mine. A forgotten Soviet writer.'

'Why forgotten?'

'We don't talk about that.'

'I honestly can't imagine my uncle as a melancholic, I mean he ... Well, for example, he and his new wife go to tango classes, she keeps him on his toes.' She laughed.

Itzik, the long-lost Mendel brother, the devil child of long-ago Riga, was himself immune to surprises having seen everything. So Jossel had taken another wife, they went dancing, he would get to the bottom of it in a minute, but she was asking, 'Was it you who sent me the invitation? To this dreary-sounding lecture?'

'It was me, yes.'

'And what have you to do with it? Are you something to do with a university?'

She had an arch and challenging manner, she seemed to him seventy-five per cent fake. She should live in Buckingham Palace with a voice like that, Mina Mendel's girl, who spoke like the class of persons he categorised as the Parasites. Now he had seen everything.

He could not precisely answer her question. Not now, not yet. He wanted her to think he was in a more exalted position than the one he actually occupied. As part of his duties at the embassy he regularly found himself having to attend these lectures, his purpose not to introduce the speaker or lead the discussion or greet the guests or offer round the meagre refreshments which the guests had hoped might be vodka and caviar but turned out to be milkless tea and concrete biscuits. He was not fostering Anglo-Soviet cultural relations through the medium of scholarly investigations into Russian folklore, the simple narratives of the peasantry with their elements of superstition and magic and absence of any didactic lessons in the service of the People. His job was to keep an eye on the audience, to listen to the questions they asked, to check their names against Party membership, and note any bourgeois deviations.

Itzik Mendel was an official snitch.

In his snitch role, with access to resources available from a network of spies and connections, he had discovered, through a Party cell in Liverpool, that there was a Mendel family from Riga, a brother and sister who had arrived together in 1914, and

Mina had three children and the daughter had recently moved to London to take a secretarial position with a firm of bedding suppliers. He would not turn up on her doorstep unannounced. He gave himself a chance to make a reconnoitre first, observing her in the queue. He had wished he had a more glamorous occasion to issue an invitation for, but the embassy did not do glamorous, or if it did, he had no input into their guest list. So it was Propp's *Morphology of the Folktale*, a lecture delivered by a comrade from the University of Hull.

He was interested in her. No particular reason, but bad little brother Itzik who had leaned over the banisters in the house in Riga and overheard the conversation, who knew all about the Bolshevik boys in the forest – had followed, found the abandoned mushroom basket – was curious to see how the story had turned out and whether there was any advantage to be obtained. He had sent the invitation only wanting to take a look at her, had been surprised by the ritzy-looking girl as easy to pick out as a giraffe in an identify parade composed of piglets. She must have known she did not belong, with her perfume and her high heels, like a piece of reproduction furniture knocked up by a cabinet maker in the East End.

They entered the hall just as the lecture was beginning. He took up his position with his small notebook and his excellent memory for faces. She sat and listened with little comprehension, her mind wandering off to the knowledge of a new uncle.

A young girl sets out on a journey, the story begins. The adventurer will confront many hardships and difficulties. She will reclaim her lost inheritance. She will recapture the castle. But this is not true. In folk tales, young girls never set out on a journey or a quest, they are passive, they are waiting, and in later years, Paula would admit, she had been waiting, and this was how her story started.

20

Inside the Conway Hall the faces of the rows of men and women, shabby, careworn, were now lit up as if they were facing the rising sun in the form of the speaker, who sent greetings from Comrade Propp himself with whom he was in regular correspondence. At these words the satellite planets shone even brighter in the reflected glow; it was incredible, Itzik thought, what a lecture could bring out in these uninteresting souls who had formed long, eager queues waiting to get in. A man with a piece of ham wrapped in newspaper in his pocket, a woman reapplying the stub of a lipstick to her chapped and flaking lips for it was a clammy evening when the leaves were slimy underfoot. And there, idling on high heels, the elegant figure of his niece Paula, whom he had summoned from her bedsit, sparkling around the lapels.

So far Vladimir Propp with his formalist insistence on structure had survived the incessant change in fortunes of the Soviet intellectual classes. The folk tale, with its origins deep in the oral histories of the peasantry, contained elements of magic and talking animals, it was childlike and primitive also, but the reason everyone knew these stories: they heard them on their mother's knee, so even the most rigid of doctrinarians became enchanted or lachrymose and retreated back into infantile memories. Yes, everyone liked a fairy story, as they were called here in England, and was able to immediately recognise the structural elements that bound them together. It was easy to understand Propp and far less of a headache than Hegel or Marx's *Theories of Surplus Value*, which personally bored Itzik, who was of the type who sees any political philosophy through the lens of what is in it for himself.

Every folk tale is one great bourgeois deviation, a blueprint for personal advancement and survival rather than the collective endeavour of the Masses. It begins with the departure of the hero from his home with a purpose. Now we have an adventure. Then the donor turns up, an agent like a talking bird or some such, who tests or interrogates. The hero is given a magical prop: a bean that grows a stalk that reaches the sky, or a hen that lays golden eggs. Next the hero is guided to a location which will change everything ... On this all goes, the villain is punished, the hero marries the princess and ascends to a throne. The end.

The ending is always happy, the hero is never thwarted, though he may be discouraged. The task will be accomplished.

Standing in the back of the hall in his double-breasted suit, with that smile of complicity which hoodwinked people into thinking that they shared a delicious secret (if only they could remember what it was), Itzik raked the room harrying and winnowing like an agricultural implement.

After it was over he came and took her arm. 'We won't be missed if we leave now,' he said. 'Or do you want to stay for the reception, though I wouldn't recommend it? It's just tea. Unless you placed some hope in it as a social occasion?'

She had. She had hoped to meet young people but the ones she had queued up with, bundled-up pamphlets ruining the line of their jacket pockets, were untidy in their dress. There were no intellectuals in the Polack family unless you counted the rabbi, they were all members of the aspiring bourgeoisie, immigrants, not exiles or émigrés. Uncle and niece walked across the square.

'That was ...'

'Yes? You enjoyed it?'

'Up to a point, I suppose. He did go *on*, I mean, two hours, and all the questions. I've really no idea what they meant by them, they seemed to be trying to, oh, I don't know, prove a point. Yes, that was it. They all had tricks up their sleeves one way or another, as if they wished to be noticed, to be cleverer than the lecturer. Though I liked the man who asked about chess, why the Soviet Union is so keen on the game with its kings and queens and knights and clerics and the pawns, who are the peasantry, sent out like cannon fodder. And when you send people away to camps they're made to carve chess sets. I thought it was a good question.'

'I know that man, a troublemaker.'

'But what kind of trouble?' She laughed. 'You people are such sticklers for always having to say the right thing. And think it too, I suppose. Are you going to put *him* in a camp?'

'We need not speak of camps, they are largely a myth.'

His English wasn't bad; they had sent him on a language course before he arrived. But his accent was that of Mina and Jossel, she could hear her family in him, it made her homesick and she clung to his forearm as they crossed the square; she was an inch taller than him. So strange to share her blood with this funny little man and all the questions she would be obliged eventually to ask about the unknown family whose letters to her parents had stopped dead just before the war. Things had been chaotic after the peace, people moving about all over the place, trying to get home, when sometimes there was no home to return to, and maybe that had happened to Rivka and Solly; they were trying to make their way back to Riga and were still in transit. They would hear from them sooner or later. The candle flames burned in a glass on the man-telpiece, 'to remember my mother and father, olovashalom', Mina said, 'though I never heard when exactly they were taken from us or where they are buried or whether they even had a proper Jewish burial or—' And she could not stop herself from breaking down into tears that she had run away and left them, never thinking they would not somehow be reunited because they were all she had ever known. 'That good-for-nothing ship.' But no yahrzeit candles for

Rivka and Solly, they were young and strong and had no reason not to be alive.

They reached the door of a public house. 'They know me here. We will find a warm welcome.' The barman nodded as they entered, it was hardly a cry of greeting, she thought. Poor Uncle Itzik, thinking people liked him. The bar had an air of waiting for more interesting customers, ones who spent more freely and gave the place the atmosphere of somewhere you might want to go to have a good time. It was the very first public house she had entered and it seemed like everywhere else she had been in London, not all it was cracked up to be. She had come to the lecture straight from work in her office suit, only adding the diamanté clips as she came down in the lift to the street.

He ordered himself a whisky and she asked for a gin and It.

So this was it, what all the years of waiting had led to, and the learning to type and take shorthand at the secretarial finishing school and the acceptance of a position in London which came directly from the proprietor of the school itself, who had 'my connections'. A stifling evening followed by a cocktail of sorts in a dingy pub in the company of a gnome-like individual who claimed to be her relation from beyond the seas. And probably was, unless it was a case of mistaken identity. She had escaped from suburbia for *this*? I am green, she thought, I know I am, I've been nowhere really and seen almost nothing, but *honestly*. Could there be a deadlier evening?

The lecture had started at seven, it was now a quarter past nine. I'll give him half an hour, she thought. Then she would return to her bedsit with the wireless and her library book and a hot-water bottle and the silk-shaded lamp that cast a sulphur glow over the pages. Wait for something better to turn up, surely it had to? She turned her attention to him while thinking of a hat she had seen in a window. It had a bottle-green feather which stood erect like a small flagpole.

'I remember your mother very well and the day she ran off to the forest to be with her boyfriend, or boyfriends, shall I say. Who knows how many she was attached to?'

'I beg your pardon?' she said, stopping herself from blurting out the common *What?* She must not be thought of as common, as her brothers Harry and Benny were. She could not afford to be mistaken in her class.

'The boys, the Bolshevik boys, she never told you? She was a great activist, until my dear brother dragged her away from that danger.'

'I think you'll find you are quite wrong about that. *Quite* wrong.' She managed the last two words in imitation of that air of condescension only the English upper classes can pull off. And didn't, she thought, do a bad job.

'But I hear she is a little bit of a socialist. That is her reputation.'

She could not remember when she had not known about the forest. It was only a story to her, a fairy story to fall asleep to, and a slim thread holding together the past in the *hame* to her mother's peculiar political tendencies. Always on the side of the underdog, full of pity when she heard of the suffering of others, full of fire when others rose up against their chains. When Hitler opened his second front, she said, '*Now* he'll get what's coming to him. The Soviet soldier is unbeatable. I knew the Bolsheviks, I mean the originals, right back at the beginning when we still had the tsar. They were fine young boys. I don't say they were right about everything but, you know, in their *hearts* they were good. To each according to his need, from each according to his ability. That is the golden rule. Does that sound bad to you? What's there to argue with? But life has painted me into a corner, life has made me what I started out as, a bourgeois. What can I do?'

Paula was exasperated. There was a finality to her next words as if she'd won the argument, like the chess question man.

'Well yes, a socialist who collects *toby jugs.*'

'And what are toby jugs, please?'

'Well, they are funny little men with hollows where their heads should be and ... Oh, why are we talking about toby jugs, they're hideous, and she has willow-pattern plates, ghastly things.'

'A mother and father do not necessarily tell the child everything. The mother and father have a responsibility to protect the child from harsh reality. Maybe your mother all this time is a secret sleeper cell for our country.'

'What on earth is a sleeper cell? It must be very secret because I've never heard of it.'

He was enjoying talking to her. He had had no idea what line he would spin her when they finally met. Her denials were beginning to sketch out a rough portrait of his sister, who had succumbed, it seemed, to the most ordinary of possible outcomes, neither in the Soviet Union nor in America but in this porridge land, this beige country in the middle which flattered itself into thinking it had won the war. Its self-aggrandising myths riled him. They told him they had suffered. They didn't know the meaning of the word. He hated all of them. They were not fully human. Only a person who had lived through the blockade was a real person, someone who had seen everything. He walked among them as if they were a fog. Unreal, insubstantial. Yet here he was, he had been assigned.

But oblivious to his loathing, Paula went on talking about her mother. 'How she and my father get on I've no idea because they have *nothing* in common, and how they met is such a well-worn family story, you must have heard it, hasn't everybody? No? Well . . . ' And she rattled off the account of the battlefield, of her father's near death, of him arriving at the door with the carnation in his lapel to woo her.

'Some story,' said Itzik, who felt drawn back, for a moment, into a long-lost real world he remembered. 'What I find the most surprising about it is my brother's role. He was always such a dreamy type.'

'Yes, everyone says that, but I suppose the war must have knocked that out of him. It was before I was born and I don't remember him any other way.'

She told next the story of the wedding and its consequences for those concerned. Itzik listened carefully.

'What a mamzer!' he said. 'His wife must be heartbroken, and the poor girl going through what she went through. And now he is an outcast; I'd never have known.'

He did know, it was his business to know, the Liverpool comrades had filled him in on everything. But the way she told the story was something else, this svelte girl in what he broadly recognised as fashionable clothes, smoking her cigarette like an amateur with no browning round the index finger as his was brown all the way down to the second knuckle, her air of having seen it all, but between the lines she had seen almost nothing. Where did she fit in? He had no idea, yet.

'But you,' she said eventually, 'what's your position?'

'In relation to . . . ?'

'Your position at the embassy? Are *you* a spy?'

'No, I am not a spy. Our mission is quite open. We would like to bring England under our sphere of influence but it must be done the English way. Which means the introduction of a Soviet system may not be necessary. An intermediary form of socialism could be enough.'

'Such as the government we have now? How convenient.'

'Are you interested in politics?'

'Not in the slightest.'

'What do you think of your king?'

'What should I think? He's just there, like wallpaper.'

'Don't you think it's unfair that he should sit in his palace with his gold goblets and gold forks and priceless paintings on the wall while the people starve?'

'Who is starving? I'm not.'

Now the first members of the Conway Hall audience were entering the pub, still talking about the lecture, about absentation, interdiction, departure, first function of the donor. They gasped through pints standing at the bar, unrefreshed by embassy tea and dry, dusty biscuits.

'Well,' she said, 'no one can say your evening hasn't been quite the success.'

'What do you mean?'

'Look at everyone, they're still discussing it all. I suppose he could have gone on all night and some of them would still be there, hanging on his every word. Wait till I tell Mummy and Daddy where I've been and who I have met, they'll never believe it.'

'And when will you tell them?'

'I expect I will ring them tomorrow night; it will be a surprise, they normally expect my calls on Thursdays.'

'But why ring? Why not save your sixpences and send them a letter?'

'Well, Daddy worries, he needs to hear my voice to know I'm still alive. There's a phone box downstairs, it's quite convenient.'

'Yes, but you will have so much tell them! You will run out of change. No, a letter is best. And when you receive an answer we can meet for coffee and you can show it to me. I am very excited at how my brother and sister take the news.'

'Yes,' she said, 'I'll bet you are.'

Yet I wonder, she thought, why you didn't write to them yourself, your long-lost— But at that moment a young man approached the table.

21

'And who do we have here, Comrade Mendel?'

'This is what you call a niece, Mr Quinn, the child of my sister I have not seen for many years. Flesh of my flesh, blood of my blood. Can you believe it? I hope you did not think she is a *girl-friend*, ha ha.'

'Never entered my head.'

'You think she has better taste? So do I. Did you enjoy the lecture? And thank you for coming, by the way; I was hoping I would see you.'

'A little dry and formalist. The French are taking things in another direction these days. It all seemed rather old hat. And you, Miss ... ?'

'Phillips. And I ... ?'

'What were your impressions of the world according to Comrade Propp?'

'As you say, dry. The questions were quite ... but I liked the one about the chess sets.'

'Well, that was *me*; I asked that. Never quite had an adequate explanation of why those feudal societies still scuttle around the chequered boards in the brave new world. And why it is always the capture of the queen that brings triumph, and why the pawns are expendable, and why the decayed aristocratic class move about in such interesting ways, back and forth and to the sides. You'd think they'd have replaced the pieces by now, given all the power to the more numerous members of the proletariat, rethought the whole thing from top to bottom.'

'I hadn't considered that.'

'I mean, how committed are they in the long run to this grand experiment?'

'So you're not yourself . . . '

'A member of the Party? No. Not even a fellow traveller. I'm the annoying type who is interested in new ideas, not that Propp is new, but he's new to me. I'm what they call a dilettante. Flitting about like a butterfly. But you, I presume, are a student of some kind, at the university.'

He had sat down on the chair next to her without an invitation.

'I'm just a secretary, personal assistant to the managing director.'

'And what exactly does he direct?'

'*Bed* linens.' She scrunched up her nose and mouth into what she liked to think of as a French *moue* but you need a button nose to pull it off, a nose like a little mushroom, and hers was nothing like that. Quinn's nose was – she searched for the word – *aquiline*, whatever that meant.

'How useful. One can never have too many sheets.'

'Really? I think two pairs are quite sufficient, one on and one in the wash.'

'You have a traitor's soul. If only your managing director could hear you now. Good job I'm not a spy, like some people I could mention. Then you'd be in hot water.' He laughed. He felt a spasm of humour pass through him uncomfortably, his ribs ached.

'Who is a spy?'

Itzik had had quite enough of this banter. Roland, taken up a couple of months ago in good faith, had proved a dead loss, neither recruitable nor a conduit for intelligence. He was a playful fool. Now he was interfering and interrupting. Itzik had wanted the satisfaction. The satisfaction that Mina and Jossel would know that not only was he still alive but he was in fact a big shot, a bona fide member of the Soviet delegation, that he had not died or come to nothing. He could have communicated this to them himself, but coming from the mouth of the next generation was double the satisfaction, for they could not throw everything back in his face, as they would if he turned up at their door. He wanted to hear the reaction through the medium of this beautiful young girl, a *daughter*, to whom Mina should not be entitled, *not entitled*. All this fermented obscurely in his mind. He was conscious of something wicked forming down there, like the old days when he had taken pleasure in collecting secrets and tormenting rodents. Those desires had died down and been replaced by the need for love, but love had come and gone, no one would love him now. That was all finished. And he did not want to see Mina and Jossel, to have a glass of tea with them, to kibitz about the old days, and generally catch up on whose fate was better or worse. He just wanted them to *know*. And for them to know he knew, and that their girl was within his orbit now.

The pub was thronging, it had transformed itself into an extramural gathering of the Soviet studies society. The regulars were marginalised and annoyed. It was always like this when there was a meeting at the Conway Hall, and how was one expected to have a quiet drink surrounded by yapping and gibberish?

'Mr Quinn, old chap, be a dear and run away while my niece and I have this private conversation.'

'Oh, don't be such a dog in the manger.'

'What is this expression?'

'She knows what I mean, don't you, Miss Phillips?'

She did. But she thrust up her chin silently and haughtily, not wanting to seem too eager or available.

'Well, I shall look up bedding supplies in the directory and come and surprise you in your lunch hour one day. You'll see. Count on it.'

'I have my sandwiches at my desk.'

'How dreary, could anything be less fun? I *mean*, sandwiches, the heart sinks.'

And somehow, before he had moved away from the table, gathered his hat and gloves and left the pub, she had given him the number of the phone box in the hall of her digs.

'A typical type, that,' said Itzik. 'What they call an aesthete, I believe. Well connected, mixes with radical elements, artists, freethinkers. But, as I say, a troublemaker, I suspect him of anarchism.'

'What is that?'

'No rules. Complete disorder.'

'I like the sound of it.'

'It's nonsense; you can't achieve justice like this.'

But Paula was very young and selfish, and had no interest in justice.

'Getting back to what we were talking about, you will pass on my best wishes to your mother and uncle?'

'Of course.'

'Tell them no hard feelings, I hope. Maybe when they come to visit you in London we will all meet up.'

'Maybe. Well, thank you for a lovely evening.'

And while hardly being lovely it had been better than she had imagined it would be, given that she now possibly had what in American films they called 'a date' with a young man. And what a young man, she thought. An aesthete, a word like scarlet satin she rolled round her tongue.

22

'Willows whiten, aspens quiver, little breezes dusk and shiver . . . '
Paula recited as the Lady of Shalott came into view on the gallery
wall, floating, eyes closed, russet hair flowing down her back, bosky,
doomed, deathly. 'How *marvellous*.'

'My God, you don't like this awful muck, do you? It wants burning down. The rotted, decomposing Victorian soul that blights us
half a century since the old grandma breathed her last.'

'But, the colours!' Paula cried. 'That little spot of green that—'

'Oh, gawd, you've been reading a *book*, art appreciation by
numbers.' He laughed. 'And how green *you* are, my dear. How
provincially new.'

Roland took her arm, steered her out of the room through to
another gallery where the Turners hung.

As if a knife had rent the canvas of *The Lady of Shalott*, Roland
had slashed through the memory of those Saturday afternoons with
her father at the Walker, where, companionably together, they had
sighed in front of the beauty of the Pre-Raphaelites. And she had
not known that his love of them was foolish, crude, common.

Roland had met her on the steps of the Tate. It was an arrangement designed to reassure her, because looking at stale British art
was the kind of genteel thing girls liked. He was late. She stood

looking across the river to its southern shore. *Terra incognita*, he would call it when he eventually turned up, looking pale and bruised under his eyes, but smiling, glad to see her because she was ten times sexier than anyone else he had passed that morning. She knew what she was doing with a lipstick and a vial of scent. And even buttoned up in a coat she had a promising shape.

He had not meant to humiliate her. Her greenness was kind of adorable. She had a plasticine quality he was sure he could mould to his own wishes. And related to old Itzik! What a turn-up. Amongst the Turners he took her hand, raised it to his lips, kissed it. It was the kind of old-fashioned gesture girls fell for, and one that was totally misleading. But cheaper than a bunch of flowers.

He took her to lunch at 'a little Italian place I know, down some steps but the grub is decent', where she drank a glass of Chianti which seemed strong, and learned how to impale bootlaces of spaghetti on her fork, swivel it up the tines and lever it messily into her mouth, her chin spattered with tomato sauce, feeling inelegant and even dirty, watching him laughing at her across the tablecloth, and sticking out his tongue, saying, 'I could lick that off if you like; I could be fairly unobtrusive, it's quite dark in here.'

And did she want to be licked by nose-boy, as she thought of him, aquiline, goyishe nose-boy, sitting across the table from her in a tweed jacket and striped tie with some kind of small crest on it, so at ease with himself, with her, with the place, with the situation? Inside she was morphing into the kind of girl who allows herself to be *licked* at a restaurant table. And doubtless thrown out immediately by the outraged waiters for creating a scene. It seemed to her like fun. But he had withdrawn his tongue and was smiling, like the cat that's got the cream, she thought.

She felt the pull of her sex appeal. She could reel him in from across the table if she wanted to. Men were so stupid, a little cleavage and they were babies crying for the nipple. You crossed your legs and the gesture looked like a lottery.

She felt his hand reach beneath the tablecloth and brush along her leg, she shuddered with pleasure while she was jabbering about bed sheets and bolsters and what an awful bore it all was, and how everyone kept clear of her, and her boss was the dreariest man in England. And somehow it all kept coming back to bed linen, so no wonder he had gone so far up her leg to have felt the nubs of her suspender belt, pressed them gently into her flesh. How could she let him do it? Why did she not angrily swat that hand away, as she had actually been taught to do at the college, because they knew all about wandering palms there, and the definition of a man who was unsafe in taxis and those who were *too* safe? But she didn't, because she was drunk on a glass of Chianti, and Roland suited candlelight at lunchtime, and appeared younger and more film-star-like. In profile, he resembled a canteen of cutlery, all angles, his nose and chin cutting through the clammy winter day. There was little flesh on him, he was a scarecrow, but facing her across the restaurant table lit by a candle's low-wattage glow he was softer, kind of rubbed out, she thought, as if he might begin to evaporate in the warmth of the wine. Oh, he was what her father would call a so-and-so, of course he was.

They said goodbye on the street. 'Toodle-pip,' he said. 'Got to go to work. See you later.' And he legged it across the traffic to jump onto a bus to Oxford Circus. She had forgotten to ask him what he did for a living and now she didn't know why he was going to work in the middle of the afternoon on a weekend. She supposed she had not given satisfaction, with her humiliation over *The Lady of Shalott*, and he was making a quick getaway.

Mina did not reply to her daughter's letter introducing the curious evening she had spent with Itzik, which Paula had relayed with uncertainty, not knowing whether to be tactful and evasive or tell it as it happened, amusingly, including the arrival of Roland at the table. Which necessitated revealing that she had been inside the premises of a public house, which no one from her family, as far as she knew, had ever stepped foot in. In the end, she left in the crack about the boyfriends in the forest, thinking it was some kind of in-joke between the siblings which might amuse her mother and bring back old times.

Mina did not believe in committing words to paper. She was self-conscious about her handwriting, the alphabet was a thicket of prohibitions, letters could be written two ways, according to a set of rules she did not get, could not commit to memory. P's and d's presented their own problems, bulbous faces that could go either way.

Mina rang the telephone in Paula's digs, where her daughter came running down three flights having been called up over the banisters by the landlady, thinking it must be Roland, for it was not the usual time her mother rang from the telephone stool in the hall alcove beneath the rows of ornaments at home.

What did he say, what did he look like, what did he say about me and Jossel, what does he want from us, what did he mean I had boyfriends in the forest, I never had a boyfriend in my life till your father came to the door, what is the poison he is planting in your mind, because it is poison, believe you me. Ask your Uncle Jossel about him, he knew him better than me, for years they had to share a bed and he tells me terrible things. And is he married, does he have his own children, and if not, why not, why is he all alone, what did he do to deserve such a fate? And after the waves of agitated sound had washed over Paula's lug-holes, she managed to get a word in edgeways to say, 'Any message?'

Mina hesitated. A message could be misinterpreted. The words could come back to hit her in the face like a wet flapping fish.

'To him? To that mamzer? Nothing!'

When she got off the phone, the ivory Chinaman trembling on the shelf from the torrent of speech, Mina made herself a glass of tea and tried to remember her brother. Maybe she had been too quick to write him off. He was a big shot now, he had a position, he was adjacent to greatness, though the Soviet Union's shine had somewhat worn off for her and the photograph of Joseph Stalin was closed up in a trunk in the spare room with a lot of other paraphernalia which did not seem to pertain to post-war life. She had stopped her subscription to the communist paper. She supplied trays of egg-mayonnaise-filled bridge rolls and cakes and poured tea and glasses of whisky for the Wednesday-night clandestine meetings Louis held in the lounge to raise money to buy guns for the Jews in Palestine.

She rang Jossel.

'You'll never guess who has turned up after all these years. We thought he was dead, he wasn't dead, he's an important man, it turns out.'

She outlined the edited version of the strange meeting Paula had relayed to her.

'He told her the boys in the forest were boyfriends.'

'Same old Itzik, wanting to cause trouble.'

'You were right about him.'

'Of course I was right.'

'Still, what does he know?'

'About what?'

'The family, where they are, what happened to them; he's all we have left of the old world, the old life, don't we owe it to . . . '

But Jossel's mind turned to stone when he thought of his brother, how one time, on the street, he had . . . But why did he even have to remember all the evil Itzik had done to him?

He described Itzik to his second wife as 'that little shit', but then Louis, talking to him on the telephone after he had calmed Mina's shock, said, 'Don't you think many little shits went into the camps and never left and don't we count them among who we lost? Terrible people went in, terrible people up the chimney as well as the beautiful children and the balabatish housewives and the doctors and the violinists. I think there are so few of us, each life must be held precious. Wouldn't you still have saved my life on the battlefield if I had been an embezzler?'

'What are you telling me? That we should say it's okay for Paula to see him, that we should invite him for afternoon tea, that Mina should entertain him?'

'If she wants she wants.'

Jossel felt that his brother-in-law was an innocent, a native-born Englishman with no memories of the old times. A good man, he was kind, he was always doing the right thing. He was a pillar of

133

the community. As Jossel had been forgiven, so, Louis implied, Itzik could be brought back into the world of Mendel.

Still, Jossel felt, hadn't the wrong Mendel survived? Why not his mother, that uncomplaining woman who had stood between him and his father? And if the old ones were not to be spared, what about the unknown fate of his little sister Rivka and her husband and three children, the silent ones. She had sent a photo in 1933 of herself as a young mother with a smudge of a husband next to her, his face obscured by the brim of a hat, wheeling a pram, a sleeping baby under a cover, and in the background a street, cars, passers-by. What of the half-remembered Solly, also married? They might still be alive, there were no graves, but who had a grave? Now a brother who was not so nice had re-emerged from the great wound of the century and wanted to be in touch. What right did he have, he told Mina, *what right?*

Mina said to Louis, 'All my life he has looked out for me when I no longer had a mother and father to tell me what was wise and what to do. Why shouldn't I listen to him now?'

'If that's what you want, my dear, we'll have nothing to do with him.'

23

In her digs on Montagu Street there was a residents' lounge. It was decorated with drooping palms and housed a small library of popular novels, the morning's *Times* and *Daily Express*, a radiogram in a walnut case and a semi-private telephone kiosk concealed beneath a metal hood with a stool, a ledge and the two volumes of the London telephone directory.

She occasionally went down to borrow a book and would find a fellow resident reading the newspaper and listening to the BBC, a finger held to a shushing mouth. Her father, who had brought her down in the Humber and installed her in her new home, had looked around it and said that there were bound to be card games and conversation with the other guests, but they were a middle-aged lot and it had proved hopeless for launching a social life.

She felt as though she was vibrating between two lives. It was looking likely that if things didn't pick up (and she had heard nothing further from Roland, that Pre-Raphaelite gaffe must have sunk her) she would have to go home. She could hold her head high and say she had survived London but found no further use for it, a point proven. Then do a closer survey of the eligible young Jewish boys of Liverpool; perhaps there was one she might have missed. There were a few boys not yet discharged from the army, serving in glamorous situations abroad, one was an army doctor. There was the 'Ringo' boy she had danced with at Bernice's wedding. According to her brother Benny, he was branching out from the family garment business to open up a high-class gown shop on Bold Street. But all she could remember of their encounter was being sick on a French cigarette.

Voices streamed through the mesh grille of the radiogram, rebounded about the walnut cabinet and took up a commanding presence among the room's knick-knacks, muting the tick-tock of the mantelpiece clock. The sound of the wireless reminded Paula of her childhood, of its early presence in her life, and words that were spoken in a way she had never heard anyone in real life speak, so the people in there seemed to her to be magical creatures, invisible forms that could extend their range far beyond the secret place they inhabited. She had heard the stuttering King, she had heard the sonorous Prime Minister, she had received news of battles and retreats and victories, and also the gaiety of dance bands and the seriousness of high-brow plays she did not understand. She had asked her father to explain the word 'felicitous' to her, he had taken her into town and bought her a black, cloth-bound dictionary.

'With all the words you'll ever need,' the bookseller said, 'and then a few more again!'

Yet what right did she have to these words, to this great language, which the bookseller had also told her 'is not pure, like Latin, it's a mongrel tongue, you'll find French and Latin and Anglo-Saxon all mixed up in there. Have you ever wondered why there are two words for the same creature? Cow when it's in the fields, beef when it's on your plate? One reflects the tongue of the serfs who tended the cattle, from the Old English, *cu*, and the other the Norman landowners who ate it. Beef, from the French, *boeuf*, do you see?' She had gone home with her dictionary and studied it. Learned the true meaning of the words she had heard on the BBC. Pusillanimous. Rebarbative. Olfactory. But on what occasions might she ever need to actually say them? None had yet arrived.

There was a class of person, Roland was amongst them, who did not have to buy this knowledge; they grew up in its understanding. She could pass as one of them, but knew she wasn't, not really; the abrupt appearance of an Uncle Itzik demonstrated that. She had always felt like an actress and was attractive enough to have become one, with a calm inexpressiveness in school plays, not lively, an air of disdain which suited parts written for women of a greater maturity. That seemed to be what she was acting here in London. Her father had the belief that people take you for what you say you are, how you seem to be, and so one must be careful about outward appearances. Apparently she looked exactly like the secretary to the managing director of a firm of bed-linen man-ufacturers. But then Itzik turns up. It was all so confusing. I'm only twenty; how should I know how the world works? she said to her mirror reflection.

When she came down to the sitting room one evening to return a half-read book, she heard Roland speaking to someone, a mono-logue without interruption, or the other person's voice was too low to hear. Now what is he doing here? she thought. He does hold the attention, that boy needs interrupting from time to time. He was talking about talks, about a series of talks on the modern novel, self-confident, perfectly enunciated, with a deliberate precision which was not quite how he spoke in person.

'Oh, the wireless,' she said to the empty room. 'He's *on* it.'

She had sometimes tried to imagine the actual people, the faces to whom these radio voices were attached, and had come up with a general idea of a man with fair hair and pale blue eyes, such as the fathers of some of her school friends whose names were preceded by titles such as Captain or Major and, once or twice, Flight Lieutenant. They were the only people in her orbit who were not large of lips and nose, or rather short, inclining to mid-life bulk, and gold-rimmed glasses, food stains on their ties. She had imagined the BBC voices like a row of tin soldiers, a platoon of such men, all identical. They were the King in various guises, only without the stutter.

*

He had not given her his telephone number and she would not have rung him if she had it. A girl waits, she is taught to wait, she does not initiate, she does not act, she hangs around in hope of being animated. She tracked his presence throughout the evening. Sometimes he was there, sometimes it was someone else. She began to form a view of him at variance with the louche rule-breaker, the anarchist she had met only twice. Maybe he was quite nice after all. He announced plays, talks, musical recitals, readings, serialisations. Would he be entrusted with imparting such significant information if he was untrustworthy or subversive? The BBC was more or less the government, after all.

After a week she started to be bored by the idea of him; boredom was her condition anyway, why should he not be added to that state? He had been a short explosion of excitement in her life in London, which had reverted to the same routine of the Friday-night family dinner in Finsbury Park and keeping at arm's length her uncle, at the request of her mother, who had been very odd about him, as had Uncle Jossel. Something to get to the bottom of there, but her questions had been deflected. She could still hear her mother's voice on the subject of forest boyfriends. Paula found it all quite amusing and enjoyed the barely credible notion that her mother of all people had a racy past. Why not? She was allowed to have had her fun, up to a point.

Itzik dropped round one evening with an invitation to another lecture. The landlady was dispatched to her room to get her. A gentleman had called, 'not a young man, I'm afraid, a foreign gentleman'. He had already turned on the radio when she got down there. Roland's voice spooled through the room like a satin ribbon. 'Why, here is our friend Roland,' Itzik said. 'Wouldn't you say he knows everything?'

'He does seem to, but I'm sure he's just reading what's written down, he can't make it up himself.'

'Only obeying orders. I believe you had lunch with him, was it successful?'

'Quite successful, thank you.'

'I won't enquire. The man has a reputation but I am sure you can look after yourself. Mina Mendel's daughter will never get lost in the forest.'

'There are no forests here. Well, the New Forest, but that's just ponies.'

'Ponies?'

'So they say, I've seen pictures of them.'

He was holding a bundle of leaflets. 'Our latest venture,' he said, 'after the success of Comrade Propp. Perhaps I can leave some on the table.'

'Is this how you advertise?'

'Yes, we put them where we can. We even have people who will leave some for us at the BBC. We hold lectures, people hear about them, they attend. Sometimes you get to know the people who come, it's our business to get to know them. The BBC is a very interesting place, full of ideas. Very open-minded individuals, some of them.'

'I see. How long have you been here, by the way? In England, I mean.'

'Oh, no more than a few months. The bare tick of a clock.'

'And how do you find it?'

'Full of bourgeois decadence, what do you want me to say?'

'I've no idea. I don't find it decadent at all; it's terribly respectable from what I have seen, here and at the office. Bourgeois, though, that's probably right. What's the Soviet Union like? Very different, I suppose.'

Merchant seamen with red enamel stars on their caps and pea coats had often been seen strolling through the streets of Liverpool. Mina had accosted a pair and shouted, 'Where are my mother and brother and sister? Do you know them, what happened to them, are they still alive?' Louis had to pull her away. The sailors looked bewildered, smiled, held their fingers to their mouths and mimed smoking a cigarette. 'They want something,' he said, 'they're not going to give you any true information. Come on, walk fast, they might follow us.'

Now Itzik began a rehearsed speech about the superiority of the Soviet system, of factory production and harvests. Paula shut her eyes and thought about a boy in Liverpool called Marvin Goldberg and the latest news of his courtship of the beautiful, wealthy Gloria Brassey (Sammy's niece) of Queen's Drive and whether she would be nabbed right under his nose by Bernie Abelson who was muscling in, the last time she heard. For Gloria, it was agreed, could marry absolutely anyone in Liverpool, including the son of the Lord Mayor if she wanted.

The telephone rang and as there was no one else there to do so, she answered it, hoping it might be for someone on the top floor so she could run up to fetch them and by the time she returned her uncle would be gone.

She had heard Roland's voice so often on the wireless it was shocking to hear it reverberating down through the receiver into her eardrum, as if he had jumped from the wooden casing into her own head.

'Hello there, Miss Phillips, sorry I haven't been in touch, you know, one thing and another, but I enjoyed our morning together, I'd like to see you again if that's possible. Are you free tomorrow evening?'

'Aren't you at work? You didn't tell me you were on the wireless, I've just heard you!'

'Didn't I? I barely remember myself half the time and I suppose I expect people to just know anyway. I've just come off shift.'

'How funny that that's what you do for a living. I think I must have grown up hearing you.'

'Not really, I only joined last year.'

'I have no idea how you would get into that sort of thing. Where do you start?'

'It's more a word-of-mouth arrangement; my tutor put me up for it.'

'I see. Not that different from the principal of my college getting me my job, I suppose.'

'Oh, yes; it's all connections, one way or the other.'

'People have very different ones, though. Connections, I mean.'

'Nobody is going to recommend me as a secretary.' He laughed and assumed a high, mincing tone. '*Oh, Mr Quinn, shall I take a letter?* But will you come?'

'I suppose I might for an hour.'

'As long as you like.'

When she put the phone down, her uncle was still there.

'So, you see him again? A nice boy, do you think?'

'I wouldn't have said he was *nice*, he's probably very unreliable.'

'You see him because your mother would not approve. Of course she wouldn't. And she will blame me if it all ends up in trouble. How could you do this to your dear old Uncle Itzik?'

'That will be my lookout.'

'Send my fond greetings to the family, particularly to the second Mrs Mendel. I'd like to hear more about her.'

What a figure he cut, in his too-long trousers, the turn-ups frayed, that goblin face, she thought. And yet he went home to the embassy and sheltered behind its high white, implacable walls. He was important. He was as close to her in blood as her Uncle Jossel.

24

Roland thought his own story was run-of-the-mill, but as it slowly leaked out, it sounded exotic to Paula. He had been brought up in Herne Hill. His father was a senior civil servant at the Treasury. He was all rules and regulations and went to work in striped trousers and a bowler hat. Took the train every day to Whitehall. Released money unto the nation like balls of constipated shit.

When he met Itzik, he heard how he had ended up in the embassy of the Soviet Union. Roland whistled. It was all a bloody long way from the Bank of England and interest rates and capital allowances and national insurance contributions and the distribution of ration books and the line of men crossing the river every morning. And it seemed to him that with a man like Itzik as an uncle it was surely inevitable that Paula would drop her knickers for him in the fullness of time, an expression of his father's, steepling his fingers together. 'In the fullness of time, I believe the government's policies will . . .'

Which in Roland's mind translated as 'I'll fuck her sooner or later, but probably sooner. I just have to get rid of that tedious provincial morality she's bound to have.'

He would take her to the York Minster on Dean Street. She might as well find out about Soho, it had the habit of loosening people's fastenings: they came, they saw, they dropped their undies, if you were lucky.

He picked her up at her digs and walked her down Charing Cross Road. It was a busy Thursday evening. Everything was in full swing and the war behind them seemed to Roland like a hallucination. They passed a stocking tied round a lamp-post, a few steps away a pair of ointment-pink silk knickers clung to the slats of a drain.

'It seems very bohemian in here,' she said as they came into the pub. 'Are these people artists?'

By the door a woman was being sick in her handbag, it was only seven thirty. She stumbled out onto the pavement and sat down on the concrete slabs.

'Don't pay her any attention,' Roland said. 'I'm afraid she's a regular.'

'How very sad.' She had never seen a drunken woman before. 'Why on earth did you choose this place? It's rather horrid.'

'The pubs round where I work are full of bores. I listen to their voices all day, I could do with a rest when I knock off.'

He found them a table. The bar was hemmed in by standing men, no women. They leaned their elbows and barked opinions at each other. The publican appeared to be French with an extravagant moustache. He has a kind face, she thought, why on earth does he put up with this rabble? And yet here she was in London, drinking a small glass of Dubonnet in the company of raffish types while at home in Liverpool her cousin Bernice would be settling down beside the wireless with Lionel and talking about nothing. While she was out at night in Soho with a man who was actually *on* the wireless.

Roland attempted to pump her for information about Itzik but she had little to add.

'My mother said he had a sneaky nature when he was a child, always eavesdropping over the banisters. He was supposed to have overheard when she told my uncle about the Bolsheviks she met in the forest.'

'Bolsheviks? In a forest? What forest?'

143

'Oh, I've really no idea, it's just an old family story. My lot are full of them, there's nothing they like more than gabbing. But they don't tell me everything, and frankly one never knows what to believe.'

'How marvellous. You really are the most remarkable girl, you know. I've never met anyone like you.'

There was a word she would not use in his company though it remained lodged in her vocabulary, stubbornly refusing to fade out and be replaced by something one could find in the Oxford English Dictionary. *Schmoozed*, that was what was being done to her. She must be careful, she thought, not to let it slip out. And she had never told a soul about the Bolshevik business and would not have told Roland had he not already met her reprobate ('good word!') uncle.

She smiled and said nothing. An enigmatic smile, she had learned from going to the pictures, was a credible weapon in a girl's armoury. And wished she was somewhere with a white tablecloth and shining cutlery and a waiter in a bow tie flourishing a menu. Not this dingy spot. One never quite got what one wanted.

A drunk lurched over to the table.

'Have we met?' he said to Paula. He was American. 'I'm sure we met at the Harrises' party. Didn't we chat in the kitchen?'

'Not me.'

'Oh, surely we—'

'Surely you should go home to your wife and take a good bath while you're at it, you stink of drink and tobacco.'

'Tongue like a armadillo's pecker, don't envy you.' He reeled off in the direction of the lavatory.

'Nicely done, very nicely done indeed. I like a girl who holds her own.'

'Do you? Lots of boys hate it. I try to rein myself in a bit, if I can and if I remember. I'm a repressed volcano at the office.'

'Oh yes, the office, how are you getting on?'

'I hate it. I don't think I'll last until the end of my probationary period. Three months of tedium. If I didn't have to go to bed at night, I'd ban bed linen from my life altogether. The unit price of a hundred pillowslips is a sum I will not forget for as long as I live. You've no idea how awful it is.'

'Well, get another job, how hard can it be? You got this one easily enough.'

'I was recommended. It was all out of my hands.'

'What a bore. Still, I bet I could find you something else.'

He had no idea how to find a secretary a position. One said these things, and then there were sometimes mild consequences. Still, he would probably think of something. He wanted to have a crack at her. There had been a handful of Jewish girls in the women's colleges at Oxford, a couple were refugees, but they wore gold-rimmed spectacles and inclined to tricky subjects like mathematics and physics. Not his type. He liked a straight seam on a shapely calf, and why not? But then what did you say to them? The brainless pretty fools had no conversation.

It was time to woo her with dinner.

The pub was getting louder. She reached across the table to hear him.

'What did you say?'

'Do you fancy a bite?' he said.

'Oh, yes.'

The drunken woman was still sitting on the pavement outside. 'Poor thing,' Paula said, as they hurried past her. 'Does she have no friends? Someone should see her home, at the least.'

'And tuck her into bed with a hot-water bottle? Not those kind of friends. Forget about her, she's just rubbish.'

He took her to another Italian restaurant. The secretarial college had taught her that there was no really elegant way for a young lady to eat in the presence of a young man. She had been educated in rules for asparagus and strawberries and what came in between, how to eat peas and string beans, but there was no class in the neat consumption of spaghetti. It was hard not to make a mess and end up with sauce on your face.

She said as little as she could while she was navigating the strands, let him talk about the news he read, the programme intervals, the actors who came in and out of the building. She recognised some of their names. Her father had taken her once to a production of *An Inspector Calls* at the Playhouse. He had presented her with a box of chocolates. But when she mentioned it to Roland, he burst out laughing. 'Is that really your taste?'

'I don't even know what's wrong with it? What's so funny?'

'Have you never heard of Christopher Fry?'

'No.'

'He's the latest thing. *The Lady's Not for Burning*? Marvellous.'

'What's it about? Who is in it?'

'It's a romantic comedy set in the Middle Ages, with a war-weary soldier who wants to die and an accused witch who wants to live. John Gielgud, surely you've heard of him?'

'He's not a film star, though, is he?'

'It's *not a film*.'

'I know, you said, but it sounds most peculiar.'

'How young and gauche you are. Green. Greeeen. Straight out of the provinces.'

'I know I am, but honestly ... you just ... '

But she did not know what to say. She could simply leave, get up from the table confident that he would deal with the bill, and get the bus home to her bedsit. Refuse to answer the phone if he rang, though she doubted that he would call again after such a dismissal. She was out of her depth. At that moment, her face distracted, Roland took the opportunity of reaching forward and putting his hand on her leg, reaching up and twiddling the buttons of the suspenders.

'Your face,' Roland said. 'If you could see yourself. You'd think you haven't been touched up under a restaurant table before. What a sheltered life. I can see I'll have to take you *in hand*. I think you'll like that.'

He smiled and called over the waiter. 'You know what we'd like now, don't you?'

'Has the lady ... ?'

146

'No, it's her *first time*.'

He said something in Italian. Roland laughed.

'It won't be here straight away, we'll have to wait. But it seems to me we have all the time in the world, why I could eat you all up.'

After a while the waiter brought two bowls of a dessert with a difficult name, zabaglione, he said. She plunged in her spoon and brought it to her mouth.

'How is it?' Roland said.

It fell out of favour on restaurant menus in later years, she sometimes asked for it, but the waiter would recommend oranges in caramel or the new thing, tiramisu. Zabaglione was just three ingredients – eggs, sugar, marsala wine – one could make it on the hob over a pan of simmering water, so simple.

'You think you can do what you like with me. You think I'm . . . '

'Well, I can't leave you amongst the pillowcases, can I? I'd have a heart of stone.'

'But what do you intend to do with me?'

'Here's a thought. If I find you another job will you sleep with me?'

'Good grief, what a transaction.'

'It's a worthy exchange, I'd have thought. I suppose, by the way, that you are a virgin. I'd love to pop your cork, so to speak.'

'That sounds *marvellous*.'

'Are you being sarcastic? I think you are.'

'Now where on earth do you think they got all these lovely eggs?'

25

She heard his voice every day on the wireless. There was a formal style to the way he spoke, clipped and precise, what her brothers would call a mouth full of plums. He had told her that once one had been on air one developed an addiction to the microphone, one preferred it to the back room, but she now wondered if he felt stymied, being a kind of manservant to the people who actually made the plays and concerts and talks. It was odd. He was famous, that is, *everyone* must know his voice, but not a soul knew his name. He was anonymous, correct, informative. 'Next, we bring you ...'

When he rang her a few days later it was to say there was a position coming up that might suit her, on the nail, actually, and was she interested? Listening to him she experienced a strange sensation of doubling, of a voice ringing in her head that ought to be echoing round a room. (And it's almost like an instruction, she thought. I'll have to be careful about that. A person could go mad.)

'At the BBC?'

'Oh, no, far more glamorous. A pal is working for a new film production company, it's called Harlequin Pictures and they shoot out at Shepperton, but the head office is on Regent Street and they're looking for a Girl Friday. I've put you up for it. They're expecting you to ring and arrange an interview.'

'Look, is this above board?'

'Of course. Would I send you anywhere that wasn't thoroughly respectable? And it certainly is all that. I heard they were doing a Dickens next, all a bit old hat for my taste. Do you know Eisenstein's little book about Dickens?'

'No. Will I be expected to?'

'Of course not, it was just a tangent.'

'I don't know what you mean sometimes.'

'You've heard of Dickens, surely?'

'I'm not completely ignorant. I did go to school, you know.'

But what had she learned there? Evidently not the same things as Roland. She did not know who Eisenstein was. She felt ignorant and annoyed with her herself for being so uninformed. One came to London expecting one thing, and it turned out to be a shove back to the classroom. She had not been aware before of her limitations. Her reputation at home was that of a wayward local beauty, *the Polack girl* with her hoity-toity voice and her dismissal of all the available beaus. And she had a shameful uncle who had run off with his shiksa secretary. One escaped suburbia to the metropolis and thought one would fit right in, but in London one needed to know about plays and actors and concerts and paintings and how to eat foreign food. She felt hollow, like a set of Russian dolls, containing only smaller and smaller versions of herself.

'And if you get it,' he went on, with something that sounded to her like a smirk, 'well, we have a pact, don't we? I'll definitely take you up on it.'

'Oh, don't be absurd, do you honestly think . . . ?'

'We'll see. Let me know how you get on.'

Robin Rose said, 'Oh yes, Roland's girl, can you get down here today? Will four be all right? You can make that, I hope.' She said she could not, she could come at quarter past five, after work. He said, 'Well, I suppose we'll have to manage until then, but honestly, you've no idea what it's *like* here and it's not what I got myself into this game for, answering the bloody telephone.'

149

On the bus to Regent Street, dawdling at traffic lights, she thought how easy it was to lose one's bearings in London, how you could never leave the house without your copy of the A–Z map book in your handbag or pocket, for even a walk to the corner shop might take a sudden wrong turn and then you didn't know where you were, the unfamiliarity of the buildings and the sense that you would never find your way back to where you had started took hold and you panicked. If she was going out of the small central core of the West End she preferred to take the tube, for at least the name of the station told you where to get off. She recognised very little. London was a few random dots of familiarity; she had no idea how the sections fitted together. It rushed straight at her, a stampeding crowd of streets and alleys and great landmarks.

The office was undistinguished, a side door, a bell, a handwritten sign announcing its presence on the third floor. It was above a shop selling luggage. It was not a first-class, luxury shop but a place where one would hope to find good quality at a reasonable price. She couldn't imagine where its trade came from, for who had the money to travel these days? Still, a couple were buying a set of matching suitcases so the lure of abroad was still alive. She overheard them speaking eagerly of their train crossing the Alps, descending into the heat and light and sensual colour of Italy – 'The fruits, the vegetables!' they cried and Paula had no idea why one would rhapsodise about the products of a market garden, gnarled apples, wrinkly carrots.

The door was answered by a pinkish young man who lived up to his surname, blushing at nothing, blushing at the sight of her, blushing at the sound of her shoes tapping up the stairs behind him. Blushing when she patted her hair and licked her lipsticked lips.

'They'll be back soon, they're on their way back to town. I'm not interviewing you myself, I'm just supposed to show you into the office and have you wait till they're here. I'm sure they're on their way. They'd better be. I can't hang around for ever.'

'Who am I waiting for, exactly? I was only given your name.'

'Didn't he tell you? It's Mr Agnew and Mr Fulton. They run the show.'

She waited for an hour. She redid her face in her compact mirror. She read yesterday's paper picked up from the floor. She heard Robin next door pecking fretfully at a typewriter with a pair of uncertain forefingers. There wasn't a single picture on the wall to look at, only piles of paperwork haphazardly dripping off the desk. The sofa on which she sat was made of the skin of long-dead cows stuffed with the hair of long-dead horses. Everything stank of tobacco and very strong coffee. Was there the faint trail of a woman's perfume that was not her own or was she imagining it? Was there a streak of lipstick on the mirror as if someone had kissed their own reflection? There were scuff marks of heels on the skirting boards. The whole place was terribly dowdy and could not be associated in her mind with the glamour of the cinema. Out of such squalor, dreams could not be spun. She heard steps, it must be them, then a lavatory chain sounded and water flushing. It was impossible to believe that motion pictures could emerge from this cramped, chaotic environment.

Eventually they turned up, barging in, she thought, like they owned the place, then remembered that they did and that it was only that she had been waiting so long that she felt disturbed by their presence, flinging their hats onto the sofa and throwing off their coats. 'So Robin was right,' one of them said, 'she *is* here, hurrah!'

Agnew was in his early thirties: short, tweedy, already balding, a slight stutter on certain consonants, flapping in in an old Burberry mackintosh and taking off leather driving gauntlets as if he were a chauffeur. Fulton was a completely different type, an air of hastily assembled opulence clung to him, in a slightly shiny silver-grey suit and a maroon tie embellished with tiny silver moons, as if he was destined to be in front of the camera not behind it. He was lighting a cigar as he entered the room. Unlike Agnew he had an accent.

The two men sat down in rotating wooden chairs behind adjacent desks. Nobody seemed to have emptied the ashtrays for

151

days. Together, talkative, they came across as a comedy double act, making incomprehensible in-jokes to each other. Apart from the wild variance of their appearance, it was difficult for Paula to work out where one ended and the other began.

'So which role are you auditioning for?'

'I beg your pardon? I'm not here for—'

'Is it saucy secretary or downtrodden office dogsbody?'

'I'm here for—'

'Yes, yes, we know, but we like to have at least a *hint* of how you'll play the part.' The one with the accent winked. The one with the stutter picked up a half-smoked stub from the ashtray and lit it.

'Ccccan I offer you . . . ?'

She ignored him.

'I'm secretary at present to a managing director, a bed-linen company.'

'*Bed* linen! Oh my.'

'My shorthand and typing speeds are—'

'Yes, yes, I suppose you must have certificates, we won't need to see them. We just need someone who will run around after us. Type up the contracts, make sure they're signed and whatnot. They turn up behind the sofa, covered in coffee stains, and that's no good. We ourselves tidy up after big egos and wayward souls. You wouldn't have to do any of that. You're not thinking of getting married in the next few months, are you?'

'No.'

'Oh good, we really can't accommodate a pram in the office.'

'Young Robin might take a fancy to her.'

'Well, he'll have to keep his sticky mitts off. No fraternisation between the ranks, out of the question.'

'You might, from time to time, have to place a trunk call to Los Angeles.'

'I'm sure I could do that.'

'And we might as well get it out of the way now, do you want to be *in* the pictures?'

'I'm not an actress.'

'That's not in itself a barrier, but such self-awareness is refreshing. So it's all excellent, because we need a secretary more than we need a starlet. And can you start, say, tomorrow?'

'Are you not seeing anyone else?'

'No time, no time, we have to be back on the lot in the morning. I could spare an hour first thing to show you the ropes.'

'He's mixing you up with the gallows scene in the next picture. *Tale of Two Cities.* We've got a marvellous young man for Sydney Carton. Quite the sensation.'

'We're not doing that one.'

'So you say.'

'Henderson is just a pretty face.'

'We'll talk about this later. Can you be in by nine?'

'No, I have to give notice.'

'Oh, sod that, give them a bell and tell them you've got polio or something. Get here first thing, bring your pencils and whatnot. The typewriter is brand new. Robin is hopeless. He gets through the ribbons like nobody's business and puts the carbon sheet in the wrong way round but he's an Oxford man, you know, can't expect him to be practical.'

Abruptly, the two men rose to their feet and each extended a hand. She was bundled out of the office down onto the street without actually having said she was accepting the position.

On the bus she tried to disentangle the two men from each other. Who had said what? Why were they so like Tweedledum and Tweedledee?

She told Mr Topping her mother had been taken ill and she must return home at once to look after her.

'Oh, yes, you must hold the fort,' he said, sounding as though he had somebody already in mind to replace her. Had her work not been satisfactory? she asked. 'It was top notch, the best, it's just . . .' But he changed the subject abruptly. There was a hint of something like relief in his voice. She couldn't quite put her finger on it. Later she wondered if he had been slightly let down when she had arrived with her excellent recommendation from the college, something

153

that did not quite suit. As if behind her name, Miss Phillips, there was something he had not expected. Or she was imagining it, and he was one of those old-fashioned men who believed a woman's place was always to be a helpmeet to others and that to tend at a sickbed was the highest calling.

26

Until she met Roland, she had never heard of psychoanalysis, a six-syllable word you could get completely lost in and trip over the consonants and mangle them in the wrong order, but it was to psychoanalysis that Roland said he went (without expecting any surprise or disapproval) twice a week. To do what? To sit in a room in Swiss Cottage and just talk about himself. When she asked him to explain what he said, and he spoke about trauma, loss, inhibition, transference, she was even more in the dark. 'But what on earth do you have to be troubled about?' she asked him, for she was only ever upset about trivial wounds and slights and disappointment.

'Oh, just listen to you, who pays far too much attention to hats and backchat,' he said, smiling for once, looking at her almost fondly, as if he was envious of her superficiality. 'That's a quote, by the way, from a poem I quite like, and I always wanted a girl who could live up to it, and now I suppose I do. But when you've a father like mine, you're born to trouble. I started out with bad dreams, now I have full-blown nightmares, but that's progress, apparently. I'll take her word for it. I don't have much choice, for I do believe in the process, you know; I think she'll get to the bottom of it all in time, it's just a matter of patience.'

'She? It's a female? A woman doctor?'

'She's not exactly a doctor, unless you count doctors of souls. Is that an expression and why am I asking you of all people? How would you know? Don't worry, she's just a grey shape in a chair. Grey hair, grey dress, grey shoes. All designed to soothe, I suppose. Soothe me into a state of relaxation so I can be startled back out of it by the contents of my unconscious. Your uncle, by the way, thinks psychoanalysis is a bourgeois deviation, not that he really understands it, he just toes the line.'

The father sounded an absolute fright. She guessed that Roland had been beaten as a child, which was something she had heard about, an act of cruelty and sadism like attaching tin cans to the tails of cats. No one at home used their fists; it was goyish, common, beastly. But when she asked Roland if he had been hit, he said, 'Oh, you know, if only it had been that easy. No, he never laid a finger on me in that way. It was more what you would call psychological warfare. Except I was not the opposing army, I was the battlefield. Do your parents love you?'

'Yes. Obviously. I'm their princess.'

'Well, good for you. Bully for you.' His mouth looked very mean, like a slit of a post box, wide, narrow, empty.

Her face must have fallen into the preparation for tears because now he relaxed, reached out his hand. 'No, don't be sorry, no need at all. I'm just jealous of you, come here.'

In her defence, she later thought, shuddering at her innocence, everything was a novelty in those days. She had no way of making judgements or comparisons. This exchange took place in a café on Frith Street, where Roland had just introduced her to a type of Italian coffee with an airy hat of foam on the top and a dusting of cinnamon, said to be good for the digestion. When he asked her if she liked the cappuccino, she said yes, but knew she had no informed opinion about anything, not even knowing what she did not know. The cup of coffee was delicious, strong, foreign, that was the most she could say about it. Unordinary life was being lobbed towards her too fast to take it all in. One could only catch so much.

So Italian coffee was digested, Roland's trips to Swiss Cottage went unexamined.

For there seemed to be such huge tracts of ignorance in her upbringing. And it was not just intellectual matters – plays, films, novels. It was a whole mass of daily rights and wrongs and that was before one had even got into politics, a subject which Roland said was *terra incognita* for her, two words she could not even find in the dictionary. Not being able to say what station was on which tube line, or the merits of different ways of dressing a Christmas tree when she had never had one. The lights on Oxford Street, the Father Christmas grotto at Selfridges, the pantomime at the Palladium – everyone had an opinion. 'Oh, I hear *Aladdin* wasn't as good this year; I really prefer *Puss in Boots*, anyway. Don't you?' The list of things she had no idea about was inexhaustible.

What *was* Roland doing with her? Or not exactly doing with her, but phoning her, taking her out, to pubs and restaurants, finding her a job.

I think, she said to herself, he just wants to deflower a virgin. Perhaps they aren't two a penny here in London, at least not when you're his age. All the girls have gone off the rails already or are married. That must be it.

His flat was in Primrose Hill. He could walk to work through Regent's Park. This afternoon the sun was lowering in the December sky as if it were being dragged by winches and ropes and cables down into the earth itself, where it would be imprisoned. A green mound ascended into the murky grey sunset. She ran a gloved finger across the windowpane. 'You should get a window cleaner in,' she said. 'They're absolutely filthy, you can hardly see out of them.'

'What's to see? What should I be looking it? Just other people. A street, a lamp-post, a bench, a car, a motorbike, a line of trees. I have seen enough.'

'Well, I'd never be bored looking out of a London window, though mine is just the sight of roofs and chimneys.'

'You will, I promise you; you'll be completely fed up by spring. I really have got to get out of this fucking place, though where to, I've no idea. Would New York suit me, do you think?'

'I think New York would suit anyone. My uncle's father-in-law is in the Bronx, or was; I've never met him, but he's a kind of presence. What could have been. We should have gone to America, you know. My mother said we got stuck. What a strange arrangement you have here.'

'That's quite the non-sequitur.'

'Oh, there you go again, another bloody word I don't know.'

'How your mind runs about; it's the lack of education, I suppose.'

'And does the lack of a duster and a broom account for *this*?'

It was not mess and untidiness that fazed her. At home in Liverpool the house was loaded with upholstered furniture from Waring & Gillow, antimacassars, ornaments, decorative pelmets, dinner services for milk and meat dishes, silver candlesticks, Wedgwood ashtrays, willow-pattern serving dishes, canteens of Sheffield steel cutlery: everything it seemed to Mina and Louis that a suburban home must have if it was to survive inspection by the authorities, and only the mezuzah on the door frames and the menorah in the cupboard the giveaway. Roland's place was nothing like that. He called it a flat, but it was, she thought, just a jumped-up bedsit, for the bed was the first thing one saw when one came in, or it was the first thing Paula saw; she could not avoid its attention-seeking presence. It was a curious arrangement without blankets or eiderdown, only a great down-stuffed quilt which he had purchased at a Scandinavian shop in South Kensington. 'You'll like this,' he said, pointing a narrow finger at it, 'it's almost weightless, as if you're lying under a warm snowdrift.'

'What on earth is it?'

'It's a duvet.'

'A duvet.' She felt like a child learning to talk, repeating new words as she heard them.

He applied a match to a thin brown stick which flamed yellow, then smoked and smouldered, emitting a strange strong scent like a box of spices. There were many things Paula encountered for the first time in Roland's flat, years before anyone else she knew had heard of them. In the sixties, she said to her daughter, 'Oh, a joss stick, I haven't seen one of those since nineteen forty-nine.'

She wondered if there were to be any preliminaries or if they were to be straight to it.

'Aren't you going to offer me a cup of tea?'

'Or something stronger? I have a few bottles in.'

She considered the choices. Alcohol would release her inhibitions. They must be unchecked or she wouldn't be able to go through with it. And did she actually have to? No, she did not. She could preserve her virginity. But what exactly *for*? For what and for whom? Your wedding night, her father would say, as Bernice had saved herself for Lionel, and had made him wait until that room at the Adelphi when they were both half dead with stress and too much champagne and her girdle must be digging into her soft stomach and his erection by now at half-mast.

'Tea or whisky, which is it?' he said. 'Oh, for God's sake, you sit there like a great alabaster monument brooding on your fate, but it's just sex, that's all. Just do it, or don't do it, but spare me your provincial excuses. Or are you a suburban prick-tease?'

If I cry, she thought, then it will be over, then he would probably bundle me out of the room and tell me to get lost. She would not see him again; there was a test she would have failed, had not prepared for, didn't understand the questions. She was too proud to cry, to fail.

'I'm sorry,' he said, 'that was hurtful, I didn't mean it. You're a terrific girl, you just need not to be so damned uncertain about everything.'

'You don't know what it's like being me.'

'Well, of course I don't, how could I? I mean, you're an exotic, like a cheetah at the zoo.'

'A *cheetah?*'

'Something like that. I do find you quite out of the ordinary, you know.'

She thought, I must have it out with him. He has to know, I can't keep up this façade much longer. He *might* understand.

'Roland, listen, I'm not what you think at all. I'm not one of your nice middle-class girls you probably went to tennis parties with. I've never been to a tennis party in my life; the private courts, the clubs, won't admit us, we'd have to start our own. And nobody in my family talks like me, certainly not my brothers, you'd think them terribly common and loud, uncouth. My father tried to teach them how to be young gentlemen but it didn't take at all, they have a lot of energy but they express it in rather strident ways. They're opinionated and rough, and my father tried to make sure I didn't go the same way because if you're a girl then you couldn't make a good marriage. My mother didn't know how to help me because she's an immigrant, so I learned how to speak from the wireless and how to dress and how to do Pitman shorthand and I thought I would come to London and my polish, which Daddy calls it, would mean I'd fit in, but I don't, because I've no idea what a duvet is, even though I just stopped working in bedding. So when you call me a cheetah, when you say I'm out of the ordinary . . . well, yes, but not *that* way.'

'So you're working class? How exciting.'

'How dare you? We aren't working class, we're Jewish.'

'That's very funny. I don't understand but it doesn't matter. You're *sui generis*, one of a kind, doesn't that count for something? And I'll confess, I find what you just said slightly thrilling, to be able to pass like that, to spy on us, learn all our secrets, you really are a secret agent, aren't you? I mean, you don't *look* particularly Jewish – that's a compliment, by the way – and I would never have known if your uncle hadn't introduced us. Don't you understand? You can be anyone you like. Most of us have no choice, we can't escape from our destiny of minor public school and a gruesome nanny. I envy you, actually. What a lucky girl you are. Now look, the sheets are clean, fresh on this morning. I know you must be fussy about bed linen.'

'Not especially. It was just a job.'

But she was still digesting his observation about her being a spy. It was the first time she had considered this unique position, which, when she thought about it, she did actually have, and the idea came over her like a newly found power, such as being able to see in the dark or render herself invisible or vault over high walls like Spring-Heeled Jack.

Roland had evidently lost interest in her personality and had turned to seduction. 'Come here.' He gestured her to come and sit on his knee in the leather armchair. This is it, she thought. This is actually it. 'And now you're here, properly here, not a stretch away. I'd like to undress you myself, do you mind? *Slowly.*'

'Like a striptease?' Her voice trembled slightly.

'In a way. Now how does this bloody frock unfasten?'

She turned her back to him. He eased the buttons through their eyelets.

Her skin flinched then relaxed against his touch. Now he was undoing her bra.

'Nice nylons and nice knickers. You really are a lady, aren't you? Some arty girls don't bother with lingerie at all. Not anything pretty, anyway. Now let's be having you, as the common folk say.'

In bed, a few minutes later, she made small plosive sounds with her lips which increased in force and volume. Her body seemed to gather itself up then lose control, like a sneeze. It was all very surprising, not that she hadn't found ways to practise in advance, using the handle of her hairbrush which she soaped and thoroughly rinsed afterwards. But the weight of a man on top of her, kissing her, licking her, lightly biting her earlobe, his stubble grating the cheeks of her face, his hands now cupping her bottom, her breast in his mouth – all of these sensations aroused her in different ways.

And the only thing she found unsatisfactory was the smell of the slimy rubber thing that lay on the bedside table, limp, wet, full, safe.

'I can see,' he said, 'that this is right up your street. I'm sorry about the first bit, you did bleed a little, I wasn't honestly sure whether to expect that or not. I couldn't quite believe that it was going to be your first time, you see. I suppose I should have asked, to make sure, and when you took to it with such enthusiasm it would have been hard to have made that assumption. You have a bit of a rash on your face, by the way, that's always a good sign.'

She did not suppose he would tell her that he loved her but he had cried out 'Darling!' at one point. And finally, he had kissed her, pushing his tongue into her mouth which tasted of cigarettes. *Darling*, she dared to call him back and he smiled at her. 'Oh, I'm your darling now, am I? About time. One might have thought you were emotionally frigid, as my Swiss Cottage woman would put it. She finds it fairly surprising that I'm not. Now for a smoke, *darling*.'

Which this time sounded sarcastic. She wouldn't be surprised if he never said it again, that they had crossed an unseen boundary and she was in another place, even more unfamiliar than the last.

'Watch this.'

He took a cigarette from a packet, and neither offered her one nor put one in his own lips but started to peel the thin paper away, using his long thumbnail to score down its length.

'What *are* you doing?'

He began conducting a reassembly with a packet of cigarette papers and a dark brown smelly resiny lump he took from a Swan Vesta matchbox.

'Now here we are,' he said. 'We'll share it, half is quite enough. You must inhale, though, no blowing smoke about, take it right down into your lungs to get the benefit. Worlds will open up to you.'

'What *is* this?'

'You'll see.'

Ten minutes later she said, 'I don't feel any different.'

'Yes you do, you're staring at things. You've been staring at the same spot on the wall for ages.'

'Oh.'

'Darling.'

27

Paula did not go home to Liverpool for Christmas. There was nothing to mark or celebrate there; for Louis it was and always had been a normal working day at the office when he gave the staff the day off but came in himself, for he always went to shul on the high holidays leaving his employees to carry on as best they could, and he didn't want to be thought of as a hypocrite taking holidays that were no celebration for him.

But this year he and Mina came to London. It was not their first visit but the first since the war, from which the business had done well – they had government contracts to supply chamois leathers to air force bases. They booked three nights at a well-recommended hotel near Marble Arch. It had, according to Louis, 'quite a write-up, first class, couldn't do better, eight storeys high, bedrooms and suites on every floor', and included in the tariff a Christmas Day lunch, open also to non-residents drawn from the streets and squares behind Selfridges and extending down into Mayfair.

They reserved a table for three and were excited and nervous about what to expect. None of them had ever pulled a Christmas cracker and were intrigued by the concept, the explosive snap, the paper hats, mottos and mysterious gifts inside. The menu had been posted to them and they anxiously scanned it looking for dietary pitfalls. What are pigs in blankets? The name was the clue, and a trap easy to avoid, but what about bread sauce, which forbidden ingredient might be concealed in it? As for the Christmas pudding, they satisfied themselves that mincemeat was not meat at all, in fact dried fruit, but what fat was used to bind it together they could not be sure of. Lard inveigled its way into everything. A note at the bottom of the menu said that an alternative to Christmas pudding was available, ice cream, choice of three flavours, or fruit cocktail served with fresh or artificial cream. So they hoped for the best and were resigned to some accidental lapses because the whole business was so foreign and exciting and made them feel that they had stumbled into a country, of a sort, where for just an afternoon they could pretend to be genuine English people who took these traditions for granted.

There might, Paula warned them, be carols and probably a visit from Santa, whom they found a slightly intimidating figure whose origins and meaning they could not be sure of. At home Christmas cards (which they only received from tradesmen) were kept on the mantelpiece folded shut behind the clock, as if even a snow scene with a robin perched on a twig or a sprig of holly was enough to be a narrow portal through which Christianity could squeeze its way into the room brandishing a crucifix and ranting about a certain people who murdered Our Lord.

The whole expedition was fraught, transgressive and thrilling. They hoped that it would all turn out okay and that on Yom Kippur, when they were subject to judgement and the indifferent gaze of justice, the verdict would not be too harsh, though Mina privately thought, It's all a load of hooey in the end; you're born, you die, that's that. For she had tasted already forbidden fruits in the munitions canteen for which there had been no divine consequences but her husband didn't know about that.

Roland went to his parents in Herne Hill. 'You look like you're setting off on a death march,' Paula said. 'It can't be that bad, can it?'

'My sister will be there. She always makes everything much, much worse.'

'I didn't know you had a sister. You've never mentioned her.'

'Pamela. She's of a spinsterish disposition, could sour milk with a glance, lives with her friend Elspeth Midgely, blonde cherub, rosebud mouth, simpers.'

'Will she be there too?'

'Who?'

'Elspeth?'

'Oh no, Dad wouldn't let her in the house. Common accent. And she's fat. He hates fat women, thinks it's a weakness. Once, before the war, we went on holiday to Bournemouth, miles of golden sands, top-class hotels, that was what we were expecting, and we had to come home again after a couple of days, too many corpulent Jews taking up the deckchairs.' He laughed.

'He sounds very prejudiced.'

'Oh, he is. And it could be anything – a wart on the nose, a double chin, the wrong accent, the wrong job. He's a seething wiggle of pet hates.'

'I see. And what would he think of me?'

'They're never going to find out. I've never taken a girlfriend home and I don't plan to. If I ever get married it will be with a pair of witnesses pulled in from the street and no announcement until the deed is done.'

Paula could not think of anyone who would want to marry Roland, it would be a catastrophic mistake. He was who you misspent your golden youth on, not formed a permanent attachment to. She imagined him joining her parents for Christmas lunch at the hotel, decked out proudly in their paper hats, exclaiming over the novelty of roast parsnips, feeling a whinny of fear as they defied the Almighty and selected the ice cream, even though they'd have been safer with the fruit cocktail. She and Roland were a complete mismatch, but he had brought her through the doors of *sex*, that would not be forgotten. He is mad, she thought, but he's all I have. He was my first so I'll always remember him.

She didn't love him, whatever that meant. She had no idea what it was supposed to feel like and he of all people wasn't going to teach her. But she had found no evidence of other girls in the flat, no earring or handkerchief or crimson smoking stub. The girl in the poem was often on his mind, ' ... *hats and backchat*'. She asked Robin in the office if he recognised it. 'Of course,' he said, 'it's MacNeice, *Autumn Journal*. He works at the BBC so Roland probably knows him. Does talks, things like that.'

Your words could hurt because they were so honest ... So easily hurt, so readily responsive.

That's what he wants, not reserve and putting up a front like English girls. But that did not include him meeting Mina and Louis, and she did not impulsively suggest that they get together at Maison Lyons on Boxing Day for an early afternoon tea, another reservation Louis had made before they took a taxi to Euston for the journey home. For though she loved her parents, particularly her father whose only princess she was, and though they would be impressed by the familiarity, in person, of his radio voice, she knew perfectly well that he was not who they had in mind for her and would agitate for her return home. And while he would probably not regard them with the same curiosity as Uncle Itzik, they would still be specimens – alien, foreign, overdressed, a little overweight, too impressed by luxury and prone to a schmaltzy sentimentality that welled up at songs like 'The White Cliffs of Dover' and (she cringed when she thought of it) 'Daddy Wouldn't Buy Me a Bow-Wow'.

The Christmas crackers were a success. Mina put her paper hat on at once, it was a silver crown. 'Look at me,' she cried. They debated whether there was any reason not to have Christmas crackers at home in Liverpool, for they didn't seem to serve any religious purpose but were more like children's toys. An excavation of their contents revealed no hidden baby Jesus surprises. Louis' contained a miniature penknife, Paula's a tortoiseshell comb, Mina's a little iron, a charm for a bracelet.

The band, got up in mustard jackets with black satin lapels, played a Christmas medley. Several tables burst into song, the

166

unfamiliar words of carols. Mina and Louis smiled down at their plates. They did not want to be noticed not singing. The waiters ran back and forth with platters of turkey and troughs of vegetables. There were hundreds in the ballroom, the men in lounge suits, the women the new fashions from Paris: the cinched-in waist encircled by vicious corsetry, the peplum, the full skirts. The chandeliers irradiated everyone with a tinselly glow. A Christmas tree decorated with fairy lights and baubles ascended to the ceiling. The whole occasion lacked the austerity of their own religion with its intense pressure to always be doing the right thing in this world without even any hope of everlasting life in the next, for ideas of heaven were infrequent and sketchy. This secular Christmas occasion was proving to be all Louis and Mina had hoped for. It could hardly have gone better. They felt, for the first time, *included*, welcomed at the feast.

Some tables were seated with eight. At others grim silent couples sat sipping glasses poured from half-bottles of wine. At a handful of tables someone sat alone trying to exchange smiles with a neighbour, failing at sparking conversation like a damp match against a damp box, reminding Paula, shudderingly, of her own pre-Roland life in London and how there really was no going back.

A waiter, racing past, lost his footing and spilled a tureen of roast potatoes into a woman's lap, spattering her grey silk dress with fat. She had only just managed to attract the attention of a wan, elderly couple who evidently had many years ago worn out each other's company. She left the table and did not return.

'What a shame her day was spoiled,' Louis said.

'And what a life,' said Mina, 'to have nobody in the world, nebach.'

'And not hide in your room either,' Paula said, 'but come out and sit stoically by yourself. I couldn't bear it.'

'I suppose you must have many friends you go out with in the evenings and weekends, though we do not know their names. Won't you tell us?'

'Oh yes, piles of friends. Louisa and Harriet and Mary and Rosamund, and Ralph and Roland.'

167

'Very glad to hear it. Nice boys and girls?'

'Very nice indeed.'

The invented names came rushing to her head like starbursts.

'Itzik writes to us. I didn't know how he got our address, he seems to know everything. He mentioned this Roland.'

'Did he?'

'He says he works for the BBC; we were impressed,' her father said. 'He wanted to see us, to meet up.'

'Roland?'

'Itzik, of course, but your mother said no. I said I was curious, and after all, he must be a powerful man. It couldn't hurt.'

'It *could* hurt,' said Mina. 'He's trouble. Always was, like Jossel says. A polka doesn't change its dots.'

'A leopard, Mummy, a leopard doesn't change its spots.'

'Same thing. And when did I ever see one of them to know from?'

At that moment another powerful man approached their table and was introducing himself. It was Eric Fulton, Tony Agnew's film-producing partner, the one with the accent.

A flurry of delight on her parents' part – better than a shabby man from the Soviet embassy was a bona fide person from the Pictures, someone who was on first-name terms with film stars, rich, glamorous, their daughter's employer, who had deigned to come over to their table from his own where he was dining with his wife.

'How very nice to see you here, Miss Phillips, what an unexpected surprise. Your daughter has got us organised, we're very grateful, what a find. We haven't looked back since she joined us.'

'But surely you're not staying at the hotel?' Louis said.

'Oh, no, we live not a stone's throw away, though I don't recommend throwing stones, barbaric, they always do it in the Bible, and it ends badly. He who is without sin, as the gentleman whose birth we're celebrating today would say. We're in Manchester Square and we come here every year to eat our Christmas lunch. It's convenient to give the cook the day off so she can see her family and I don't want to miss out on a traditional Christmas, so exotic, so primitive, yet so very cosy.'

'We think exactly the same. It's our first time,' Mina said, 'I hope you understand.' She had unerringly clocked this 'Eric Fulton' was not what the name implied, easily identifiable as one of their own.

'Mrs Phillips, I understand *everything*. Would you care to join us for coffee in the lounge a little later? They will serve us there and bring our petits fours.'

'What a charming man,' Mina, said, when they had agreed to this assignation. 'Very nice; his name, what was it before?'

'I don't know, I don't suppose it was anything before.'

'Oh, it was. Don't worry, we'll get to the bottom of it, I think. And don't tell a soul back home, but I'm going to have the ice cream. If the Lord smites me down, then they'll hear all about it, if not, it's our secret.'

Paula thought her mother seemed skittish, girlish even. She was clearly enjoying herself and the day was going to be marked down as a great success. Her parents had come back from that post-war holiday in Paris with a new, springy quality to them. They seemed to feel that they had lived, and this gave Paula the confidence to believe that they would stop making plans for her, and start making plans for themselves instead. There would be no going home to Liverpool now. When no hand of God struck Mina as she ate a strawberry ice after the un-kosher turkey, though the day of judgement might be another matter, they filed out to the lounge through the double doors where the waiters were handing out Christmas presents.

'This is worth every penny,' Louis said, looking round at the glass-topped tables each with its vase of silk flowers, the whole scene twinkling under chandeliers. 'We should do this every year, you certainly get your money's worth.'

'Now *she's* a lady,' Mina whispered, as they approached the table where the couple were waiting for them. Fulton's wife was a striking blonde woman. (Not platinum, Paula thought, not brassy either, sort of pale straw colour – can't be natural, can it? Or can it? Some people have all the luck.) A triple rope of pearls with a diamond clasp brushed her throat and she wore an eau de Nil silk dress which had,

Paula said later, Paris written all over it. It was a hard colour to pull off unless you had skin with bluish veins near the surface. But Mrs Fulton, intimidating at first sight, was charming, friendly, squealing with delight as they all sat at the coffee table opening their gifts.

'How lovely, embroidered handkerchiefs, they do pull this off rather well.'

Mina said to Eric Fulton when the coffee and petits fours arrived, 'If you don't mind me asking, where are you from? I don't think you were born here, am I right?'

'You are, of course, correct. Let me introduce myself, Elias Flüsser.'

'I call him Eli, it's our little joke,' his wife said.

'I'm from a terrible town, way out in the sticks, you'd never have heard of it, it produced nothing but rabbis and thieves. And carp from the river.'

'And *you*.'

'Yes, me! So you see, your daughter is among friends, so to speak. I will make quite sure she is looked after, she's one of us. If you'll excuse my wife, who has *chosen* to be one of us, whatever the inconvenience.'

Mina thought this was very beautifully done. She asked how he had come to be in the film business. It was a long way from fish and rabbis.

'Well, good question. I suppose you could say I was a restless soul. I found myself, as one did in those days, in Berlin and started out first in the theatre with Max Reinhardt, then one thing leads to another.' He gave a heavy wink. His audience nodded knowingly. 'Scarpered in 'thirty-four. A pessimistic disposition, which was a life-saver, wouldn't you say? But you will have your own similar story, I'm sure, or we wouldn't all be sitting here on this delightful afternoon full of Christian delicacies. My first port of call was Paris, then I "legged it", as Tony puts it, in early nineteen forty, skin of my teeth, you know what I mean? I had some connections in London, met Tony, luckily, found we had nicely aligned minds. And he introduced me to Diane. Didn't want to inflict a name like Flüsser on a native-born Englishwoman.'

'How glamorous. And Mrs ...' But Mina did not quite know by which name to address his wife.

'Call me Diane, please.'

'I'm Mina or Millie, whichever you like.'

'I like Mina, I'll call you that.'

'Are you also in the films?'

'She was. She—'

'Don't listen to him, he'll only over-egg it, I *was* an actress but I lost my nerve, stage fright, couldn't remember my lines, froze on tour as Ophelia in Wolverhampton, the prompt had come down with flu and they forgot to put someone in his place, sheer carelessness, but when I looked across the stage for help I realised there was no one there *to* help. I was quite on my own, I started making up lines, can you imagine? A few boos from the gallery, ran off in tears at the end of my scene. So that was that. End of my career. Got a job as a continuity girl in the pictures, still do it, actually, only for my husband, of course. And here we are, isn't this nice?'

And it seemed to Mina and Louis that yes, it was very nice indeed, and that Paula had landed on her feet, and there was no need to worry about her, having been told, abruptly and without preamble a month ago, that she was turning her back on bedding and going to work for a couple of movie men. Had she planned this meeting? Was it really so accidental? But Paula, who sat more or less silently, was clearly in awe of her employer, whom she still addressed formally and would have to take instructions from the day after tomorrow.

Elias Flüsser ordered a brandy, inviting Louis to join him.

Diane said she would have a snowball. Mina asked, tentatively, 'What is that? It sounds so pretty.'

'It's Advocaat and lemonade, have you really never tried one? But you must, both of you. Even if you don't like it, you can eat the maraschino cherry.'

'Cocktails,' Mina said, 'whatever next! I must say, I'm having the time of my life. We'll do this again next year now we've got the hang of it. To hell with the cost, you can't put a price on memories.'

171

It was a third way between the drawn curtains of the suburbs (Louis always wanted to close them too early in winter, when there was still some light in the sky – 'Don't let the cold in, dear') and being on the outside like that doctor from before the war, tramping the streets with his leaflets. And Paula seemed to belong here, in a new, chic dress and diamanté clips, looking years older than her true age, now taking out a cigarette and bending across to the click of their new friend's silver lighter. The girl is a flame! she thought. This I made with my own body.

Finding a brief gap in the lively conversation, she said, 'Well, you know, I also have a story,' and embarked on the tale of the forest while her husband sat back and thought of the paintings he would see the next day at the famous Tate art gallery, and Eric Fulton leaned forward with glittering eyes and said, 'How old did you say you were when this happened?'

Paula could not believe it had all gone so well but was anticipating the next time she saw Eric Fulton in the office and what sort of relationship theirs had morphed into, or had it stayed just the same and he might regret this lapse of formality? It was hard to tell; she seemed to be on first-name terms with one boss and not the other. Something had been breached, in her parents' lives and possibly in hers. It was unnerving and odd and required, she felt, a radical readjustment. She had no idea how she would explain the occasion and all its consequences to Roland, and perhaps better not, to be on the safe side, God knows how he would make a song and dance about it, and ask all kinds of tricky questions to which she had no well-formed reply. He would be bound to trip her up.

Eventually Mina and Louis, slightly drunk, made their excuses, returned to their room for a rest, and Paula walked back to her bedsit. While she was changing, she was called to the phone.

Roland said, 'Where have you *been*? I've had the most awful time. I suppose you've been *enjoying* yourself like a normal person.'

'I don't think you should be so put out about that. We can't all suffer because you are having a bad day.'

'How can you be so selfish? Mummy tripped over the cat – drunk, of course. She's broken her bloody ankle; we had to take her to hospital. I've had nothing to eat but a piece of toast when I got home. No Christmas dinner at all. As far as I know it's still in the oven, she forgot to turn it on. Stone cold. Can you come to see me, maybe cook me something?'

'I'd better not, Mummy and Daddy will probably ring later.'

'Can't you say you're with a pal? I'm a pal, after all. Darling, please.'

'I have to be at the hotel first thing in the morning, we're going sight-seeing and things, I'm in their hands.'

'But I thought we'd spend the day together, go for a walk or take a boat out on the Serpentine.'

'Well, I can't. What about tomorrow night?'

'No good, I'm on air.'

'I'm sorry, darling.'

'*Darling.* So you say. Bitch, I should give you a good thrashing.'

She laughed.

He hung up.

28

After she had started at Harlequin Pictures, Paula had made herself familiar with its back catalogue. The company was only getting started and had just a couple of releases out there, neither of which she had seen. Roland had, of course. He said the first, a biopic of Nell Gwynne, was wearily typical of the stagey, romantic melodramas that everyone was making these days, and he wasn't sure how seriously one should take 'this bilge'. But the second, *Ad Astra, My Darling*, was 'interesting'.

This was one of Roland's words, which could denote genuine curiosity or the precursor for a tongue lashing.

'It's certainly slicker, and the fascination with mountebanks and fairground hucksters shades into, I don't know ... It's all very *heightened*, varnished, if you like. Are we supposed to believe that place along the river actually exists, or even *could* exist? But then the shot of the girl applying her lipstick in tight close-up, it was rather influenced by the surrealists. You have to make up your mind what you're doing and this is all over the bloody place. Why are some parts in black-and-white and some in colour? It's a distraction, a bit of a mess, I'm afraid. But there's certainly some talent there, I don't think it's a total write-off.'

'They long to shoot only in Technicolor, but the stock isn't easy to get hold of and even when they can often it's just too expensive for the budget, so they have to make do.' She had typed and filed many letters to film stock manufacturers, so this aspect of their forthcoming production she was familiar with.

'They should stick to black-and-white, it has purity. Colour is like a lurid dream.'

'Funnily enough that's sort of what Mr Fulton said last week. That – I think I've got this right – cinema is a highly organised hallucination which mimics real life, but a real life full of visions and ghosts.'

'Oh, did he now? And what did you reply? Or did you just clatter away in respectful silence on your typewriter? Girls have no opinions worth listening to. What are you all *for*, exactly; it's a mystery to me.'

'You know perfectly well what we're for. Or what you think we're for, you filthy beast.'

'Oh, that.' He ran his hand along her thigh. She would have liked to have brushed it away but she never did. It was all too arousing. He kissed her. She lay back on the cushions on his old leather sofa and waited, gazing up at the ceiling rose, a whorl of plaster ivy leaves. They might stand and move over to the bed, or do it here, among the fraying cushions. She preferred the bed, he liked the danger of toppling onto the floor and dragging her down with him. Sex, in those days, was terribly easy. Sex was around all the time, waiting for an opportunity. Roland was only punctilious about his bedside drawer of rubber johnnies. 'No surprises coming, if that's what you're hoping for, and then an engagement ring. There'll be no more Quinns marching out of *my* loins.'

But now he drew away and said, 'Well, come on? How did you respond?'

'I don't know why you go on at me like this. You could just leave me alone if you think I'm so unsatisfactory.'

'Not *you*, it's all the girls. You're not properly human, you know. Especially you, you've no education to speak of.'

'Then find a girl who has.'

175

'I don't want one of those frights. Never can keep their seams straight. You're like a mannequin, very beautiful. Normally you'd be out of my league. So, so fuckable. Now I want to hear more about this conversation. Continue.'

She was flattered, she was conceited, she was pleased to be both out of his league and fuckable. Outside the window snow had fallen on Primrose Hill, the sunset turned it pink like a Christmas card. 'Nature can be utterly vulgar and clichéd,' Roland said. Dark was coming in, she stood up and drew the curtains. She bent to turn on the lamps.

'You seem at home here,' Roland said. 'Are you angling to move in?'

'Of course not, don't be silly, that would be ... '

'Would be what?'

The phrase 'living in sin' came to her and she swallowed it, it was tiresome being called a provincial bourgeois.

'I'd really like my own flat. I think I could afford it in a few months.'

'I'd have quite liked you to have moved in, actually.'

'So I could cook your meals and do the housework? No thanks.'

'Where will you live?'

'Oh, I don't know, Chelsea?'

It was the first place that came into her head.

'You'll have to ask for a raise to afford that.'

'I might get one. Mr Fulton has something in mind for me.'

'What on earth ... ?'

'Mr Fulton is interested in my mother's story. About when she was a young girl in Latvia and she was wandering in the forest with a basket of mushrooms and met a band of Bolsheviks.' She giggled.

'And what is Fulton's interest?'

'He thinks, or I think he thinks, that it might be their next picture.'

'Extraordinary. A fairy tale, of course.'

'I suppose so. I wonder how he thinks it might end, but then he rushed off before I could ask. How funny, my mother's life portrayed in film.'

'A *highly organised hallucination*. Which is what that story might actually have been, when you think about it.'

'Really? Why on earth would she make that sort of thing up?'

'I assume her subconscious had an agenda of some sort, I don't know. You go into the forest and who are you when you come out again? That's what my Swiss Cottage woman is trying to find out.'

'I don't think my mother has that much of an imagination.'

'You don't need one, darling, it's all going on at another level. I expect she was just expressing the desire to be fucked.'

'You go too far, you can't say that about Mummy! She was only fourteen, for heaven's sake!'

'Are you never going to grow out of your provincial bourgeois phase?'

'*Stop saying that.*'

'I'll give you provinces. My sister was fucked in a railway carriage between Bournemouth and Weymouth. By a clergyman. She was seventeen. Or so she *says*. What do you think? Is such a story just a mask for her adolescent sexual fantasies?'

'How horrible, did she go to the police, report him?'

'Of course not, which is why it probably never happened. Now your mother and these Reds, she makes up a whole crowd of forbidden young men to populate her fantasies.'

'Oh, stop, please stop.'

'All hot and bothered, are we? Upset because Mummy might be a bit of a tart?'

She could leave now, or they would have sex, and to her shame in the years to come, she would remember that she had stayed and they had got up and gone to bed in the winter afternoon. Roland remarked afterwards, 'Well, you came like a fucking steam train, darling. What was it that so turned you on?'

177

29

The Story of the Forest was Harlequin Pictures' fourth feature and, after a stuttering start, its breakthrough movie internationally. When it was first released it was dismissed in the British press as 'a joke that the makers don't quite pull off', 'a romantic fantasy that veers off into obscurity', 'thin, pretentious'. But by the time it reached America, where the Yiddish-language writer Isaac Bashevis Singer was already publishing his fiction, it had acquired an audience of young Jewish intellectuals hungry for stories of the old world, its superstitions and symbolism. A largely admiring review in the *New Yorker*, making allusions to Cocteau's *La Belle et le Bête*, brought a quick re-release in Britain.

In those months between the first and second releases its young star, 'Introducing Jennifer Patterson', who had played the fourteen-year-old part of 'Hannah' with her breasts bound with bandages and hips suppressed by cruel corsetry, had reached her twenty-first birthday and had started to go to Mayfair nightclubs, photographed oozing out of the boned oyster satin bodice of her gown. She had been originally cast for a wavering quality on the cusp between innocence and vampishness. It really depended, Tony Agnew said, on how you looked at her. An innocent mind saw an innocent. But there were other ways of looking. So when she walked into the forest with her basket, you could believe that she was both a fairy-tale innocent and a girl just asking for trouble. The Board of Classification could not put its finger on what was so iffy since there was, as Eric Fulton said, 'absolutely no monkey business with the boys onscreen' and awarded it a U certificate, suitable for all ages.

Throughout the making of the picture, Paula told herself that all would be well, that her mother would accept that her story had been turned into an innocent fairy tale (a metaphor, for the more sophisticated): her temporary metamorphosis first into a snow-bird, her adventures in the sky, then the return to the forest floor and her second, vulpine transformation, before being restored to human form, setting forth on the ship to the New World, as if it had been a dream.

Mina had conveyed her story to Eric Fulton, as she had told it many times. She expected him to challenge her version of events, to demand more detail, to interrogate its contradictions like a police inspector: 'How could that have happened? Do you expect me to swallow this? No, the information is of no use to me at all.' But he seemed to have absorbed the story as if it had happened to himself. Soon he was telling it back to her. 'It never was like that!' she said. 'No, maybe it wasn't but this way is better.' 'Better how?' 'A better story.' The tale, this piece of once-lived first-hand experience, was his now; what she had was scraps and remnants of the original memory. She no longer knew what she believed and it seemed to her that if Eric Fulton thought she had turned into a snowbird then a she-wolf, maybe she had grown feathers and fur after all. Who could contradict him? For he had written her a cheque for £500, and he now possessed world rights in the story of the forest. If she was a wolf, then, God help her, she was a wolf and that was the end of it, she wasn't going to argue. The man was a gentleman. He was a shayne Yid, a beautiful soul. And his wife was a dreamboat, a lovely lady, such beautiful skin for one thing, and manners from heaven.

Mina did not know what to do with the money. She wanted to

divide it between her three children, though maybe Paula should have more, for she had made the introduction.

Louis said, 'The kids are doing fine. After all these years, why don't we take a holiday, don't we deserve it? Why not go to the South of France, stay in a top hotel?'

That is what they did, though Mina said she had nothing to wear. She bought her first bathing costume and, at the chemist, a bottle of tanning oil. Never, she said, had she suspected that when she went out to gather mushrooms it would end up like this, a wicker handbag in the shape of a sunflower.

They spent two weeks in Cannes, where they encountered no Bolsheviks at all but Belgian and French Jews who came down to dinner with wary eyes and a kind of flinching quality to their expressions when greeted by the maître d'. She purchased a gold-capped Helena Rubinstein lipstick and a pearl necklace and Louis bought himself an Omega watch with a tan leather strap. They strolled along the Croisette and Louis said, 'It was only a few years ago that the Nazi beasts were here, and look, all washed away, as if they never were, the sun is shining for us now.'

'Is it?' said Mina. 'You think?'

Five months after the Christmas Day lunch Paula had her own flat in Chelsea.

Eric Fulton's wife had fallen pregnant, there had been a stillbirth years earlier, then a miscarriage. On the advice of her doctor she had had her fallopian tubes tied and yet somehow one little wriggler had made it through. 'I can't help feeling,' Diane said, 'that if it's made it this far, such a tight squeeze it must have had, and the odds were really so many millions to one, that I should at least give the thing a *chance*, though it means lying on the sofa like a bloody invalid for months. What a bore.'

This news created a vacancy for a continuity girl, a repository for all the tedious detail of the picture, a vigilant memory bank with a sharp eye for hats and shoes and trees and cups and saucers and the ability to type it all up and keep immaculate records.

'It would save us an awful lot of trouble if you'd step in,' said Tony Agnew. 'Easier to find a secretary at the last minute. Diane will show you the ropes, you'll soon pick it up.'

He liked continuity in his continuity girls, said Bobby Orr, the key grip. Seamlessly, the show went on.

The flat in Chelsea had been taken in a hurry. She had not accounted for how far it was along the King's Road, a long way from Sloane Square tube. Shepperton Studios were even further out, not in London at all, Paula had not understood that. Every day the train took an hour to pass through Clapham, Wimbledon, Kingston, Hampton Wick, Teddington. Sometimes Eric Fulton picked her up and drove her out in his car but most days she was alone, gazing out of the window at unfamiliar Home Counties scenery, bucolic, quiet, picture-book vistas she had only seen in the films. The gap between London and the studio was a green and gold backdrop behind glass, punctuated by old villages. She could not imagine life carrying on there in any way she would recognise. What did people *do* all day when there was hardly anywhere to shop, no cinemas or restaurants? There were farms, thatched cottages, inns, and between, bulky cows, heads down, eating, mooing. She passed a field of pinkish pigs let out to go mad amid the clover.

The studio was a mile from the station. Sometimes she walked, sometimes a studio car would meet her. The day was very long and film sets were not glamorous. It was mostly waiting around, waiting for the right light, waiting for the rain-machine to be fixed, waiting for scenery to be built, waiting for costume changes, waiting for make-up to be applied, waiting for actors to recover from hangovers and tantrums, everyone playing cards, playing practical jokes. Where was the forest? Oh, we'll paint it in later, Agnew said, as a papier mâché tree was wheeled into place. The wolves were dogs in costumes, the birds came in cages with a trained handler. Jennifer Patterson was having an affair with Tony Agnew. Dressed up in her childish forest clothes, it seemed obscene when she came up behind him and nuzzled his ear, taking the lobe between her teeth and nibbling, as if he were a biscuit. He shuddered, 'Do it again! Harder.' Closer, through the Max Factor, you could see she did not have a child's skin. Pimples erupted around her hairline. She was dark and sulky and petulant and gave off whiffs of expensive scent.

Behind a cardboard tree shedding paper leaves due to poor glue adhesion, Eric Fulton grabbed Paula's wrist. 'Stop, I have something to say to you.'

'I'm listening.'

There was a sheen of sweat on her forehead, she smelled ripe, like a pear in the fruit bowl. She smelled to him as someone who had had sex recently and had not washed. Beads of perspiration dotted her upper lip. Tony had already taken Jennifer, he was entitled to something for himself.

He kissed her.

'That was what I wanted to say. What is your answer?'

'I'm not sure what the question is.'

'I think you do.'

'But what about your wife?'

'She does not require my attention at the moment, she is resting. It would be unkind to bother her, and also, I believe, unsafe, too much agitation of the womb. These are medical considerations, I put my wife's health above all else.'

It was strange to her to have his tongue, which had just been in her mouth, saying these words. Men were crazy, that's all there was to it. They were selfish beasts, one could never understand them, but one *wanted* them. He smelled of cigars and a masculine skin preparation, woody, boxy, arousing. He had a gold signet ring on his pinkie, it had brushed her face. He was twice her age.

'What arrangement do you have in mind?'

'Do you want a contract? Is that it, do you expect me to put something in writing?'

'No.'

'Well, suppose we say that for the duration of this picture we have a little fun together. Would you mind?'

'I have a boyfriend.'

'Then now you have a boyfriend and a lover. I'm not asking you to be my mistress. That's another thing altogether, my wife would not approve of such an arrangement.'

Eric Fulton smelled sexily of wealth, it came from the starched collars of his shirts and the careful way he combed back his hair and put a preparation on it. Above all, she thought, there was plenty of amusement, a lightness about him, and God knows you got none of that from Roland. She knew that the sex would not be so *charged*, so intense, but he might be a laugh in bed. He would come to the flat in Chelsea, she would make him delightful little suppers, she could manage an omelette, at the very least. And a glass of wine. It seemed harmless and, as he said, temporary. So why not? She kissed him back.

'Excellent! Now just don't say a word to your wonderful parents.'

'As if.'

30

All roads lead to and from Itzik. If Itzik hadn't invited Paula to the talk at the Conway Hall she would not have met Roland, without Roland she would not have heard about the job at Harlequin Pictures, would not have gone to work for them, would not have taken coffee in the hotel lounge on Christmas Day and Agnew and Fulton would not have made *The Story of the Forest* and Paula would not have begun her affair with Eric. These frail strands of coincidence were being pulled as an unbroken thread by a man with his own story.

One that begins with his nasty sneaky nature, earwigging over the banisters of the house in Riga and following his sister into the forest. How he ended up in the embassy of the Soviet Union in Kensington was a tale both melodramatic and romantic. Events had piled onto events and by 1917, still a teenager, having deserted from the army and fallen in with 'undesirable elements, though their hearts were in the right place, being of the People', he was shot robbing a store. Was wounded, delirious, nearly died, nearly had his leg amputated, lay in a slumber between life and death, like Louis on the battlefield, survived, came to as a citizen of the Soviet Union a long way from Riga and how he got there he wasn't about to say. All but the most truculent members of his outlaw band found themselves absorbed into the new system while the authentic ruffians preferred to go out in a shower of bullets. What mattered was that as a fish does not notice that it is swimming in the sea and a land creature is not aware of oxygen, Itzik very quickly forgot that communism was anything but the natural order of how things were done, because the communists now did everything so what was the point of arguing about it? He was of and for the People, because the People were the majority, they alone were the route to power. And his exterior presentation, coming from that short unimpressive body, lent to him the air of a man who could be of use, who would not argue with orders or sigh but would nod and you heard later it was 'all done, boss'.

This account had its origins not in the actual events of Itzik's own life but in a taste for reading which he acquired in his twenties when he fell upon some stories by Isaac Babel. The tales were of the fictional Benya Krik, the gangster king of Odessa. The curse of being a Jew was that people took you for a weakling and Babel might have been (probably was) talking about himself when he described the type with spectacles on his nose and autumn in his heart. But in every Jewish community there was a shtarker, a tough guy who was the fists for everyone else. No one wanted their son to be a shtarker but you wanted *someone's* son to be one.

'Tartakovsky,' Babel wrote, 'has the soul of a murderer, but he is one of us. He originated with us. He is our blood. He is our flesh, as though one momma had born us.'

Isaac Babel had a foot in both camps. He had done his military service on horseback in the cavalry. A Jew riding a horse shooting a gun. Mowscha Mendel would never have thought of that.

Riga was a port and ports are not the same as inland cities, they smell different, different types of people live there, but Riga, situated on a northern waterway facing Scandinavia and the Arctic, was a poor relation to Odessa which reclined on the edge of the Black Sea and was, in those days, one of the most famous Jewish cities in the world. In lawless, anarchic Odessa in the years before the Revolution you could get your hands on anything you liked and Odessan Jews were known to have acquired a taste for wine and luxuries – Jamaica rum, oranges from Jerusalem, cigars from Cuba, silk from Japan. It was ruled by the machers, the Top Men, and their authority was briefly consolidated after the tsar was taken out.

For as the gangster Benya Krik observed, 'Where there is an emperor there can't be no king.'

What Itzik would have done to have been Odessa-born and grow up to be a macher with a spicy nickname: Mishka the Jap, Sonya the Golden Hand. He read these stories with joy and exhilaration. The glamorous world brought to life those young Jews wildly brandishing machine guns while sporting chocolate-coloured jackets and raspberry-coloured top-boots. 'And Benya Krik got his way because he had passion, and passion rules the world.' Itzik wished he had that kind of natural, easy fervour. How he longed to discard his sneaky nature and be a free and fearless gangster who knows what he wants and takes it with pleasure, no devious machinations. Why couldn't he be forthright and strong? Well, his height told against him: he was only five feet four inches with a wide forehead and a loose curly mouth. His whole figure was foreshortened, his head too big, his legs too short for his torso, looking as though they could barely hold him up, though he was not without strength in the hands and forearms. He was no weakling, but he looked like one, Goliath trapped in the body of a monkey.

The truth about the years Itzik spent between the events which overtook the rest of the Mendel family during the war and his re-emergence as another kind of macher in a food procurement unit was unknown to anyone but himself and he told no one. The times were chaotic, there were few records. He *might* have been hiding out with the outlaws in the forest but if he did his compatriots were all dead and not available as witnesses. By 1925 Itzik found his present situation unsurprising and uninspiring. The son of a Riga grain merchant had wound up as a provincial Soviet government grain merchant. What was the difference? In his bitterest moments he wondered if a snowy miasma of flour would ever leave him. He knew about flour by osmosis, all those evenings spying on his father's conversation hoping to hear something to his advantage. Which turned out to be an understanding of the relations between the millers of grain and the bakers of bread. And in such a position he thrived, for he was a conduit between two spheres of activity. He heard things, he picked things up, he passed them on to the authorities. He acquired a nickname: Itzik the Worm, for the way he wiggled his way into greater and greater positions of responsibility.

He had always felt he was a type naturally unlovable because of his appearance; Jossel had fairer hair and dreamy eyes, or so the girls were likely to say. Itzik congratulated himself on his isolation from the human heart with its easy capacity to betray and condemn when it feels aggrieved. In thirties Leningrad, where he ended up in a certain job in a certain place under a certain somebody's direction, to have an intimate friend was to risk revealing one's secrets or be betrayed for reading a pamphlet too early before it had been adopted as Party policy, or too late when it had been denounced – all the crimes you could be accused of, including ones they hadn't thought up yet and which could be applied retrospectively. But at night in his bed he felt like his insides were clouds. He would never be a gangster in raspberry-coloured top-boots, that time was over, and what else could fill the painful hollow in his chest, for he felt as if he was nothing but stale air. In this period of his life, like Paula much later, he was waiting, waiting for the day to be over so he could go to bed and escape into dreams where everything seemed real and they couldn't touch you. Dreams were messages of hope and happiness. Asleep he was invincible.

He dreamed of the house of his childhood, the bustling rooms, the voices and footsteps passing in and out, his mother in the kitchen, saying little, understanding everything, the country maids shaking out the bedding, the iron stove, the row of dolls in his little sister's bedroom. Mina and Jossel talking on the stairs about the forest, their subsequent flight on a ship to the New World, their father's face blackened for weeks as if by fire. His mother never

187

expressing that she loved him, as if she wished he had been still-born, that's what he read into her silence. Was he right, or was she just a natural non-talker? He woke up from a dream of her singing him a lullaby ('*Schlof, mein yingele schlof*') and doubted for the first time his sense of grievance. His parents were dead, that he had been able to find out. His father shot in the street, his mother gone quickly of a fast cancer in her breast. He would have liked to have asked her, 'Did you love me, love me just a little bit, a thimbleful of love to wet my newborn head?'

But that whole world had disintegrated into dust and was lost for ever. The house in Riga might be still standing but if he ever returned there he would find it inhabited by strangers and no friendly faces to greet him. The past was a dead, cold planet.

And this led him to two conclusions about his life. That he would remain in this isolation for the rest of his days, waiting for the nails in his coffin to close over his face, or he must take a chance and make a new family: the family of Itzik, with wife and children and in-laws and cousins and nieces and nephews. All his instincts were for the first course of inaction, not to risk everything that love promised and threatened you with. Better to lie in the dark, preparing yourself for the perpetual darkness. But the heart wants what the heart wants, it has its own agenda, he could not help himself. Who could stand this loneliness? Who could bear to live so long with your body untouched? Some have cats and dogs, they stroke their pelts, but did the animal ever stroke you back? His heart wanted to be thawed out, could it? Even in the coldest Russian winter spring arrived eventually, and the birds sang their incessant high-pitched mating calls and the plants sent forth blossoms in the warmer air. It all started up again, out of death, and if it was possible for snow and ice to melt even in Siberia, then the heart of Itzik Mendel could also be touched. Against his nature he went looking for a wife.

The time of the shadchans was over. Still, the general principles applied when you came to look for potential matrimony: a girl from a good family bringing not a dowry but opportunities for an ambitious man in the prime of life. And so Beyla appeared on the scene, twenty-four and small, almost dwarfish, she reminded him of a china doll with reddish curls and a happy smile. He first saw her walking in the Summer Garden with her friends, panting along behind them like a small dog they adored, and made it his business to be there the next weekend and to catch up with her and detach her from her group. How charming she appeared to him, how easy it turned out for a man to be captivated by the way her cheeks bunched up and shone when she laughed. Her button nose and black nostrils, she snorted like a piglet when she laughed. He thought you could pick her up and take her down from the shelf and put her back again, and she would be waiting for you when next you were ready for her.

Beyla took the courtship by this shabby young man with a pragmatic resolve that she would have him. She had always known she was destined for a short person and by the time she was fifteen she had cottoned on that shorties tended to have an inferiority complex, some try to punch above their weight, are ambitious beyond their natural reach. Itzik was such a man; Napoleon, she had heard, was another. Another thing, she was a doctor who worked in a medical laboratory and came home odorous with chemicals. Some men might find this off-putting but Itzik had a poor sense of smell. Roses were a closed book to him, but so were dung hills. Her father said, 'If you marry this one, he'll go far. Whether he loves you or not, I can't say, it depends on whether that kind of thing matters to you.' Beyla said, 'He'll come to love me, why not? Am I not lovable, doesn't everyone say so? He is not, so just showing him some affection will bind him to me. I'm not afraid of life with him. Also, no in-laws, no mother-in-law looking around for corners I haven't cleaned. He's all alone, our family will absorb him.'

Itzik thought he had chosen Beyla, as Jossel thought he had chosen Lia on board ship, but Beyla was the one who decided, she was the one who had figured it all out, her mind unclouded by emotional longings and pain and loneliness and dreams.

Itzik was reborn, he was a new man, a family man with two small

189

daughters like little imps, full of energy and having inherited their mother's laughter and smiles. Finding a bird pecking in the street a cause for uproar and pointing and chasing. The sight of them on little legs trying to catch the bird now in flight, rising fast into the sky to the safety of a tree in leaf, caused in Itzik a stab of joy when he recalled it. And would they always be joyful and loving when they grew up or would life beat it out of them? Would they turn into sombre and sullen women with bad husbands and dubious thoughts? He hoped he did not live long enough to see it, but if he did, at least *he* would remember.

But his memory was the only place they survived. The times killed them, history assassinated their brief lives. Aged nine and seven was as far as the girls got; under the harsh conditions of the war they did not survive their childhood illnesses. Beyla had died of hunger during the siege. He had watched her yellowing skin as she starved to death. And he had come through intact; the smallest, the runtiest of the Mendels, needing little, was unaccountably still alive and walking the earth.

He knew the fate of Rivka and her husband and children who were still alive up to 1943. He knew the name of the camp. No one came out. Now it was just a clearing in the forest. She and her family had been driven there and murdered and the evidence destroyed. The quiet leaves were the only witnesses. Solly, the kid, the baby, had fared better; how he had done it Itzik did not know. But he guessed that when you have your back to the wall and a gun pointed at your head you behave like Benya Krik, be a shtarker, not a martyr. Enquiries released a bad smell around him, he consorted with evil elements and was said not to be loyal to the People in ways that Itzik couldn't afford to be associated with.

On a bus in Moscow he had suddenly burst into tears and cried out, My *family! I have no one!* And a comrade took pity on him and gave him the sleeve of his own coat to dry his tears. Itzik felt something had cracked inside him, he was a leaky jug, no use. Love did this to you. Better he had never laid eyes on

Beyla, and enjoyed the pleasures of a solitary bed for the rest of his life in peace.

Another one who was dead was Isaac Babel, the imaginary Benya Krik could not save him. He was arrested, imprisoned in the Lubyanka and executed in 1940. Ashes and ice in the mouths of his admirers. Itzik had seen men dead one minute, ghosts come back to life the next during a temporary period of rehabilitation, no longer shadows and mist but corporeal in the world. But in the case of Babel it could not be in person as his body had been cremated and his ashes buried in an unmarked mass grave at the Donskoi Cemetery. For a long time the authorities would lie and tell his family in Paris that he was alive somewhere in the Gulag. The French intellectuals like Sartre and de Beauvoir who Roland admired were warm towards the Soviet Union and would not have wanted to hear that it had murdered one of its greatest writers. Itzik knew, he stayed shtum; what else was he supposed to do? Truth was a worthless currency, a bad coin. A man was not entitled to an inner life, it belonged to the State, the truth belonged to the State, it was whatever it said it was. And in the end, Itzik thought, how do you tell the difference between your own spontaneous feelings and the ones the State has created for you? For he should feel glad that his little family had stood up to the Nazi Beast, preserved the integrity of the People and the Soviet Union; he should be proud of their martyrdom. And sometimes this was what he did feel and other times he thought, *To hell with that.*

He had thought he had no one, not a soul in the world; the last he had heard Mina and Jossel were waiting for the guns to stop in France so they could sail on from Liverpool to America, which was a country for which he had no remit, no connections. But they were here, still here. There was a sister and a brother, nieces and nephews, the whole mishpochah of relatives, the ones who had got away to safe shores, away from the intense reality of history. *These people*, Paula in particular, who turned up looking like a mannequin with jewellery, a mouth drawn in with red paint.

Mina had sent him a letter in the end. She defied Jossel. Was she not the one who felt sorry for cast-offs? Why should she not drop him a line, make nice, what would it cost her after all? It was just words, words she wrote with Harry's help.

So she told Harry to say that she was glad her brother was still alive, and how strange everything had turned out, when it was her who had met the Bolshevik boys, and shouldn't they all be proud the way Stalin had held the line, how the Russians had won the war with their sacrifices, but where was everyone, where had they gone, did he know? Did he have any information? Maybe they would meet one day, take a cup of tea together and reminisce about the old times, about their mother and father and how happy they had all been in the house by the harbour, though their father was a proud unyielding man and what good had it done him?

Which Harry wrote down in short staccato sentences, starting with 'I am in receipt of certain informations – such persons known to you – wartime expediencies . . . ' and concluding with 'Yours sincerely', which was the proper way to sign off. Making his mother's voice sound like a bank manager, because that was the only kind of letter he knew how to write, how they'd been taught in school, leaving no hostages to fortune.

Mina said, 'Can I see what you wrote down?' He handed her the letter.

'This is the correct way?'

'Yes, this is how it's done, Ma. Businesslike.'

'I'm not so sure it's right; he's my brother, after all.'

'I know, I know he is, but remember where it's going, to an official address. You got to be careful. We don't want any trouble.'

'From who?'

'You never know who is going to read it before it gets to him.'

'This is true. But you don't even mention some things I said, about the boys.'

'Better not. I'm just taking precautions, Ma.'

'Whatever you say, son, you know best.'

'I can get the girl to type it for you, if you like.'

The letter was put into the typewriter, entered an envelope, a stamp licked and affixed, the King's head looking sideways like he did on the money giving it all the necessary authority, sent to the embassy where numbers of people read it and copies were taken, and filed in more than one place until it eventually reached Itzik who felt that sense of foreboding when one knows that *no good can come of this*. The wording made no sense to him, this was not a letter from a sister. Who had dictated it, and on whose orders? And why no mention of that business in the forest? It had all started there. What was she trying to hide? And who from? Out of his paranoia grew a desire for revenge.

31

The last time Paula saw Roland they took a bath together. It was his idea ('Darling, would you like to hop in the tub with me, I'll give you *such* a scrubbing?') and it seemed for a moment a sexy, sensual proposition. To wash his chest with its meagre hairs, soap him down until he was slippery and perfumed with the bar of lime-scented Floris she had bought him for Christmas. The bathroom at home was the place of the airing cupboard, her father locked in, straining over his bowels, the smell of him and her brothers, the seat left up. It was a realm of privacy defended against intruders. The idea of sharing a bath with another human being was one of Roland's modern thoughts. It depended on there being enough hot water and the room not too chilly.

'There's a heater, darling,' he said, 'have you never noticed? It's on the wall. I can put that on if you'd like.'

'You really want to do this, don't you?'

'Yes, why not? Just get undressed if you're going to or we'll have to think of something else to do.'

She remembered how little Roland usually bathed – once a week, if that – and how the bar of Floris soap was still unopened from its tissue paper, and actually, now she thought about it, how unerotic it would be lying with him in the scummy water. She might have turned back, but she thought, Oh, well, if he wants to do something nice for once ... Lately he had become impossible, not completely so, she calculated, but irrational, starting fights, picking at a scab of jealousy. She knew he knew about Eric. He said his name with a pulse of hatred. She assumed Robin Rose had told him. He hadn't. It was Itzik who had said, 'My dear old friend, we are friends now, aren't we, and we must look out for the young lady, we must not allow her to be taken advantage of by an older, powerful man in a position of authority. We must save our little Paula from that.'

Roland had suddenly felt an attack of vertigo, as if he was peering down a lift shaft, leaning much too far over the edge. Everything seemed so thick and muddled these days. Paula breezed in at times of her own convenience with her stupidity, her lack of natural grace, her lacquered artificial finish, talking about shooting scripts and close-ups and dolly shots. He had not taken her on for her conversation. *He* was supposed to educate *her*, his little Pygmalion. And he had taught her sex, he had deflowered her. Forgetting that once he had done that, now, it turned out, anyone could have her. He imagined lines of men queuing down the street, waiting their turn like housewives waiting for the butcher's ration. It drove him mad. He must punish her for her promiscuity. Possession, he thought, was nine-tenths of the law, but for how much longer would he have her? And who or what would he be without her? He didn't like to think about it, which meant, he supposed, that he must be in love with her. Which he associated with flowers and boxes of chocolates and engagement rings and there was no way this could be happening to him, it didn't fit at all. He didn't believe in it. It was another temporary hallucination.

In the bath, he called Paula his angel. She smiled. Seemed flattered, splashed his chest, blew him a kiss. She could be proud, haughty, wasn't now. He had her between his finger and thumb.

'Am I?'

'Of course, I don't mean a Renaissance angel, you'd be completely out of place at the National Gallery.'

'Why is that?'

'You're vulgar, your face is too modern.'

'How can a face be modern? I don't know what you mean.'

'Well, your eyebrows are plucked into those very thin arches that are in fashion at the moment, completely unnatural, and your mouth has a painted cupid's bow and there's that black dot you draw in by your lip. Why do women do this? Your kittenish tricks drive me mad. I used to sneak into my sister's bedroom and smell the cups of her brassieres because she powdered them with scented talcum. What do you even need brassieres for? They're a trick, too, pushing up your bosoms to shove themselves in a man's face.'

'How revolting you are.' She splashed water in his face. He grimaced and wiped away what felt like tears.

'Me? I am revolting? That's a laugh, we both know what I taught you to do with your mouth. You went for it like a bird takes to the air.'

Her body shuddered, her chest went red. Her limbs gave out heat to the cooling water.

'I only did it once.'

'But you liked it, didn't you, that Paris whore's stunt.' He made a gobbling gesture with his mouth. 'You did it once, so do it again, go on, bend your head.' And his hand reached for the back of her damp hair.

She slapped him lightly. He withdrew his hand in surprise. His cheek bore a momentary imprint.

'Oh, is it violence you want? Well, violence you can have. If you don't mend your ways, miss, I'll whip you.'

She laughed. The things he came out with, how could one take him seriously? 'Where on earth are you going to get a whip from? Do you have a horse I don't know about?'

'There are saddlery shops where they stock that kind of thing.'

'Yes, in the countryside, I suppose, but in London? I don't think so.'

'Well, there are the King's horses, the Guardsmen must get their paraphernalia from somewhere. Saddles, and bridles and bits, that sort of thing. Now I come to think about it, there's a saddlery shop in the Strand.'

'I've never noticed.'

'When did you ever pay any attention to shops that aren't hats and gloves and gowns and jewels? No, hang on, the Army and Navy must sell them, of course they will, no better place.' He laughed, satisfied. 'Get ready for a good thrashing, young lady.'

'Oh, you are so pathetic.'

The shared bath had not turned out to be a romantic moment. The water had cooled, there was nothing left in the immersion tank to heat it. The Floris soap had sunk to the bottom and grown watery, lost. It is time to pull the plug, she thought. And yanked its chain.

'What are you doing?'

'It's over.' She hadn't meant to say that but when the words came out of her mouth she knew they were true.

'What's over? What do you mean?'

'I'm cold.'

'I know you are, you always have been. You don't care for me at all.'

'Oh, Roland.'

He stood naked on the bathmat, at half-mast. How frail he seemed. He used to be a soldier, she thought, I always forget about that. He doesn't look as if he could say boo to a goose, yet he must have fought somewhere, had a rank, a war record, bad memories, been brave or frightened. His body showed no sign of a wound, no bullet scars.

'By the way, what did you do in the war? I never asked.' It suddenly felt important to complete the picture, so the story could end.

'Then why are you asking now?'

'I just can't imagine you in uniform, going into battle.'

'I had a uniform, all right. It's still in the wardrobe, as it happens. I'm surprised you never noticed.'

'I'm going to look right now.'

'Help yourself.'

She found it, the navy blue jacket, the gold buttons, the stripes.

'Oh, so you went to *sea*. I hadn't thought of that. You in a ship, dodging U-boats and torpedoes. Was it exciting or boring and do you have medals?'

'Yes. I do. Just the usual ones; nothing for gallantry, if you're looking for a hero.'

'Show me.'

'My mother has them. I don't keep them here.'

'But you keep your coat.'

'It's warm.'

'Put it on. Let me see you in it.'

'No, *you* put it on.'

'Me?'

'Yes, leave it unbuttoned, let your tits hang out.'

'Okay.' She sniffed at the serge to see if it had a salty smell. 'It's very heavy.' The shoulders weighed her down.

'I wish I had a camera. I could sell the pictures to a dirty magazine. You'd be famous in Soho. I really should buy one. I'd take pictures of you every day and you'd be in every sex shop. I could see you any time I like, which isn't the case now, is it?'

'You think I'm a tart? Really?'

'Yes. You *are* a tart.'

'Because I have a modern face? Is that why I'm a tart?'

'If you say so. If that explanation suits you, I'm sure I can think of more.' He patted the back of his own head and giggled. Conscious he had gone too far, he tried to think of ways of going further.

Paula remembered the woman being sick in her handbag outside the York Minster. Perhaps once, long ago, she had had a modern face and it had all led to there, to the pavement, to being rubbish.

He said, 'Also, while you're still here, who exactly sent you?'

'Sent me where?'

'Here, *here*.'

'Like a letter, a parcel?'

'Stop playing with words. Are you spying on me?'

She thought, You really need to get out of here before he goes completely off his rocker.

'I'm going to get dressed now. Will you come outside and find me a taxi?'

'Where are you going?'

'Home, of course.'

'Why there of all places? You're seeing another man, aren't you, a *third* fellow. I can tell from your face, as if I didn't know already.'

'Don't be so mad.'

'Who is it? Not Robin Rose, he's an obvious fruit, but you've fucked one director, now you're going for the other one – you are, aren't you?'

He went and lay full length on the leather sofa, his arms by his sides. 'If you're going, then go, I don't see why you need my help, it's not the blackout. You'll find a taxi easily enough, they'll love a fare all the way to Chelsea. Have you got enough money? If you haven't, I'll pay you for a fuck. My little tart, you're not really going, though, are you? I might be court-martialled, you know, for letting you wear my uniform. Did you find anything in the pockets? Did I leave anything there, left over from the Battle of the ... No, I mustn't say it, they'd throw me in the clink. Or in the drink.'

'Get up. You'll freeze to death lying there.'

'Where are you going?'

'I told you, home. Roland, I don't think I'm going to see you again.'

'The hell you won't. You're mine.' But he made no effort to stand and prevent her from leaving, or even sit up; he lay back looking half-dead, she thought. A scrap of a man. A fillet of a human being, boneless, wasted. What had he made her feel that she suddenly did not feel any more?

On the street Primrose Hill was a dark hump in the distance. It was near eleven o'clock. Not too late to find her way home. There were still buses running and the lights of several taxis milled about on Regent's Park Road, returning to the West End for one last push at a fare. That was easy, she thought, as she found a cab and settled down into the seat. Easier than one might have expected. It was just a matter of asserting your rights and opening and closing a door. After a while the taxi turned into the King's Road.

'Is it much further?' the driver said. 'This road is always longer than I think; it goes on for bloody ever.'

32

Like God in the Old Testament brooding over the abyss, Itzik considered the situation and made a plan for his revenge on all who had slighted him. Roland was not important but the man's arrogance got up his nose (this was a new expression he had recently learned: the experience of an irritant in the nostril was exactly what Roland felt like).

First he dropped round one morning to the Primrose Hill flat. The place was in disarray, it smelled of spermy sheets and cigarette ash and sour spilt milk. Paula had evidently not been there in some time to do her womanish little things to the disorder. Roland did not even apologise for the mess; he seemed immune to the jumble of dirty plates and glasses in the sink. Itzik wondered how he still functioned at the BBC, but perhaps behind the wireless mesh they were all like this, with yellowish eyes, stinking of cigarettes.

'Are you still stepping out with my niece?' he said. This was another new English expression, which seemed to imply the opposite of what it meant. Roland and Paula, he supposed, spent most of their time at home, in bed.

Roland shrugged, as if to hoist the weight of a girlfriend off his thin shoulders. It had been nearly a fortnight since he had heard from her. He was too proud to nag her back to him. At night he thought of her, naked in his pea coat. He supposed he would never get to thrash her, see her skin turn pink with the excitement of it. He had been building up in his mind to bondage, none of that was likely to happen now. Unless he could put things right between them but he didn't have the strength, he was ridiculously tired, he supposed he might be suffering from anaemia, needed a plate of spinach and fried liver to set him up. He had missed two appointments with his woman in Swiss Cottage. He didn't feel like talking.

'It is a good job,' Itzik was saying, 'you intellectuals don't believe in bourgeois morality in your private lives, it would be so embarrassing for a different type of man, a conventional type, to bear the reputation of a cuckold.'

A sour possession rose up again in Roland's throat like heartburn. He had thought of her as a butterfly, impaled on his pin, reserved for his inspection and admiration and enjoyment. Damn her, damn the bitch.

'Yes, that's all so very old hat.' He raised his open palm to his mouth and patted the air, a Regency yawn.

'So you don't mind?'

'Not at all, she's free to do what she likes, with who she likes. I don't want her to turn into a bore. Heaven forfend.'

'Did she tell you who it is?'

'She might have mentioned it, I probably wasn't paying attention. We don't have those kinds of conversations. Frankly I didn't listen to her most of the time, she had nothing interesting to say.'

'Well, at least the old chap is married so it shouldn't last. Men like that always go back to their wives.'

Now he thought he should have insisted that she move in with him, she could have kept the place tidy and emptied the ashtrays and he would have slept with her every night and there would have been no opportunity for another chap to touch skin he thought of as satiny like a black-market blouse. But he'd let her move to Chelsea and she was out of his orbit now, she was spinning away from him. In fact, whichever way you looked at it, everything was. And it was his own fault, for giving her that introduction to Robin

Rose instead of letting her continue in her position of secretarial inferiority where she would be under his thumb, subservient and servile. Then he could thrash her as much as he liked. The lost erotic potential of a live-in Paula depressed him.

They talked for a while about the situation in the Soviet Union. Itzik praised Stalin in the usual terms, phrases like blocks of wood and concrete, resisting slippage and misunderstanding. They bickered and then Itzik left and walked through Regent's Park, past the nannies wheeling perambulators, looking for the ghosts of his wife and daughters running across the mown grass, wild and rambunctious and free. Why them? he asked himself. Why not these representatives of a rotten imperial power?

Next he wrote to Mina again, this time in the guise of a worried relation, stating that, and it had to be said with delicacy, her daughter was the girlfriend of a drug fiend and he was communicating this out of what he called *concern* and for the good name of the Mendel family. A name which had gone through a number of permutations to wind up as Phillips but the facts were the same.

Mina's knowledge of intoxicants and stimulants stopped at alcohol: a champagne cocktail at Bernice's wedding, the snowball at Christmas at the hotel. She had never heard of marijuana, let alone heroin. She consulted her younger son who had a reputation as a man of the world.

Benny listened in shock. He was currently courting a girl called Ruth Blackstone whose parents already did not approve of him because he had been rumoured to frequent public houses and drink pints of beer like the common folk. A sister mixed up with a drug addict would put the kibosh on that.

Benny said to his mother, 'Don't worry, Ma, let me and Harry fix this.'

'How will you do it?'

'All I'll say is there won't be any negotiations.'

They drove down to London on Saturday morning in their father's Humber. All week they had gone to business in suits with ties clamped down with tiepins and decorative folded handkerchiefs in their breast pockets like good Jewish boys in family businesses, sons with war records and campaign medals who marched with the Jewish ex-servicemen's association. Now in their father's car they turned into hooligans *itching* for a fight, practising poking the air with their fists and coming out with crude expressions about what they were going to do to that mamzer who had ravished and brought low their sister.

The English countryside rolled away beneath their wheels. Lancashire turned into the Potteries. They drove past farms and fields, cattle and, sheep; they shared the driving, stopping at a lay-by to gulp down wurst sandwiches and, turning their back to the traffic, irrigate the grass verge with volumes of piss. London eventually loomed in front of them, they hardly knew it. It was not their territory but now they had to find their way to Roland's address, a place with a hill, named after a flower. They got lost in Hendon, recovered their position in Golders Green, navigated Alexandra Palace, stopping to take a photograph of the BBC transmitter which beamed out Roland, got badly lost again in the vicinity of Hampstead Heath when they thought they had taken a wrong turn and left London altogether, then finally reached Primrose Hill which was the northern margins of the West End.

They hung around waiting for Roland to come home. From high ground they looked across to St Paul's, 'the big goyishe shul', Benny called it. Then, like fox hounds, they saw their quarry. The door of the house was usually kept unlocked, in those days when there wasn't much to steal, and the flat door was ajar, as if Roland was waiting for someone. Waiting for their sister? Neither of them was a large man, they were not beefy shtarkers like Osher Blackstone back in the old days on Brownlow Hill, but there were two of them, they had the advantage of surprise and Roland was in an advanced state of what was called in those days 'nerves'. They were able to take out his front teeth.

'Left him whimpering on the floor,' Harry said proudly when they got home late that night, stiff after hours behind the wheel. 'We didn't kill him, we just made him *wish* we had.'

'And left him a reminder that the Jews are not so weak any more,' Benny added, with a wink.

Looking down on his mouth full of blood, spitting out dental enamel onto the carpet, the brothers saluted each other, raised their hands to their foreheads as if they had won the war. Then they drove to their sister's flat. Eric Fulton had not long left, she was curled, soft, warm, kissed in all the right spots. He had told her she was gorgeous; he would, for as long as it was possible, make her as happy as he could. There would be presents, 'parting gifts', she thought.

When she heard a knock on the door of her flat she assumed Eric had come back for something, perhaps his keys or his lighter. She looked around her little sitting room for a lost object which she could give back to him, smiling at having known what he had returned for, and receiving another kiss.

Harry rushed in and started packing up her life. He threw her things into a suitcase, jumbled up together, the face creams next to the dresses. The diamanté clips skittered across the floor and fell through a crack in the skirting board. Benny, who was fastidious, said, 'Take care, you're making a right mess there, they'll come out all stained.'

'What the hell is going on?' Paula said. 'What do you think you're doing?'

'We know about that boyfriend. Has he got you on opium yet?'

'Oh, him. I haven't seen him in weeks. I'm finished with him. You can go back home and impart the news that I'm safe and sound.'

'Impart? Big word.'

'It only has six letters, Benny.'

'You know what I mean. Anyway, we promised Ma we'd fix it and that's what we're doing.'

'She has sanctioned this?'

'By any means, Paula, any means.'

'Oh, just listen to yourselves, you're absurd.' She turned her back on them and reached for a cigarette. The little drama could not go on too long, they would all go out for a bite to eat and then the boys would be on their way home. They were behaving like they were *in* a film. It was all too ridiculous.

The heel of her shoe came off as they were dragging her downstairs. The neighbours came out of their flats and stood on their doorsteps, Benny shouting, 'She's our sister, she's not well, we're taking her home.'

And she was screaming back, 'You pair of bloody hooligans. I wish you'd never been born, I wish I was an only child.'

Then she was in the car and they were driving through the night, back to the north, back to her childhood bedroom, her parents waiting up in the lounge in their nightclothes, bread and butter and cheese under a damp tea towel, a plate of biscuits, a jug of orangeade. Paula ashen, like a walking statue, her mother thought. She went straight to bed, eating nothing, and woke the following day at noon, Mina sitting at the end of the bed watching her daughter stirring from a heavy sleep.

'I'm sorry we did this to you, but don't forget, once I nearly got into trouble, my brother got me out of it, Harry and Benny were only doing the same thing. I know you're upset. But mamzers are mamzers the whole world over.'

'Mummy, you needn't have worried, Mr Fulton was looking after me.'

'Oh, was he? That was nice. What does his wife think about such niceness?'

'We were making a *picture*, your picture, that's all.'

'And we will all go to see it when it comes out. I wonder what he has done with my life.'

'It's not a biopic.'

'I know. I've got the soup on, come down for lunch when you're ready. The boys will be back from golf in a minute. We can all eat together like the old days.'

At the table Louis said, 'I suppose I should blame myself for giving her ideas. I never thought, I mean how could it have come to *this*? London is a big place, millions of people go about their business respectably, yet she has to get mixed up with undesirables.'

'Maybe she gets it from me and Jossel,' Mina said. 'Maybe we've got a bad seed we pass on.'

'Don't be ridiculous. There's no such thing. The fact is, she fell in with the wrong type of goyem, bohemians. They lead a rackety life. I took her to the Walker, I took her to the theatre, she read books. She had the taste for another way of life and I gave it to her.' He theatrically mimed banging his head against the table laid with silver-plated cutlery.

'I don't know what to think. We gave her everything, the very best, you'd have thought she could have been more . . . I don't know the word.'

'Discerning?'

'Is that a good one? Okay. This terrible man she was carrying on with, what did she see in him?'

'What do women see in any man? I don't know, you tell me. Did you ever hear the stories about the Brassey boy who had the hairdresser's on Allerton Road? They say he was quite a card with the local housewives.'

'That's just gossip, I don't believe a word of it.'

'Not you, of course, I never meant you . . . '

Mina had not thought of Sammy Brassey for years. Men, she thought, aren't very complicated. They want what they want and say so. A woman has to hide a lot away. It gets into a mess. Now there was going to have to be a story, her daughter was going to have to save face. Something happens to you, your brothers rescue you from danger, you go on to lead a different life as if it had never happened, but it *did* happen, you'll always remember, and how you tell it is who you are going to be in your future. They would find a way of telling this new story, as they had told the story of the forest and of Jossel's flight from his family into the arms of the shiksa. There would be contradictions, false clues, Harry and Benny would play an heroic role, Paula would be blameless. Yet Mina was secretly pleased and did not say so, told no one that her daughter had had her moment in the forest and no real harm had come to her.

When later in the day Paula went to turn on the wireless, Louis got up and intercepted her before her hand could reach the knob. 'Haven't you heard about television?' he said. 'I've ordered a set, it's coming on Wednesday. The Wattses two doors down already have one, it's the talk of the avenue.'

She knew her brothers had taken out Roland's teeth, they had boasted about it on the drive back, where from the back seat, watching the road signs pointing to the north, she heard them say, 'The shmuck, the lobos, he won't forget us in a hurry.'

She was fond of her brothers and ashamed. Harry proclaimed himself to be a good boy, but Benny was squaring up to be a wise guy, a Dutch Schultz type, a movie gangster. She had thought it was no more than a pose, a style, like a certain type of hat worn at a rakish angle.

'What on earth did you think you were *doing*? Who asked you to interfere? What has my life got to do with you?' She felt for the familiar seam of her glove but her hands were bare.

'You had a reputation, we couldn't stand for that. You're our sister, we gotta look out for you.'

'I was perfectly—'

'Yes, we all know you're perfect.'

'I never said that.'

'Listen, Mummy packed us a lunch and a supper, we can stop in a lay-by if you're peckish, we ate all the hardboiled eggs, but there's Cheshire cheese sandwiches and still some kichels left.'

'Oh, why can't you call them biscuits?'

She knew she sounded petulant and spoilt. She remembered when Roland had asked if her parents loved her, and her reply, 'Of course! I'm their princess.' She had taken their love for granted, thinking of it as a given, not a bond that would interfere with her life. Strong love like this could, it turned out, do what it liked. It could inflict violence on a person.

In the weeks that followed her return, she supposed Roland must be being fitted with dentures before he could return to his post at the BBC. When the television set arrived she kept expecting him to turn up on the screen which peeked like an eye from the great wooden cabinet with drawers for the *Radio Times*. Roland in a dinner jacket and a bow tie, reading the news, and she would be able to decipher all his discontents and deceptions, the glib mouth, the mad eyes. But he seemed to have disappeared. Her brothers had ruined him before he could completely ruin himself.

In the afternoons, after a lunch her mother put on the table and took away, only pecked at, she went for walks in Calderstones Park. Dead limbs dragging through the grass. Hollow mind. Eyes that took in familiarity, an old world and an old time. Her childhood. The place that was a shoulder an arrow rested on aiming at the far distance. An arrow rebounded.

But I'll find my way back, she thought, feeling a lot like Scarlett O'Hara and that tomorrow was another day. I *have* to, I can't stay here for the rest of my life, I don't belong any more. How can I be nothing more than Paula Phillips of Allerton confined to a mean little social circle, controlled by my brothers? I'm bigger than that.

She stayed in her bedroom and used her dressing table as a desk to write letters to Eric Fulton. He replied charmingly, with wit and kindness, sorry, he said, to lose her so dramatically. She thought he might turn up on her doorstep in his car. Make it all right with her parents, bring her back to the King's Road flat and the exciting, clattering, trivial life of the film business. But that was a romantic fantasy, a fairy tale, for he wrote of the new continuity girl, 'not a patch on you, my dear, but hey ho as the English say', and after a few weeks no more replies came.

A month later, an envelope with a snapshot of himself, his wife and a baby wrapped in a shawl sleeping in his arm. 'It all came right in the end,' he had scrawled on the back. 'Best regards, Eric Fulton (your dear Flossie!)'

So London's great indifference carried on without her. A few friends already had babies, and she passed them wheeling coach prams through the park, chattering to each other about teething rusks and knitted booties. The best boys were being snapped up, not that she wanted any of them but she was used to being amongst the first rank of the available choices among the young Jewish girls of Liverpool. Might she have to settle for a second-best, early-balding businessman's son her father fixed her up with, some profitable extension of the chamois trade, another business merger like the thwarted hopes of Mendel-Clumpus? But even they, she had heard, spoke of her as shop-soiled, a display model like a marked-down television set. This was what Roland had meant by provincial morality, though there was more than one bride who walked down the aisle in a forgiving empire-line wedding dress, the little hypocrites, and she could name names if she wanted.

I am in hell, thought Paula Phillips, with a segment of wider experience she was going to have to eke out for the rest of life.

Then, in the months that followed, there was Ringo, the Schwartz boy, who was opening a new gown shop on Bold Street catering for women who wanted Paris styles at north of England prices. Who knew from his time in post-war Germany how easy it was to fall in love with a survivor and be their saviour, bring a girl with a number on her arm back to Liverpool and promise that nothing now would ever hurt her, and her bad dreams were only bad dreams. A few of his army buddies had done that, and were married to fragile, difficult wives with terrible memories, girls who woke them up in the night demanding comfort. One had grown enormously fat, eating up the whole world to fill a starvation hole, and force-fed her children. He knew educated Jewish women who had had professions, written academic papers, even books, marooned in Liverpool among the vulgar Ostjuden, playing the cello at home with the curtains drawn and not daring to let the German language pass their lips when out at the shops. That was a whole basket of trouble he could do without, their hang-ups and neurosis and lack of the comfort of Yiddishkeit.

He was holding out for Paula Phillips whom he remembered as a sulky, beautiful teenager he had danced with at Bernice and Lionel's wedding and smoked French cigarettes on the steps of the Adelphi, the wedding which had begun the precipitation of the whole family's reputation. He liked that about them, he found the whole set-up interesting. (And they had no idea what they were getting into letting his cousin Lionel Clumpus into that family. They'd learn, sooner or later. Good boy, my eye. Poor Bernice, who had no idea what she had walked into.) Now, Paula seemed even more lovely, more volatile – whatever had happened in London had not humbled her, he was glad of that. She was wounded, but not scarred, he felt, as he watched her coming down the steps of shul with her mother. She walked as a princess, a proud head tilted to look above the crowd of women in their Shabbos hats. He winked at her. She was pretending (badly) not to recognise him. Women's tricks, he thought. It didn't matter, he would get her attention. She was beautiful and damned – irresistible!

'No one wants a cake with a slice cut out of it,' his mother said.

'Yes, they do, it shows it's a good cake, delicious.' He laughed. What would he want with a wedding-night virgin? From what he had heard through Lionel, who heard it from his wife, who heard it from her mother, she had had two men, one of them older, married, experienced. He would not need to pretend he didn't want what he wanted.

'If you like what you see I think we could easily make a go of it,' he said to her. 'I'll give you everything and I'll take you everywhere. It wouldn't be just this, I'm a man of the world and so are you, a woman, I mean. I believe we could make a life for ourselves that would be something wonderful.'

They were in the lounge bar of the Philharmonic Hotel. She had passed it many times on the bus but never been in it. The place was all stained-glass and mahogany opulence. Already he was taking her to new territory, that was in his favour. It was the first time she had been out in the evening since the great comeback. But she looked around at what she had been missing and was unimpressed. Roland would doubtless have said something withering about the place, a cruel put-down of his own invention.

'But we'll always have to come home, to *this*.' She looked around at a provincial crowd of insurance men and other labourers in the world of commerce, their wives and sweethearts straining to look smart but missing the mark.

'What's so bad about it? I've travelled, I've seen how people go on. Anyway, I'm in love with you and I don't like to be thwarted. You don't love me yet, but you will. And one thing I'll promise you: I won't let your brothers interfere with a thing. No repetition of that business.'

She considered him across the table drinking his gin and tonic. She took in the backs of his hands covered with dark hairs, his black eyebrows, his gold tooth when he laughed, his tie, his suit, his shoes, a disarmingly casual effect it was clever of him to pull off. A man without hesitation, who knew what he was doing. She imagined what he might be like in bed. Energetic, certainly. She thought of him on top of her, heavy, panting. Growling like a bear. Might be fun, she would have to see. No threats of thrashing but there could be other surprises.

'I know you're a little bruised,' he went on, 'but you'll get over it. I'll make sure you do.'

'You're a good talker, I'll say that.' And as if trying to present some clinching argument for or against this businesslike proposal, she said, 'Will you take me to New York?' It was the highest card she could play. America was still the Promised Land.

'Of course, how could you think any different? By aeroplane, too, no schlepping across the sea by boat. We'll be there as quick as a flash.'

'I'll think about it.'

A few days later Mina said, 'I'm hearing a lot about you and the Schwartz boy.'

'Oh, yes?'

'I have an opinion.'

'Do I want to hear it?'

'I don't know, I've never been able to read your mind.'

'That's a relief.'

'Paula, you won't do better, not in Liverpool, he's made for you. He'll give you the earth. Take him before he gets bored, a man like him can lose interest.'

'He's waited for me long enough, since the wedding. Anyway, I don't think I'm in love with him.'

'You will be. You'll fall for him sooner or later, don't leave it too long.'

'That's what he says.'

'Same with me and your father. It all worked out in the end.'

'Mummy, was there ever a point at which you thought, just because he's come all the way from Leeds I don't have to say yes?'

'Of course, I didn't give in the minute he turned up. But I knew he was a good man.'

'But what if—'

'I've had my say.'

And Paula waited for a few weeks. She waited for Roland's voice to come back on the radio, but others had taken his place. She waited for a reply to her letter of congratulations to Eric, but there was silence. By the time the picture came out they were engaged. She had thought, Oh well, I suppose I must.

The first time they slept together, at his flat above the Bold Street shop, she realised she had made no mistake. Sitting on the edge of the bed in his dressing gown, one furred thigh crossed over another, he said, 'How much would do you for a dress allowance?'

'Do I need one?'

'I'll make you the best-dressed girl in Liverpool.'

'And the best fucked, too.'

'I didn't know you knew that word, you trollop.'

'Someone once said I was fuckable.'

'Well, you are.'

'I think this is all going to work out well.'

'Told you.'

The family travelled to London for the premiere.

Mina watched it in silence; she didn't laugh, she didn't smile, she didn't cry. When the credits rolled up, she said, 'Very good, well done. I hope it makes a million pound.' Paula didn't know if she was being sarcastic, or if it had touched a nerve in her. Maybe now she wanted to turn into a snow bird and fly away? She couldn't read her at all. Eric came over, bending down to the small round woman in her satin dress and her silver evening handbag looped over her wrist. He held his hands together in an imploring gesture. 'What did you think?'

'Very good, very good indeed. You did me proud.'

'Thank God for that. Did you ever hear what Orson Welles said about stories?'

Louis said, 'We don't know Mr Welles, but we heard of him, we saw a couple of his pictures.'

'What he said was no story has a happy ending unless you stop telling it before it is finished.'

Mina looked at him, and rolled her eyes. 'So what's next?' she said.

PART THREE

33

One minute Louis is sitting in the lounge with the evening paper on his lap watching *Coronation Street*, reaching towards the bowl of sweets on the nest of tables, next he is on his knees on the floor crying, *Help me, someone help me*. The heart has a blockage, the heart is in trouble. An ambulance ride to Sefton General, an iron bed frame bound tight with sheets and blankets, hospital pyjamas, a bottle of Lucozade on the bedside table. He looks pale and startled; he dislikes the aesthetic of his surroundings. The nurses – Irish, beefy and practical; the doctors matter-of-fact remote faces. If only he had his burgundy silk dressing gown with the tasselled belt and at the very least some clean Marks & Spencer pyjamas. Then he can recuperate with dignity in the Nightingale ward full of coughers and wheezers and moaners. Then he can be himself: Louis Phillips Esq. of Acme Chamois Leathers, who combs Grecian formula through what remains of his hair; whose business has survived the downturn when others have gone under and even his very successful son-in-law got a bit of a fright for a few months and had to close down two shops.

In Sefton General Louis did not think he was going to die and Mina did not think he was going to die but the place gave him the willies; maybe he would be better off going private, they could afford it. There was discussion about being transferred to a con-valescent home over the water, run by kindly, experienced nuns. Ringo brought in a brochure. 'Top notch,' he said. 'Beautiful gar-dens, good food, views of the sea from some of the rooms. A couple of weeks there and you'll be back on your feet.' But Louis didn't like the look of the place, the nuns in their long black dresses and white wimples, the bedrooms each with a wooden Jesus bleeding wooden blood above the bed.

No, he would recover at home. 'My wife will look after me,' he told the doctor. 'And I have wonderful children and grandchildren.' But the doctor insisted he must stay in hospital a while longer.

'Make me look a mensch, please, Mina,' he said. 'You know what I'm after. The silk dressing gown from Simpsons. And when I get out of here, maybe we can take up ballroom dancing.' Because that's what he's overheard one of the nurses say to a fellow three beds along. *You'll soon be back on your feet and doing the foxtrot.* Why shouldn't he and Mina take up a hobby now he is semi-retired and Harry pretty much running the whole show? Exercise is important, he's been told. He must give up his cigars, start playing golf, be his own caddie. And he has always been light on his feet so he sees a future for them doing ballroom classes and taking to the dance floor at weddings. Showing off. And why not?

'And what about in the bedroom?' he asked the consultant. 'Do I have to take it easy there?' He managed a slow wink.

'There's exercise, and there's exertion. We will have to have a man-to-man chat about it when you're discharged. We'll leave it at that, for now.' And hurried away down the ward, escaping smells and sick bodies and unemptied bedpans.

Louis remembered the teenage girl he had courted in his best suit and bowler hat, red carnation in his buttonhole. Sometimes he looked at Mina and here she was, a tangle of dark hair, currant eyes, a mischievous expression. Sometimes she was an old lady with thick ankles and hands distorted by arthritis. Her neck had collapsed in, a flap of loose skin wobbled below her chin like a turkey gobbler's throat. He didn't understand the passage of time, if the Minas were the same person or she had been usurped by an imposter. If she went first, who would be left who remembered him as a young man with light brown hair? For he felt, against all the odds, in this hospital bed, looking round the ward at the old men, that he was not one of them, did not belong here; that he was going to live for ever.

Mina said, sitting by his bed with half a pound of grapes in a paper bag in her lap, 'You've had a lucky break. But like Ringo says, what doesn't kill you makes you stronger.' She saw their old age together with great clarity: comfortable in each other's company, bickering, fussing over their grandchildren, spoiling them. 'And we could go back to Cannes; do you remember the time we stayed at the Martinez and we saw that Arab sheik arrive and that slave or whatever he was crawling backways in front of him?'

'Will I ever forget it? What can you do with people like that? But they have the oil and oil is king these days.'

'I know, in our day it used to be coal and factories and electricity.'

For a few days Louis lay in all his pomp in his silk dressing gown with his Reader's Digest condensed books, his grapes, his Lucozade, his tentative conversations with the other patients, the pleasurable sight of the young nurse straight off the boat from Cork last month who gave him a sponge wash and he tried not to get an erection as she felt under his armpits with her soapy water.

Where was she when, in the middle of the night, he had another coronary? In the nurses' station reading a magazine.

'In a *hospital*,' Harry said, who was in a mind to sue for medical negligence. 'What were they all doing while my father was lying there fighting for his life?'

The young nurse cried and went to church to confession and told the priest she had as good as killed a man while she was reading an article about David Essex.

In the afternoon, Matron handed back to Mina the silk dressing gown and M&S pyjamas wrapped in brown paper and string.

'I gave that nurse a man, she gave me back a parcel,' she said to Paula, for it was a universal truth among widows that hospitals took husbands and returned them as something you put in the post.

She went home on the bus with Louis in her shopping bag to an empty house. Hung his dressing gown back up on the bathroom door. From the toilet seat she thought any moment he might turn and say, 'Mina, will you be long? I'm desperate for a wee.' Such a romantic, my husband's ghost, she thought.

Now she was in sole possession of three bedrooms, a lounge, a dining room, a morning room, a kitchen, a matching bathroom suite, a garden with a locked shed for which the key had been long lost, a disused coal hole and a garage with Louis' car in it which she couldn't drive and would give to Harry for his youngest daughter who was taking lessons.

She had never lived alone. From her father's house with brothers and sister and maids, to Brownlow Hill, two families under one roof. To Allerton and three children messily growing up together. To her and Louis watching the telly together in the evenings. To silence. Where a spoon left out on the countertop and an unwashed mug in the sink were still there when she came home from shopping, untouched. There were only so many times you could wipe the Formica counter, straighten the cutlery in the drawers, dust the ornaments, clean the oven, hoover the carpets, polish the Friday-night silver candlesticks, rearrange the crockery so the patterns matched. By the time *Coronation Street* finished she was in her nightie and dressing gown and slippers. She was watching the mantelpiece clock until the hands reached nine and she could go up the stairs to a bed warmed for half an hour by the electric blanket. She cleansed her face with cold cream, brushed her teeth, kissed the shoulder of Louis' dressing gown and trailed the hem along her fingers. Then the boxer's knock-out blow of sleep.

Her children took it in turns to have her for Friday night dinner. Ringo had hired an architect, not a run-of-the-mill jobbing builder, to present his wife with a modernist plate-glass mansion behind the Allerton allotments, a house of dreams. She had a dressing room and a walk-in closet. He had a room for his cigars. Under his energetic direction he had expanded the family schmatte business to a chain of boutiques extending from Liverpool across to the wealthier suburbs of Cheshire. They had a daughter they named Shelley. From the sixties to the late eighties they went every year to the Caribbean. Ringo grew his hair over his collar, they became vacation hippies, dressed in sarongs and smoked grass, returning home deeply tanned, relaxed, ready to place new orders with Mary Quant, Ossie Clarke, Foale and Tuffin. Paula and Ringo ate steak tartare and salads. They had introduced into their kitchen the concept of an hors d'oeuvre avocado pear, its hollow swimming with a pool of vinaigrette, eaten with a teaspoon. They were modern people who held dinner parties. Now Paula made chopped liver, chicken soup, roast chicken, stewed apple to tempt her mother's appetite.

To Paula, the sight of her mother sitting behind her plate, barely touching her food (and really, it wasn't *that* bad) brought out in her the rash urge to take on the role of being a parent to her parent. Which was bound to end badly, she didn't have that kind of touch. But as Paula insisted, 'Somebody had to do something, and if I hadn't stepped up I'd have got the blame anyway.'

For though she had been worried about her mother's depression, she had thought at first it would pass. Years after she had last seen Roland she had begun to take an interest in psychology. Mina, she reminded Ringo, had not been able to mourn the deaths of her own mother and father. It was years before she learned the fate of her little sister in that terrible camp. Nobody had known graves and she must have been sublimating all the sadness and uncertainty for decades. What she needed was closure, the stone setting that would finally seal the graves and memorialise an internalised trauma.

But before that could take place Paula had been shopping in Hargreaves when she had overheard one of her mother's friends, Hettie Chalkin, say, 'It's been seven months since Louis Polack died and Mina has to realise that there are newer widows than her, she needs to get over herself.' Then noticing Paula enquiring whether the shop stocked olive oil, she quickly said, 'Have you got trouble with your ears?'

Paula, putting a drumstick onto her mother's plate, said, 'Mummy, have you considered Valium?'

'Yes, the whole world takes Valium!' said Ringo, who had not swallowed any of the happy pills himself. 'It's like penicillin, but for your mind. A wonder drug.'

'Drugs?' Mina said. 'You'd know all about that, Paula.'

'Not those kind of drugs. You get them from the doctor, on prescription.'

'What do doctors know? I gave them a husband, they gave me back a parcel.'

'Yes, Mummy, but you mustn't keep saying that, it's started to get boring. I don't mean to us, I mean to other people, your friends. You know there are plenty of widows who throw themselves into activities, you could—'

'I never did an activity in my life and I'm not starting now. I was too busy bringing up three children. That was your father's department, going to see his pictures and taking you with him and look where that led.'

'Okay, Mummy, if I come to the doctor with you will you at least give the Valium a try?'

Mina wanted to say no, but it was not easy to stand up to the combined might of her daughter and son-in-law, who led the good life and were talking about digging down below the foundations to install a swimming pool. Ringo had saved her daughter from a false start. She could not have wanted for a better son-in-law, a man whom everyone liked. And gave his wife everything she had ever wanted. A dishwashing machine. A powder-blue Jaguar convertible. An emerald eternity ring. How could you say no to him?

Mina had always been a restless woman, quick in her actions, busy on her feet, impatient reading a book or watching television. She would get up on a sudden impulse and put on her coat, tie a headscarf round her hair and run out of the house for a walk in Childwall woods. Not deterred by a flasher showing her his gross pink thing held plumply in his hand, smiling at her, and she had shouted, 'I've seen bigger and better than that in the forest, believe you me.'

Now she sat. She sat with her hands in her lap, dead fish-eyed, a head full of cotton wool. Is this supposed to be happiness? she asked herself. What a con. She felt – and struggled for a word which was not in her everyday vocabulary – placid. Uncaring, muffled, she might as well be a corpse. A few times a day, when she could be bothered to stand up from the armchair, she went and looked in the bathroom mirror to check that she still had a reflection. She saw in an unflattering fluorescent light the turkey wattle in her neck, the dewlaps on her chin. Who would look at me now? she thought, thinking of the time her husband-to-be turned up at her doorstep. This is a punishment. But for what? For leaving my mother and father and my little brother and sister? Could be.

Jossel, nearly eighty, completely bald, shabby, content, still in love with his wife, would come round to visit and try to make her laugh. Had she heard the one about—

'I'm not in the mood for jokes.'

'All right, let's talk about old times, remember—'

'All I *have* is memories, is this supposed to be a life?'

'Life is what you make it, Mina.'

'Like you? Am I supposed now to run off with a young gigolo?'

'I never said—'

'Better you never say anything, if you're going to start.'

'Start what?'

'I don't know. Stop bothering me, I can't think any more.'

'If I'm not welcome, tell me to leave.'

'I'm glad you have a home to go to, a wife to make you a cup of tea when you get in. What have I got?'

'Mina, it's the pills. I have the greatest respect for your son-in-law who gave you such advice but you're taking poison. If you carry on like this you'll top yourself. Give them to me, I'll put them in the bin. You'll thank me for it when you're back to your old self.'

'Maybe you're right. But I don't know.'

'I'm your brother, I only want what's best for you. Where are they? In the bathroom?'

'In the cabinet.'

Up there he lifted the toilet seat and pissed painfully and slowly in the bowl. He dropped the bottle's contents down the pan and flushed. They raced down to the river to pacify the fishes.

At night, the little animals came, snouty, tiny-eyed, they pushed their way out of the bedroom wallpaper. No species she recognised but they were not rats or mice or hamsters, they were particular creatures that lived behind the walls of the suburban semi-detached houses of depressed widows, waiting for a chance. She pulled the blankets over her head. 'Louis, where are you? What have you let them do to me?' she cried to the empty twin bed.

In the morning she rang the doctor. Who rang Paula. 'I think you should go and get her, she's having withdrawal symptoms. Coming off the pills needs to be done gradually, I told her that when I put her on the prescription, but they forget, these old ladies, and they start hallucinating.'

'I'm so sorry, Mummy, I accept full responsibility for what's happened to you. I didn't know Valium could—'

'Little animals,' said Mina. 'What did I ever have to do with an animal? One time I fancied getting a cat, but my Louis said he wouldn't have one in the house. He said you have a cat to keep the mice away and a house with mice has got to be unclean in the first place. He was very fastidious, your father. But he had a sweet tooth, did I tell you he was reaching for an Everton Mint when he was struck down?'

'Mummy, you're babbling. And why are you wearing Daddy's dressing gown, you look . . . '

34

It was cousin Bernice who saved Mina – poor Bernice Clumpus, whose marriage the precocious Paula had observed from the outset as doomed and not just because they had returned from honeymoon to the uproar of Jossel's desertion.

Years later, Louis had gone into the gents in shul during the Rosh Hashanah service, his bladder full of morning tea, and heard muffled noises coming from one of the cubicles. He assumed someone had been taken ill and might need him to get a glass of water or call an ambulance. He looked at the gap at the bottom of the door and saw two pairs of shoes. He recognised the tasselled loafers of his nephew-in-law Lionel, noisily ran the taps in the basin to wash his hands of acquaintance with sin and warn the miscreants they had been spotted, banged the door and waited in the lobby, examining the notices for various fund-raising events – card evenings, sponsored walks, the perennial campaign to buy trees to plant in Israel to make, he assumed, the desert bloom. (It turned out they had planted the wrong kind of tree, which caused soil erosion. 'You can't win,' Mina said.) After a short interval Colin Grabman, the best man at the wedding of the year, emerged and, straightening his tallis, went back in to rejoin the service. When Lionel poked his head out as if looking for the all-clear, Louis collared him, said, 'I knew Colin was a feygele, you can tell that type straight off by the pink shirts and signet rings, but for crying out loud, Lionel, you're a married man! What's got into you?'

Lionel tried to express himself. Why not get it all off his chest? If not now, when? Bernice's uncle was a sympathetic, cultured character, always beautifully dressed, he had what Lionel thought of as a soul, in the sense that he was bound by the conventions of the community while knowing deep in his heart that there was more to life than chamois leathers.

'I'm in love with him! I think I always have been, since we were at junior school. I just never knew it until—'

'Until after you married Bernice? Made a fool of her?'

'It was the wedding night. A disaster. I've never been able to make her happy. I *wanted* to, I did my best, but it just wasn't in me.'

'What do you mean? You have *children*. How do you explain that? Andrea and Judy, they're living proof you're not—'

'I managed, but I had to think about something else. Someone else.'

They were talking man to man, as Lionel had only ever spoken to Colin, the confessions erupted from his throat, and not even the thirstiest towel could wipe them away from the world. How am I even saying this to Louis Phillips? he asked himself. How do I have the chutzpah? But I must, I must.

'At least I suppose it was quick,' said Louis, who was thinking of poor Bernice, all these years with this schlemiel for a husband.

Lionel looked around. The vestibule was still empty. Secrets were flying around their heads above the piles of prayer books.

'Uncle Louis, are you going to tell her?'

'Me? Why should I have the burden? I'm telling nobody, not even Mina. You've got to tell Colin to go away, leave Liverpool, put yourselves out of temptation's way. Be a proper husband after all this time. You can get magazines at the newsagents these days with saucy pictures. Buy a couple, you never know, you might get excited after all. You're a nice boy, Lionel, everyone knows that. I don't want to see your reputation ruined.'

226

But the nice boy stood there in his navy suit and yarmulke, his tallis round his shoulders, and thought, *To hell with that.* For in the thrill of their discovery, as he later told Colin, 'something in me snapped. I thought, It's over, finished. I'll take my chances.'

He walked back in to shul and sat down next to Colin. Their dark-socked ankles touched.

'What kept you?' Colin said.

It was time to blow the shofar.

'I'll tell you later.'

Six months later the two men had set themselves up in a flat near Sefton Park, 'like they were husband and wife', said Mina, 'but I can't work out who does the housework, they must get a daily in. You can't expect a man to do the hoovering.' She had always liked Lionel, poor boy, who she saw now had had the kind of forced marriage that her father would have pushed her into if Jossel hadn't got her onto that ship.

Jossel, an increasingly threadbare figure tramping along Scotland Road with his battered briefcase doing the books for chip shops and pawnbrokers, was shocked and ashamed. He had thought Lionel was a harmless sacrifice in his own journey to happiness with his true love. He had assessed the boy, could see no defects; he was self-evidently a provider in a successful family business, a good boy, a nice fellow.

'But you of all people should know about secrets,' Mina said. 'Didn't you suspect?'

'Why should I? He never tried to kiss me.'

'Well, it's all a mess, I don't know what to say.'

By the start of the seventies Bernice had somehow risen above the horror and shame of her situation, the social disgrace, and reinvented herself in ways that no one could have predicted. Her mother was the catalyst. Lia took on the humiliation of her daughter's situation with a ferocity that turned her into a holy mess of grievance and crying until she started to get on Bernice's nerves. If she had wasted twenty years of her life on a husband who was not a real husband as everyone understood it, lukewarm in bed and they hadn't had sex since 1957, then she would make the next twenty years count for something. She had the model of her mother's incessant cries of *I'm the only one*. Well, there were more divorcees now in Liverpool, but only one wife abandoned for another man, she really *was* the only one and she wasn't going to let this unique position ruin her life.

She threw herself into activities. She raised money for Jewish charities, she took up painting in watercolours, she joined a film society. Ringo offered her a position as a sales girl in one of his boutiques – she had, after all, a charming smile – but Bernice said she didn't need the money, give it to someone who did. Lionel still paid the mortgage on the house and a generous allowance to support his abandoned family.

There were fund-raising coffee mornings, card evenings – the housewives of south Liverpool kept themselves busy, but busyness for the sake of it did not seem enough to Bernice. Where was the *purpose?* Colin Grabman had become the first homosexual to come out publicly in Liverpool, they interviewed him on Radio Merseyside when the law changed. He was one of the solicitors who advised the campaign group. Yes, Colin had been brave, he had earned the right to be happy, Bernice thought. Her husband not so much. She read an article in the *Daily Mail* about men like her husband and the word for wives like herself was *beards*. The shame should kill her, she thought. But only if she let it.

Back in the USSR, Raiza Palatnik, a Jewish librarian, was arrested for distributing an anti-Soviet samizdat. She wrote, 'In my trial I will cry out against all anti-Semites in the Yiddish I was taught by my mother and father!' She was imprisoned with a daily diet of rotten fish and cabbage soup made from water and bones. Word filtered out. A group of Jewish housewives from north London demonstrated outside the Soviet embassy. They rigged up a van as a mobile protest vehicle with a mocked-up cell on top and a picture of the imprisoned Raiza behind its bars. They carried placards painted with the words PLEASE HELP LIBRARIAN RAIZA PALATNIK SHE IS INNOCENT OF ANY CRIME SHE ONLY WANTS TO BE JEWISH. Raiza was eventually released and the women's attention turned to the other millions of Jews in the Soviet Union who could not practise their religion or their culture: doctors and scientists and musicians who could apply to leave, but when they were inevitably refused would lose their jobs and be reassigned to lowly positions as janitors, coal shovellers, stokers and lift operators.

Bernice had found all this thrilling. She joined the Women in Black protest group. She told her aunt all about it. This was her purpose. To save the world, one Soviet Jew at a time.

Mina considered the information she had received from Bernice. She had never forgotten the vivacious optimism of the Bolshevik boys. It was a breath of fresh air to be with them after the house of her doomed mother and father. The brave boys of the Red Army had helped win the war; some said that without them it would have been unwinnable, a shaft opening up into darkness if Hitler had got across the Channel – and who among her neighbours would have been the Resistance, and who the collaborators? How could you know who to trust until they were tested?

But then there was Hungary in '56 and Prague in '68. So all along it was just might is right, Louis had said. He had liked Mr Heath, when he became prime minister. 'A harmless soul, not a socialist bone in his body.' Mina had to agree that the Soviet Union maybe had lost its way a little, become calcified, hardened, inflexible, no longer in touch with its own dreamers. 'The dreamers are dead,' Louis said, 'those types wouldn't have lasted five minutes.'

The Red Cross had finally informed her and Jossel of the fate of little Rivka and her family on what remained of the funeral pyres of Treblinka. Shot, gassed, died of disease or starvation, it came to the same thing. She was a yahrzeit candle in a glass on the mantelpiece. But what of Itzik, who had already caused so much trouble, and had done well for himself, who was one of the higher-ups, though nothing at all had been heard from him since those letters from London petered out eventually. She could not help but be curious about his fate. In his seventies was he now leading a life of comfortable retirement in a government dacha? Or was he still in harness, part of some Soviet delegation in a far-flung country – China, India? She could not imagine that he had not done well, it was in his nature to squeak through any eventuality. True, she had not laid eyes on him since the day they left Riga, but Paula had seen him, observed his busy officiousness. Had reported on his demeanour, his runty shabbiness, his cynicism, and his love of revenge.

And what of Solly, the baby? The Soviet Union was a vast place, stretching from Europe to Asia, and somewhere in it he might still be alive and flourishing in that penal colony of a country, his wife fearfully lighting Shabbos candles every Friday, him putting on a frayed old tallis, eating pork because there was no access to kosher food, speaking their mother tongue only in secret. Solly had grown up, she had heard, with all the attributes lacking in his brother Itzik, a sunny, energetic, manly personality who knew how to make things happen, to charm and flatter and be liked. Of course, his death might have not been recorded: perished on a death march, or thrown from a train and buried by peasants in an unmarked grave beside the tracks – there were so many ways and opportunities to die in those days, but what if he had survived?

Mina had found a cause, an activity, when as a seventy-five-year-old widow, she was part of a coach party bound for London to take part in a protest against the Bolshoi Ballet at the Albert Hall or to dress as ghosts and jump out at a visiting Soviet delegation to Marx's grave in Highgate Cemetery, to be altogether a nuisance and a catalyst and to get members of parliament talking and forming an All-Party Committee.

Mina thought, If my Louis could see me now. He would be torn, she concluded, between support for the great cause and the desire of his family to stay at home and mind their own business, not to draw attention. He had changed their name to Phillips, and all for what if she was going to run around town with a placard and a demand and a slogan?

Bernice said, 'Auntie Millie, you can't get on the coach with ladders in your tights and food stains on your blouse, you'll make a show of me. Get Paula to take you into one of Ringo's shops and buy you an outfit. You're a handsome woman, or were in your day, but you've let yourself go since Uncle Louis died.'

'Who should I dress for?'

'The world, Auntie, the world! Let's start with a new lipstick, my treat.'

Mina didn't have the energy to be taken in hand by her bossy niece and daughter, so she went into town to George Henry Lee's under her own steam and bought a new dress and a new winter coat and four pairs of tights, which were the latest thing. In the accessories department, she saw a red silk scarf with a pattern of roses. Held it up to her neck, thought, When I go to the Russian embassy they'll see this and maybe they'll think I'm a little bit on their side.

She was London-bound on the coach with Bernice and Paula and all the other middle-aged Jewish housewives who had been born in this country and weren't afraid of the police. They were dressed up to the nines, perfumed, excited, knowledgeable, chanting, singing, carefree, temporarily liberated from the leash of the washing machine and the dishwasher and the hoover and the Friday-night roast-chicken dinner. They headed down the motorway, travelling south to pick a fight with the representatives of Leonid Brezhnev.

'My kids think I'm round the bloody bend,' said Adele Bernstein, turning round to address Paula, in the aisle seat behind her, dressed not sensibly, in slacks or Crimplene skirts, but in a bottle-green suede trouser suit, because, Adele thought, she just couldn't help herself from having to be different, that Schwartz swagger she'd picked up, the two of them lording it over Liverpool and seen eating *lobster* at La Bussola on Bold Street.

'Why? What's it got to do with them?'

'I *know*, I told them that, but Myrna said to Harvey, "Daddy, are you going to let her do this?" I said, "Who's he to stop me!" And she came right out with, "Oh, are you getting into women's lib now?" Teenagers, what can you do? They think they know everything.

"And what if I am?" I said, but she went berserk, as if I'd stolen her best dress – one of them what's-her-name, Laura Ashley get-ups, like a milkmaid, all the rage. Because it's just for them, this feminism, like we'll show them up, us old ladies, if we get involved. But here I am, anyway.'

There was a scattering of applause from the adjacent seats. The women felt brave and free. They thought they could teach their daughters a thing or two about getting off their actual backsides and going out protesting, getting into trouble, even facing a night in the cells for the cause.

Paula wanted to tell them she had had the opposite experience. Her earnest daughter Shelley had practically goaded her to come, to rouse herself from what she called 'your bourgeois lifestyle'.

'And what is so wrong with it?' Ringo had said to Shelley. 'Because if you've come from nothing it's good to have nice things. My father fled from Romania with just the clothes on his back and look what he built, out of zilch.'

Shelley had countered, 'Then you'd think he would stand in solidarity with the workers, dispose of his surplus income.'

But Ringo couldn't contain his laughter, put his arm round his daughter, said, 'Little Miss Lenin.'

'Trotsky, if anything.'

'And look how he ended up, an icepick in the back of his head,' he said, having, as always, the last word but with too much amusement at these battles to find her, as Paula did, a bore and a nag.

'My daughter is a Trotskyite on Mondays and a feminist on Wednesdays,' Paula told the coach party. 'She lectures me when I wait in the car until Ringo comes round and opens the door.'

'And why shouldn't a man open the door, it's just acting the gentleman,' said Lorraine Solomon, on the other side of the aisle. 'It's worse being married to a lout.'

Adele Bernstein said, 'Mrs Phillips, this is going to be quite a day for you, it must bring back all kinds of memories.'

'Oh yes.' Mina began to reminisce about her father and mother's house, the maids, the children, sitting on the stairs. The miasma of flour, the sacks of grain, the rye bread. 'And you know, sometimes I needed to get away from all that.'

The story of the forest was recounted once again, this time to a new, avid audience who laughed and gasped. The elements in the narrative were repeated and relayed up and down the coach.

'Wasn't that a film?' said Lorraine Solomon. 'I'm sure I saw that at the Rialto just before I got married.'

'They paid me five hundred pound for my story, then they did what they liked with it. Who am I to complain? Me and my Louis went to the South of France.'

'What were they really like, those boys?'

'They were gentlemen, like in the picture. Explained everything to me. It's no secret in Liverpool that I was always sympathetic to the common man. I thought the Soviet Union was a great ally to us, and Stalin was a good person. Now, I see he was just a murderer. I have a brother, or maybe had, I don't know. I don't mean Jossel, another one; in fact, there were three, but this one, he was something to do with the Russian embassy after the war. I don't think he's there any more, we haven't heard from him for a long time, he was always trouble, but you never know, maybe he can help us out.'

She pulled her shopping bag up from below her seat and took out packets of cheese sandwiches and home-baked macaroons.

'Now, who wants a bissel to eat? There's enough to go round.'

By the time they reached London Mina had become the star of the expedition, and Paula thought, Good, she doesn't need me to chaperone her, I can light out on my own, for she had her own agenda that afternoon.

Climbing down from the coach Mina knew she must ask, there could be no harm in just *asking*. She did not care what they did to her, if they arrested her it would only be to an English police station with officious constables in comical helmets. She would do what she was going to do, and turning the corner, where the vast white many-windowed magnificence of the embassy bore down on

233

her, she thought, It's just a pile of stone, nothing more, and walked over to the uniformed guards.

'I'm trying to get word of my brother, Itzik Mendel, he used to work here. Do you know him?'

The soldier was young. He had a rash of pimples across his forehead which the peak of his cap could not quite hide. His rifle was a weight on his shoulder. He looked down at her. What was she babbling about? He said nothing. He was trained not to speak while on duty and to watch his words when he wasn't. The old lady was yattering away on the pavement. He couldn't understand what she was saying. He kept his eyes fixed straight ahead. It was easy to resemble a stone statue.

'Oh!' cried Mina. 'You're too young. Maybe you weren't even born then, when he was here.'

She fell back into the crowd of women marching from the coach. The atmosphere among the protestors was that of jaunty defiance; they had come all this way and they would make their point. Some had brought brooms and were sweeping the pavement in imitation of the menial tasks the refuseniks were forced to perform as part of their demotion from their previous lives. They handed out leaflets to passers-by. They had brought sandwiches with kosher fillings. A few would stay the night and go to a show in the West End. A photographer turned up and took their picture.

The gates opened and closed to let the officials in and out, Mina tried to waylay them. The protest organisers told her not to be a fool: 'That's not what we're here to do, our banners speak for themselves.'

'It's a personal matter,' Mina said. 'I have my own business with these people.'

But the stony exterior of the embassy released stone-faced individuals. Mute and unfriendly, they went about their business in silence.

'My brother Itzik Mendel,' she pleaded. 'Did you know him? He used to work here, he was an important man.'

A middle-aged woman in a green mackintosh was returning to

her office. She was also an important person, she was in charge of the embassy catering. Meals must be provided, and plenty of tea, coffee, vodka. It was a logistical challenge to keep everyone fed. Mina felt she had a sympathetic face and she stepped into her path.

'Excuse me, I have a brother. His name is Itzik Mendel, I haven't seen him since I was a child. He used to write me letters, I heard he was one of the top men here. Do you know him?'

'What are you people doing here with your banners and protests? Are your lives so unhappy that you want to walk the streets poking your nose into matters that are of no concern to you? Go home and look after your children and grandchildren. Go home to your kitchens.'

'I'm a widow, I don't eat much, I just heat up a tin of tomato soup and cut myself a slice of bread. Rye bread is the best. I come from Latvia, that's where I was born.'

'A good loaf is a pleasure, I agree. How is the bread in Latvia? I am from Ukraine.'

'My father was a grain merchant in Riga, he knew all the millers and all the bakers, we were able to obtain the very best bread, dense, chewy, full of flavour, nothing like this white rubbish they eat in this country which in your mouth turns into the pap you feed a baby.'

'If only the nations could speak of our common love of good bread. Then there would be peace.'

'I remember drinking coffee and eating bread with honey. My mother had a very pretty coffee pot.'

'Bread and mothers are the same thing.'

'You have a beautiful soul to say such a thing.'

'Thank you, I must go back to my work now.'

Back inside the embassy her boss asked her about the conversation.

'Stupid woman, weak in the head. Something about bread and coffee pots. Jewish physiognomy. Said her brother worked here, do we know him? Went by the name of Itzik Mendel.'

But no one in her office that day had heard of Mina's brother and they went about their business in the usual way, forgetting about bread and old ladies from the Baltic.

Paula did a few minutes' placard duty and raised her arm to hail a taxi. She sat watching London as if the city were a film she had once starred in. Jumble of memory of events possibly imagined, or at least embellished, so unlikely did they seem to her now. She knew perfectly well how indulged she was. Ringo had made good. She had reached the stage in her life when she was bored with everything her husband had promised and right-royally delivered: the Caribbean holidays, the overnight stays at the Hilton on Park Lane, the trips to Paris for the first look at the season's styles, the house with its open-plan living area, the picture window flooding the space with sun. The dressing room for her clothes, the jewels, the chinchilla coat she had draped round her shoulders at home during the three-day week. Her lifestyle *was* bourgeois, she had liberated herself from what Roland had called her provincial morality to be imprisoned in a life littered with its knick-knacks.

She might have an affair, had thought about it, had flirted with an actor from the Everyman, fifteen years younger than her. She was keeping him hanging on, reeling him in with her can of Rive Gauche, which smelled of wealthy women and uninhibited sex. Ringo would forgive her, he would never kick her out. The two of them were like pillars that held up some kind of unseen sky in his mind that she had never seen and which he could not describe. It was his own secret, what he aspired to, and which apparently could not be achieved without her. She had put a foot wrong and been forgiven, her past cancelled, but wasn't it here, on *this* street, that Roland had taken her to lunch down a flight of steps to that Italian bistro? But no, all bistros looked alike and they were nowhere near Pimlico or Soho, cruising now past Harrods towards Park Lane, past the Hilton, and the car showrooms, Ringo's territory, not Roland's.

On Haymarket Roland had grabbed her wrists as they were crossing the road and kissed her, stopping the traffic. Reaching the pavement he had bent down to tie his shoelace and she had mimed kicking his scrawny backside with the tip of her shoe. At Sloane Square she had started her long morning journey out to the film studios. In Bloomsbury she had died a little every day, waiting for something to happen. Past Red Lion Square and the Conway Hall, waiting in the queue to get into a talk on – what was it again? – something to do with folk tales, her lapels glittering with diamanté clips.

The taxi skirted Regent's Park, zoo animals roaring in the distance. She had once asked Roland to take her to the zoo but he had winced. 'Oh no, the poor mangy lions; I couldn't bear it.' She had thought at the time that he was not completely heartless. He had mentioned once the desire to get a domestic cat. Nothing came of it. 'I'm not a dog person,' he had said inscrutably, 'I hope that's clear.'

The taxi driver was curious, couldn't place her, she wasn't a Primrose Hill type. She had not spoken during the ride, had not taken any bait he offered to tempt her into conversation, just looking and looking and looking out of the window, not reapplying her lipstick in the round reflection of a powder compact or fiddling with her little diary as these women usually occupied themselves, alone in the back of a cab. There was nothing provincial about her, nor did she look as if she might be up from her place in the country. She was smart, wealthy, cosmopolitan, yet she stared out of the window like someone from out of town.

What was she up to? He could not fathom her.

'When you get there I'd like you to wait for a few minutes, then take me back to where you picked me up. I won't be long.'

'You should have said, I could have turned the meter off and given you a special price. Still could, if you like, do you fancy doing some touring? See the sights?'

'That's quite all right.'

He pressed on. Talkative, opinionated, thinking he might get a fingernail under her cool indifference.

'I don't know if you've been here before but this area has come up in the world these past few years, I remember when it was all bedsits. People living hand to mouth. Now they've got a whole

237

house to themselves.' He paused, she did not contradict him or pretend not to be listening.

'I see.' She looked slightly less bored.

'It starts with the houses going cheap because they're wrecks, then the busybodies buy them and drive the prices up. Quiet as the grave now, no life here any more.'

Paula thought, Well, it could have been me and Ringo. Would we have fitted in here, or are we too *trade*? But he could never live anywhere without off-street parking.

They passed houses painted the colours of sugar dragées, rose pink, powder blue, pistachio. Roland, she saw now, must be long gone, he was a radio personality, the poor relation. This was television land. The shabby had become smart, the cramped bijou, the peeling paint of the front doors turned hard and glossy, sprouting polished brass knockers and letterboxes.

Roland was and always would be dissolute. She could not imagine him walking past that columned door, hair fashionably long over his collar, kipper tie, velvet jacket, turning to kiss a wife and children goodbye. One did not grow out of that level of self-destructive neurosis.

'It used to be quite seedy here,' she said. 'I hardly recognise it.'

'You seem to know the place, did you live here in the old days?'

'Live? No, never. I did come here sometimes, long ago, I knew someone. But I was always a visitor. You can stop now.'

This was her destination, what had been Roland's front door. She hesitated, sighed. What was the point? Nostalgia and for what? For the girl she had briefly been allowed to be before she was driven back by her brothers, who would never let her forget that she had crossed over into enemy lines. She could find out what had happened to him, she might write to the BBC, or to that boy Robin Rose whose name she still saw on film credits. Or his university, they kept track, didn't they? If it came to it, she could hire a private detective, keep it a secret from Ringo, pay for it out of her dress allowance. But looking up at the front door to which Harry and Benny had gained such easy entry, now locked, and the windows hung with cream silk festoon blinds over which a hanging basket of pink geraniums and blue lobelia announced a Mediterranean taste, she thought, Some people don't make it out of their times. Or if they do, they just linger, maimed and useless like a fly without its wings.

And taking out a cigarette and lighting it with slightly shaky hands, she said, 'You know what, I shan't get out after all. Just turn back and take me to Harrods. I think I'll do some shopping instead.'

'Yes, treat yourself, why don't you? You deserve it.'

Jewelled, scented, longing, not knowing who she was, Paula remembered Roland's promise to thrash her. Well, who has beaten who? she thought. One survives, one is, as far as it is possible, intact. I have been lucky, very lucky. I got what I deserved in the end. Still, as the taxi turned and headed south, back to the strident Jewish coach party from the north, the doors, she thought, were all closed now, and always would be.

'What have you been up to all this time?' asked her mother.

'I dropped into Harrods, Mummy, look, I've been shopping.'

'As long as that's all you've been doing.'

'What else, Mummy?'

35

In the end there is only a room. Four walls, a chair, a table, a couch, a window. From this position if you fold your neck down to your left shoulder you can make out a definite patch of blue which is not the incessant colour of the sky, it is the sea which is only three blocks away. It is there, the grace note in his confined existence. He spent his childhood by the sea, a different sea, a different country, but he has always missed its presence. Once he had dreamed of Odessa, the raucous port where anything was possible. It is a good room, everything is compact, useful, sufficient for a single person's needs. The couch converts into a bed, on hot nights the breeze from the restless body of water makes its way onto his tired face.

He eats his meals out at a café at the end of the street, the same meal every day, he is a regular. The waitress does not bring him a menu any more, she knows what he will have: chicken with rice. In the evening at home he will eat a couple of slices of bread with a slice of the local cheese. In the morning just coffee. He has never been a big eater. He does not miss luxuries, they have never mattered to him.

In the afternoon he walks along the beachfront. Families are playing on the sand, the children building crumbling towers, the mothers splashing seawater on their bosoms, the fathers smoking and reading the newspaper. Teenagers taunt him, he is an old man with badly fitting dentures and the appearance of a gnome in a fairy tale. He does not speak the language well and the words and phrases he does know are not idiomatic so he has to guess at what the insults might mean, he has to use his imagination.

This country of his last residence, his final resting place after a lifetime on the move, has date palms and orange trees. It has bougainvillea, a messy, colourful shrub that crawls over walls and fences and climbs telegraph poles. The vitality of this plant, its brassy vigour, affronts his senses, he's used to a monochrome palette. There are fragrances in the air he does not recognise, and odours of cooking oil, scents of tanning creams. After an hour of plodding exercise he returns to his room: to a book, the radio, the sounds of his neighbours fighting, having sex, newborn babies screaming their lungs out.

He has been here for six years. The newborn is in school now, he sees her leave the building with her little briefcase, holding her mother's hand. She reminds him of his own girls, who had they lived would be mothers, and himself a zayde, his pockets full of little surprises. On bad days he believes that the Itzik who had a wife and children was someone in a story he had once heard, and appropriated to himself. It was too hard to believe that he of all people had been loved. The condition of solitude is a concrete overcoat from which one can never escape. Or he can't. How had he managed it back in the thirties when he had first seen Belya walking with her friends in the park? Whatever he had done, he would never be able to pull it off again.

All his life he has been busy, talking and listening. He has had work to do. He has not enjoyed the intimacy of friendship with another person but he has tried love, marriage, fatherhood, and everything came to dust. Whose fault? The times? Other people lived through the same portion of history and succeeded. His sister in Liverpool – the whole bourgeois dream came true for her. Jossel, who he remembered as a sanctimonious bore, had a second lease of life with a younger lady. Of Solly the baby he could not be sure. He used to hear things, matters which made him not so quick to claim him as a brother. Rivka had drawn the short straw. Hadn't she once broken her doll, a premonition of her own fate? He couldn't remember.

Now he is silent, there is no one to talk to. No one has anything to say to him, and he has nothing to say. The waitress in the café who wordlessly goes to the kitchen to give his order to the cook does not know his name. He doesn't know hers, he never asked, she never told him. With other customers she cracks jokes, flirts, angles for tips. With him, she just brings the food. His tongue seems to be shrinking in his mouth; his voice, when he does speak, feels rusty and disused, it needs to be restored to fluency by conversation but he goes for days, sometimes up to ten, without speaking. There is a telephone but it rings only once a month, a routine call from a bored official to ask if he needs anything. He is only doing his duty. The old man has long ceased to be of any use to them, he's been comprehensively debriefed. One morning he sang a song to a bird, felt foolish and self-conscious, but his ears heard his speech was not broken. He sang the lullaby his mother had crooned to him, and he had crooned to his daughters. Surprising himself, he cried. He has no photographs of his family, they were left behind. When you jump you carry just the clothes on your back. He had left the embassy in the suit he was wearing now. The clothes on his back and a filing cabinet in his brain. It was not an ideological decision, he had not lost faith with the communist system, he had never believed in it. He had jumped before he could be grabbed by the collar and wrenched back into a purer version of communism in the Gulag. Someone didn't like his face, that was all. And was his a face so easy to love?

He walked out of the embassy in this inconsequential country with its mild climate and the sea as a boundary. Walked out into a room.

On the other side of the city there is a cinema which screens classic movies from a bygone age, films from many countries, subtitled or sometimes dubbed into the local language. A few months ago they had a Dziga Vertov season: *Man with a Movie Camera* is one of his favourite films and he had taken the bus to the unfamiliar neighbourhood to settle down in his seat in the palace of dreams. Reliving the exhilaration of the early years of the revolution induced in him a nostalgia for the clarity of his former life. How easy it had been, *anything* was possible. Everyone was young and everyone was suddenly free: from the tsar and from other tyrannical fathers.

He folded into his pocket a flyer which contained a list of forthcoming films. In six weeks' time that old British picture, *The Story of the Forest*. He waited. Six weeks passed with no incident. It felt like sixty years. Every day the same, without incident. In other rooms families argued, children wailed, wives sang to the sea. He went back to the cinema and bought his ticket. He took his seat and held his hands together in his lap; they had recently started to tremble. Parkinson's, he thought, that's all I need, not to be able to bring a cup to my mouth, to be fed soft food by an indifferent nurse.

The audience was arriving. There were old-timers nostalgic for the films of their youth, students of cinema, young lovers, couples who had nowhere else to go on this rainy evening, solitary types like himself, their purposes inscrutable. Of everyone in the half-empty cinema, the atmosphere heavy with the smoke of cheap cigarettes, only Itzik knew how false the movie was. He had been there, he had seen everything, it was nothing like this, *nothing*. There were no magical elements, there was instead a spoilt girl and a pompous brother, a group of boys who believed in ideas that were going to crush them.

He remembered Vladimir Propp and the lecture in London to which he had enticed his beautiful niece. The lecturer had spoken at great length about the structure of stories. But I also have a story, he thought. He had told it several times to his handlers. Why here, they had asked him, and why now? To which there was no answer besides, 'Once I lived with my brothers and sisters in a good merchant's house in Riga not far from the port, and one day my little sister went out to the forest and our family was undone.'

Which was not the truth either but who says stories are supposed to be true? When you tell a story you are bound by its own internal rules. The truth is an awkward branch that will poke your eye out.

The film ended, a few members of the audience clapped. Some laughed. Some booed. The manager of the cinema decided not to screen that old thing again. It was 1977. No one was interested. These old black-and-white movies felt stale and old-fashioned. Two streets away, people were lining up to see *Star Wars*. That was the kind of fantasy people wanted these days. Plenty of crash-bangs and lasers.

Outside it was still raining. Itzik waited for his bus. The orange lights of its destination melted in the wet atmosphere. The journey took forty minutes. He watched the unfamiliar city in all its mystifying sociability. What did anyone think and feel? Was it possible for a man like him to believe they actually had these sensations? Where had he gone wrong, when was the slip-up? He got off the bus at his stop. It had stopped raining and the waitress was standing outside the café smoking a cigarette. Here was a person. A tired person in shoes with heels too high for her line of work, a person who must feel all day the discomfort of her situation. Nevertheless, a person who is aware of his existence. He allowed his tongue to move slowly in his mouth to form a greeting.

The waitress had forgotten that he could speak. Nobody knew who he was. Nobody knew anything about him. He was just an old foreigner.

'Hey,' she said. 'Look at you, you're wet all over, your coat is splitting at the seams. How old are you? Too old to be out on a night like this.'

Itzik smiled. He hadn't moved his mouth into such a formation for years. She saw his face slit into a wolfish grin. Cunning, knowing, full of pain and knowledge. It turned out, after all, he was a person!

She later told her boyfriend that she had given it no thought at all when she said, 'Why don't you come in for a cup of coffee? You look as though you need warming up.'

It was, she said, just a spontaneous act of kindness and pity, but he seemed so surprised by the gesture that he appeared immobilised, frozen under the dripping awning, the neon of the café's sign flaming red on his right shoulder until he stepped forward and felt her hand lightly touch his arm as he stumbled through the door.

36

In the end there is just a room.

Mina lies there dying. She is one hundred and two years old. At a hundred she has received her telegram from the Queen.

'So even the high-ups notice me now. God save the Queen, save her from old age, it's not a nice thing, but she still has her husband beside her. No, not beside, he has to walk behind. I should ever have asked my Louis to let me take the lead he wouldn't have known what to say. But you know I was born in another country and we had a tsar and look what happened to him, you should not count on your luck never running out. Even if you are Queen of England.'

The next year she is less coherent. She sees the Queen's face on postage stamps, the crisply waved hair, the crown, the necklace. 'Who is this one?'

Her stomach is swollen. She moans and touches it. Sometimes she cries. The doctor says the family must be called, she is approaching her grand finale. Mary Malley, who takes the bus in from Garston every day, a humble emptier of bedpans and turner of bodies prone to bedsores, says, no, there's more life left in the old lady yet. She claims to have second sight, sees things others cannot make out. Through the veil of so-called existence Death is always waiting but he has not yet come for Mina. He is sitting on the back step, but she hasn't invited him in. 'With some people Death doesn't get it all his own way,' she says; 'he'll have to hang on a bit longer, polishing his fingernails.'

And she is right. It goes on for several days, and they are long days and nights. Sometimes the light returns to Mina's eyes. She is still capable of coherent thoughts, but she cannot utter them.

I was no Queen Esther.

When you lose your zest, your excitement for living, you are nobody.

Why do I have to be an old lady, what happened to me?

The TV flickers with the forms of couples looking for an escape to the country. They speak of fields and cottages and lanes and walks and friendly pubs and village greens and express their ambition to breed llamas. Mina takes this in distantly, remembers what Andrievs said about trees.

The trees know exactly what to do, they have all their wisdom in their wood.

She still doesn't know what he meant by it. A tree is a tree, it just stands there, she has never learned to tell the difference between an oak and an ash, not by the leaves or by the bark.

Her middle child, Benny, arrives from his beach-front home in Israel, a short, tanned, suspicious man in an open-necked shirt. He has been there since 1956, married a local girl, has grandchildren in the army. Every morning when the sun is rising, and before heat crushes the land, he and his wife go for a power walk along the sand, an army of fit, brown, wrinkled retirees. Now he has come as quick as he can, driving recklessly fast to the airport through rumours of another war. On the radio the American president is banging the drum. This time Iraq is the enemy. They must be prepared for missile attack from the air because everybody knows the tyrant has weapons of mass destruction. He needs to come now, before the airspace is closed. He hasn't seen his mother for ten months and he is not going to miss the last opportunity to kiss her and hold her hand. Of all the children he has the least complicated relationship with her. He loves her unconditionally, 'She gave me life, what more can a person ask for?'

The three children of Mina Phillips sit in Matron's office with Dr Collier, who struggles to deliver bad news in a palatable way. He is a young man who is just settling in to his new practice, which includes in its catchment area this home and all its inhabitants. He is ascending the sharp face of gerontology. He wishes he did not have to take death home every night to his wife and two children. His clothes smell of it.

'I have to tell you that your mother is very weak, she has almost no resistance to the slightest infection. In my profession we call pneumonia the old man's friend, and the old woman's, too, but it's taking its time. It's dawdling.'

She is in pain, she moans in discomfort. She reminds him of an animal ready to be put down. What words she comes out with are a mishmash of English and Yiddish, language broken into unintelligible syllables of two tongues, clouds of gas from another world.

He tries to explain what he wants to do but they don't want to hear. Yes, there is an injection he could give her, this is what he wants to administer, its purpose is pain relief, he must be very clear about that, it will make her comfortable and at peace. He lays out what he wants to give her and what it will do.

'But that's heroin,' Benny says, alarmed, 'you'll turn her into a junkie.'

'Too late for that.'

He explains she will be comfortable and pain-free. This is the important thing. They can sit with her if they wish, some relatives sing, others tell stories, reminiscence or just hold their loved one's hand. Or they can go home and wait for a phone call. It's their decision. They must do what they think is best. Their mother is past deciding.

Benny, who prides himself on knowing what's what, spades

called by their right names, says, 'Am I hearing this right? You're asking us to give you permission to *kill* our mother? Our own flesh and blood? What kind of place is this? How many have you bumped off already? Because everyone should admit that our mother is going to live for ever and good luck to her.'

The doctor says, 'Let me put it another way—'

Harry interrupts. The doctor knows him as a local businessman of good reputation and an organiser of generous tombola prizes to the home's garden parties from Jewish shops. Once there was a side of beef, another time a portable television, driving lessons, a jewelled evening handbag.

'Now I'm not one to throw around accusations, I dare say this is all standard medical practice and in the old days it was a pillow over the face, kinder in the long run when you had no drugs to give them, but to ask *us* for permission? It feels to me like a rusty gate in the mind what you're asking from us. Do you know what I mean?' He looks round at his brother and sister.

Benny says, 'Not half.'

Paula, who seems to the doctor the most intelligent of the three, so far has said nothing. He has met her and her husband several times before, a glamorous wealthy couple with the year-round tan that can only come from frequent holidays in the Caribbean. He has them down in his notes as 'cosmopolitan, flashy, shrewd'. He's not aware that there is something a little prejudiced about this assessment. If challenged, he'd say, 'But it's true, isn't it?'

He turns to her, and says, 'Mrs Schwartz, what's your view?'

Putting her on the spot, he recognises, hoping to drive a wedge between her and her brothers. He has seen no evidence in her of the two men's schmaltzy sentimentality. She sits in the peach-coloured vinyl armchair, her still excellent legs crossed, her skirt an inch or two above the knee and some kind of silk – or is it satin? – blouse in a shade he thinks might be called midnight blue. Self-possessed, well preserved by the application of cosmetic surgery and expensive dentistry. Smoking a gold-filtered cigarette without having asked permission.

Paula hasn't spoken for good reason. She can tell that they are going to put it all on her, relying on her to make the decision. Then they can blame her. *Paula made us do it.*

Last year Paula had been forced to acknowledge that yes, she herself is in her seventies, because Mina keeps saying, 'Look at us, two old ladies, whoever would have thought we would have that in common?'

And that reminds Paula that she too is on the helter-skelter, that in a few years, even a silk scarf concealing a ruined neck will not be enough. That she will be infirm, incontinent, trouble with her legs, her eyes, her bladder, her bowels, everything decaying, going wrong, unfixable. Then the unthinkable, death, which is about to happen to her mother, meaning, if they go in order, Harry is next, then Benny, then herself. What a line to have to stand in. She can't bear it. So she too harbours the illusion that her mother will not die.

To try to narrow the gap between them, Paula had brought her mother a lipstick a scarf, a vial of perfume, anything to make her look younger – 'Just freshening you up, Mummy' – and Mina had started to enjoy the vanity, to say, 'Paula gets me the latest of everything.'

She had also brought news of her own daughter Shelley who is mother to Zoë Fletcher, this uninterrupted line of daughters, each less Jewish than the last. Paula, who speaks like a BBC announcer, and is rumoured among the younger housewives of the community to have had an actual fling with a BBC announcer in her wilder days, is still a recognisable suburban Jewish type. She wears gold swimming jewellery, for a start, which makes Shelley blush to think about. Shelley went in for the law, is now a silk, which is to say, a top barrister. She has always been of an argumentative disposition, which her father says is a Jewish trait, for disputation is the essence of Judaism.

'No, it's not,' Shelley replied.

She lives in a narrow, tall, old house in London with her second husband, Mike Harris, while still on good terms with her first, Eddie Fletcher, whose name she has given to her daughter, while staying Schwartz herself. She goes to dinner parties with the Prime Minister, she knows law lords and the Director of Public Prosecutions. There has been a big interview with her in one of the national papers with a photograph of her in her barrister's wig, seated on a stool at her quartz kitchen island. Paula brought the paper in to show her mother. But Mina, who can no longer tell the difference between her granddaughter and the Queen, dropped it on the floor, like a baby in its highchair learning the difference between here and there.

Paula knows that Shelley thinks she is difficult and eccentric and shallow. She reads, she reads all the time, but Shelley says, 'Only *novels*.' She reads Philip Roth and Saul Bellow and Margaret Atwood. She likes best the American Jewish big-hitters, energy like a boiler firing on the very first page. When Shelley speaks of books, she means non-fiction: footnotes, an index and a bibliography. Paula had warned her against Eddie Fletcher, her first husband. 'Men like him have a clock where they should have a heart.'

But Shelley had cried, 'Mum, at least he has *principles*.'

'Really? They won't keep you warm in bed.'

When Zoë was born, Paula said, looking at the babe in her all-white knitted clothes, 'Let's see what her story is.'

Between each generation there has been misunderstanding. Paula feels like the January god of the Romans who faces in both directions. Each way she looks there are difficult women. One of the last coherent sentences her mother has spoken was this: 'I always was on the side of the underdog, but what does it mean when the underdog doesn't like *you*?'

Paula remembers the kitchen in the old house on Brownlow Hill, the drying clothes hanging from the pulley, old songs, '*schlof mein maydele schlof*'. Then the wireless, the very English voices, the correctness of vowels, the modulation of consonants, the sense that there was an external authority which applies outside the walls of their home, and her mother did not care or know about it, because here in the kitchen was steam and safety and cooking smells, and sometimes her mother was standing by the door all dressed up, in a pair of white kid gloves, and her father with his hat in his hand and his face turned to his zaftig wife. But after Louis died she gave up keeping a kosher home, the separate pots and pans and china and cutlery, 'all a load of hooey'. So what, Paula wonders, was she really thinking all those years?

Still, whatever else was going on in her head, Mina knew how to be a mother but Paula had never learned the trick of it. Shelley, in the years to come, given the possibility of what is obviously a lethal injection, would probably say, 'Go right ahead.'

'Go home,' Dr Collier says, 'talk it over. Ask your children, ask your friends. Ring me any time, I'm always available, I'll tell reception to put you straight through and if I'm at home leave a message. I want you to know I had a great admiration for your mother, she was one of the real characters of this place, the stories she told, I never knew what to believe and what was her imagination.'

'All true,' says Benny, truculent, prickly, 'she never told a lie in her life. Don't you go accusing her of being a liar. She was as honest as the day was long.'

'Of course, of course, I didn't mean . . . but you must understand, the world she came from, it seems like a fairy tale to me, forests, wolves . . . Where *did* she come from, by the way? I always thought it must be somewhere in Russia. We never had a copy of her birth certificate on file.'

'She never had a birth certificate, as far as I know,' Harry says. 'Or if she did it was lost long ago, or they never brought it with them, they left in a hurry. She came from Latvia, Riga, the capital, a real city, I'm told, with her brother, olavasholam, who passed away in here a few years ago. Before your time. We wanted to go, look around the place, see where it all started, but it was hard to get into, or it was then. Things are different now, I hear.'

'All in the past,' says Benny. 'Long gone now. And all we have left of that generation is our Mummy.'

'Was there any significance in the red scarf she always wore?'

The care workers tied it round her neck every morning; in the last weeks she has put the points into her mouth and sucked them so they had to hide it. The dye could come out and poison her. She would look around the room for a lost object and point to her neck. 'My schmatte,' she would say. 'Where is it?'

It reminds Paula of her baby daughter's piece of blanket, the loss of which on Formby sand dunes, fallen out of her pushchair, was possibly the founding trauma of Shelley's life. Paula had tried cutting another piece of blanket but Shelley said it did not smell the same: of herself and her bedclothes, and spilt milk. 'I don't want it,' she had wept. And had learned to live without it. Paula told the care workers to give Mina back the scarf, let her die with that rag rightfully round her neck, whatever it meant to her.

'Oh, yes, there was *significance*, as you put it,' says Harry. 'You won't know this but in the old days she used to hand out leaflets for the Communist Party. On our road, full of dentists and custom house officials! They probably went straight in the bin, this was all before recycling. Don't forget she had that picture of Stalin on the mantelpiece during the war. What a moustache that man had, still gives me the willies thinking about it. What did she mean by Stalin, what could anyone mean? I'm *lucky* to be born an Englishman. It could all have been so much worse. Paula, what's your opinion? Was she really a Red?'

'I think it was mainly an affectation,' Paula says, who finally feels that her tongue is loosening, having been a stick of wood in her mouth. 'How far she believed in it all, I've no idea. I suspect it was all bound up with her vanity, wanting to remember she had once been a young girl, that old story of the forest, which must have had some truth in it, a germ of truth, but obviously embroidered. Anyway, by the seventies she had turned against Russia and began to campaign for Soviet Jewry when that was in fashion. By that time she had found out her little sister's fate but she didn't know what happened to her brother Solly, still doesn't. Then there was the other brother—'

'Itzik, that mamzer.'

'Oh, stop it, you never knew him.'

253

'I didn't *want* to know him. Look what he nearly did to you.'

'I didn't end up so badly off.'

'Doctor,' says Harry, giving his brother and sister a not-in-front-of-the-goyem look, 'my mother meant the world to us. Nothing will ever replace a mother's love. She was unpredictable, I agree, a very complicated woman. I never understood her and I won't for as long as I live. A film was made about her, did you know that? You want us to end our mother's life? Well, with that, everything is over. The Liverpool we grew up in is finished, Brownlow Hill has nothing left, and soon the Liverpool we made our own lives in will be over, the beautiful suburbs. You give her this so-called injection and what's left?'

But eventually, they seem ready to leave, to get in their cars and go to Paula's house, to drink a cup of tea and refuse a slice of cake, to say, 'how can anyone eat at a time like this?' and 'not a morsel of food will touch my lips', to argue, to throw their weight around and claim seniority, to wait for Ringo to get home because he will have an opinion, being a man who could have letters after his name if it hadn't been for the war and had gone to Berlin and passed the judgement of Solomon on real Nazis.

'Do you think we should ask your Shelley?' Harry says to Paula in the lift. 'There must be laws about this kind of thing. She'll know.'

Paula briefly thinks about calling her daughter on her mobile telephone, as she has been instructed to do in an emergency. But why put it all on the heads of the next generation? They must find a way out of this situation on their own, it's their duty.

37

It is Ringo, using common sense with a dash of Torah, who talks them into it. ('Not even Methuselah, the longest-lived person on earth, made it past nine hundred and sixty-nine years so Mina Phillips is not going to live for ever, she isn't that special.') He speaks kindly and he speaks harshly. Is it not a tribute to their great and abiding love for their mother that they could not do without her? A mother's love is *everything*, it is how the world begins, and a Jewish mother's price is beyond rubies. But is it not for themselves that they are condemning their mother to continue to suffer – their own souls they are afraid of losing?

So they all cave. Harry rings the doctor, says they have agreed, it's for the best. Make her comfortable.

At four o'clock in the afternoon, the hour when the care workers bring round the tea trolley for the bedbound, and in the day room toothless mouths masticate biscuits, Dr Collier gently takes Mina's hand, raises it and empties his syringe into her bloodstream. A small sigh.

The children sitting by the bed do not know what their mother knows. It's impossible to tell. She is so changed. Her hair is white, her throat is haggard, her face is marked with the brown blotches of old age. Benny scarcely recognises her. He has stayed away too long in his pride, having had a fight with his sister about something in the news. He is all for the coming war, she is against it. It's opening a can of worms, she says, it won't end well. Is she turning into a pacifist now? Then to hell with her and her fancy house and her fancy daughter, he won't spend another minute under her roof. (The clichés, Paula thinks, that's all they know.)

The children have argued about who would sit with her until the end. Ringo says, 'Why not draw lots?' He gets out a deck of cards and cuts them. Paula has drawn the jack of clubs. She was always the one with the luck.

Mary Malley opens the door and sees three people in there.

First there is Mina, lying in her bed, the morphine coursing through her bloodstream knocking out the pain like a boxer, a rough brute who will take down anything in its path, including its host. Mina is starting to look a little transparent, as if she is preparing to become insubstantial, to melt. It's a certain waxiness of the flesh Mary has observed in others. Some people become ghosts, she's seen them about the place, but Matron told her off for mentioning it. The Jews don't believe in ghosts, it's not that kind of religion, it's all about rules and how you live in this world. It's not a mystical faith. On her personnel file, 'Good worker, but fanciful.'

Second is the elegant Mrs Schwartz, who looks, as she always does, as if she has come straight from the hairdresser's, her powder-blue Jag parked outside (it should be a Mercedes, but obviously Ringo won't buy a German car). She's wearing a tan suede trouser suit, it must have cost a fortune, but of course, in her husband's line of work she gets everything wholesale. It will be hours yet, and Mary Malley is surprised, she didn't know she had it in her.

Finally there is Death himself, sitting now at the end of the bed in a clean black suit and high-collared white shirt, a distinguished gentle-man in sober finery, such as one used to see riding his high-bred horse down the country lanes of Wicklow. Death looks very ready, his eyes are shining. It won't be long now, a small number of hours. She'd seen the second son an hour ago, bawling his eyes out, a good boy come straight from the Holy Land to be here when he could be washing his feet in the waters of Galilee. But there's nothing he can do to stop her being carried away. The daughter neither, who is reading a magazine, dry-eyed. If only everyone could see Death as she can. Then they would not worry and debate. The priest told her she was mental. No one could see Death. But what did he know? What did any man know?

Mina is aware of movements in the room. People, shapes, shadows. She cannot see Death. She would laugh if Mary Malley told her she saw him. And why is Death not a woman? she might have said. A woman brings a person into this world and so a woman drags them out again. But she can't form such thoughts. She is walking into a forest, the sun is blocked by the canopy of trees, the others are waiting for her, her husband, her mother and father, her brothers and sister. They are singing. The music is loud and strong. The earth is fresh and fungible, mushrooms erupt from the trunks of trees. Everything is growing and decaying.

'. . . and the earth was a formless void and darkness covered the face of the deep, a wind from God swept over the face of the waters.'

The world of the narrow metal bed, the medicines, the jug of water, the framed photographs, the curtains, the sanitised plastic chairs, the magazines and the silent television is withdrawing, only the tip of the scarf remains between her lips. Paula gently withdraws it. Mina's hand moves, her mouth makes a small sound. Her breathing is different, Paula has never seen anyone die. She knows she is witness not to greatness, to a grand departure, but to something small, almost insignificant.

Mina falls like a dry leaf from a tree.

Her mouth is slightly open. Paula leans forward and kisses her face. 'Where have you gone?' she says. 'Where are you?'

Paula feels the tendons of her throat slackening, she has the urge to cry, but a sense of wonder overcomes her. It is such a mystery where the dead go, and have they gone anywhere at all? It must be why people make up stories about heaven and hell. The human mind cannot deal with such a void, a vacuum. The whole galaxy of her mother's being, from the little girl to the cackle when her Palace telegram arrived, is nothing now. And me, Paula thinks; it will be the same.

She remembers Roland's hand touching her stocking top under the restaurant table. *When I die that will never have happened.*

Outside the bedroom window the sky is shut out, no stars, no moon. Harry's wife Betty stirs. From her dreams she thinks a bell is ringing, a school bell, a church bell, she feels summoned, summoned to the terror and the beauty of life. Harry switches on the light, Betty's face looks very old in the sudden glare. He picks up the phone. He hears his sister speak to him. 'It was peaceful. She went away without any pain. I thought she was asleep but no, she'd gone. I never saw a person die before but now I've seen it, I know. There's nothing there any more. A corpse is like a tailor's dummy.'

'How can you say such a thing?'

'Well, I said it. Will you tell Benny?'

Who is along the hall sleeping in the spare room.

He knocks on the door and rouses his brother, breaks the news, offers him a cup of tea.

'Yes, I'll be an Englishman and drink a nice cup of tea; that will change everything. Maybe it will bring her back to life. Tea with two sugars please, and plenty of milk. Oh, look, she's opening her eyes.'

'Well, I'll make one anyway.'

The undertakers have been expecting her. They have been informed. They arrive at eight in the morning when the living residents are still having breakfast in the day room, crumbs of toast and splashes of cereal milk on the tables, the TV on in the corner, people on sofas interviewing pop stars barely awake, ravages of night-time on their faces. Everyone knows Mina Phillips has died in the night. Some cry, some pray, others think the natural thought, Who's next, is it me? One of the residents, Addy Goldberg, as a seven-year-old child had seen Mina walking down the Hill to the munitions factory. Her mother said, 'Mina is going to war.' Now, to the carers, Addy says, 'She had a gun, you know.' And it does not seem likely to anyone that the one-hundred-and-two-year-old would ever have had a gun, but Mary Malley, who has an imagination, says, 'I wouldn't put it past her.'

In Matron's office, the family talk about the practicalities of a funeral that will take place that afternoon, the gravediggers booked, the rabbi already preparing his eulogy, wanting some stories about the old lady he had never met.

Matron reminds them that the council had awarded a grant a few years ago and paid an oral history lady to come in with a tape recorder to capture the dying world of the old community. The transcript was available at the library. Their Uncle Jossel had told some fine tales of the world of Brownlow Hill and had such a memory for all the little businesses that thrived before everyone moved out to the suburbs. And their mother had some stories too.

'I wonder what she told them,' Harry says.

'Remember how Daddy met Uncle Jossel, on the battlefield?' says Benny. 'That was a hell of a yarn; I mean, how could you beat that, it had everything?'

'You never believed that fairy tale, did you?' Paula says, smiling, her lips like a scimitar, curved, sarcastic.

'What do you mean? What's not to believe? Daddy came courting her all the way from Leeds with a carnation in his buttonhole and changed into his best suit in the toilets at the Lyceum. And they walked together down the boulevard on Princes Road.'

'Well, you've been away a long time; these stories get worn out in the telling and they let something slip, the truth peers out through the curtains. What I heard, years ago, from someone who lived on Brownlow Hill, it was a shiddach, the rabbi fixed it up. It was an arranged marriage as they all were in those days.'

Harry makes his contribution, he's been bottling this up for years. 'To be honest, I heard something else, another story, not very nice, that's why I never told it while our mother was still alive. Auntie Lia let the cat out of the bag. Uncle Jossel owed Daddy money and he gave him his sister to pay it off.'

'The malicious old cat,' Benny says, 'she deserved everything she got. Uncle Jossel was well shot of her, if you ask me.'

'Well, all I'm telling is what I heard. The way I believe it happened was Uncle Jossel got a taste for gambling when he was in the army. It must have been the boredom of all that waiting around for everyone to start shooting at him. He thought he was so clever he could work out a system, he never knew it was all dumb luck. So the story goes that he lost our mother in a hand of poker.'

'Nah,' says Paula, 'Lia was a jealous, sour, hard-done-by bitch all her life. It's exactly the kind of story she would make up. I'm with Benny, I don't believe a word of it.'

'Margaret would know, if she's still alive. He would have told her the truth.'

'Oh, would he? Since when was the truth so important to anyone in our family?'

'What, you're saying we're all liars? That we have no probity?'

'I'm just suggesting what Mummy always said, that you tell the authorities what they want to hear,' Paula says. 'It's only common sense, self-preservation. They were immigrants, no one knew them, they could say what they liked. When you're uprooted like they were, you can *be* anything you want. Who's going to say otherwise? But now which do you believe?'

'Me?' says Harry. 'I always like the best story. I was sitting on a plane one time flying to Spain, me and Betty were going on holiday but we couldn't get adjacent seats, and I'm next to a gentleman who starts telling me the story of his life. He was a chiropodist, and what a terrible story it was, he could send a person to sleep with all the feet and toes and corns and bunions, and I had the urge to yank that story out of his mouth and retell it, except I'd make it a comedy, wouldn't anyone? The best story is the one with the longest legs, you know, like a racehorse. But what do I really believe? I think the rabbi did everything when Uncle Jossel came back from the war and found his little sister working in a factory with the common folk, the lowest of the low, ideas in her head like you wouldn't know from. Yes, the rabbi fixed her up with a Leeds boy who wouldn't have heard of her reputation – how could it have been any other way in those days?'

38

The Jewish dead must be buried within twenty-four hours. Harry has driven to the town hall to get the death certificate, muscling in at the head of the queue – 'Got to have it now, please' – because there's no three-week wait in the stone-cold morgue for the Jews, no visit to the undertaker to choose the coffin from a catalogue of garish wooden overcoats, pricing up brass handles. No invitations, no printed order of service, no consultations about hymns and pieces of music. No open casket and viewing of the body dressed up in her Sunday best to go into the afterlife, as if God is inspecting the new arrivals like wedding guests conforming to the RSVP dress code.

The women of the chevra kadisha are washing the body, wrapping her in a linen shroud, placing it in the simplest pine container with rope handles. Everyone knows Mina Phillips, or knows of her, she's the last of the last. How come she has lived so long is anyone's guess, but she has resisted Death's famous entrance until everything finally has given out. Afterwards the women, Sheila, Lorraine, Jackie, drink coffee and gossip about the funeral. The famous granddaughter, they hear, is already on the train up from London.

Shelley is in fact running late. Paula rang her at eight in the morning with the news, like a starting pistol going off for the day ahead, and she has an overnight bag packed, ready for the

Euston dash. Her daughter Zoë is coming with her; being a child of the metropolitan elite she's interested in the whole scene up in Liverpool, which is somehow the opposite of her do-gooding parents with their tedious principles. Full of relatives who loudly proclaim that Margaret Thatcher saved the country and the Arabs have it in for the Jews and always will.

But the train to Liverpool is held up outside Crewe for an hour and seventeen minutes by an injured swan on the line. The RSPCA has been called to remove it and take it to a place of medical sanctuary, then find the river from which it has wandered and return it to its family. It staggers around the track with a half-broken wing, flapping and straining to gain height. The RSPCA chases it with a large net over into clumps of rosebay willowherb. A footpath follows the line of the railway, and groups of ramblers in dun-coloured anoraks put down their sticks and walking poles to cry out encouraging suggestions. The swan is growing weaker, still it struggles to evade capture.

Everyone is on their phones. Shelley is talking to her mother. 'We haven't cut it fine, Mum, we left immediately. As I said, there's a bloody *swan* on the line. If we have to we'll come straight to the cemetery, but I'm sure we won't miss the interment.' In the seat behind them a voice at a lower but still audible volume is saying, 'When they arrive, and they will arrive, probably any minute now, deny all knowledge of a safe. Tell them you never got involved.' Shelley, the barrister, mimes cupping her hands over her ears.

Zoë is wondering what she is doing on this journey. But Shelley had said, 'I'd *like* you to come; I need an ally when I'm at the heart of that family.'

'That family? Yours, surely?'

'You know what I mean.'

'Not really.'

'You'll see.'

Zoë quite likes Paula and doesn't understand her mother's difficulties with her. But her father has said, 'Those two are sandpaper and wood. They wear each other down.'

So here she is, travelling towards that ruined port, that Jewish suburb, that clutch of relatives with political opinions the London visitors find crude and uncomfortable. What will she be witness to and what will be demanded of her? It's hard to predict. Perhaps she will be a bystander, merely an audience for all the *sturm und drang* of the Schwartz psychodrama. Or maybe some speaking part will be required of her, she has no idea what it might be.

Eventually the swan is taken, netted, in need of medical attention and in the process of being transported back to Crewe in a van. The train announcer conveys the revised and expected time of arrival into Lime Street. They are moving, they are off. Shelley reminds Zoë of the first time she took her to Liverpool when she was a child, crossing the mud flats of the Mersey at Runcorn, pools of river water gleaming glassily under an implausibly strong sun, passing the factories of Halewood, and Zoë saying, 'Are we in England any more?'

While they are swan-stalled, Harry is doing his own hustle. They need ten members of what Shelley calls sarcastically 'the male persuasion' for the minyan. Women, on this occasion, having prepared her body, don't count. Nor does Ringo. Every Jew is assigned at birth membership in one of the twelve tribes of Israel and any member of the Kohanim tribe, the priestly caste, as Ringo Schwartz and Leonard Nimoy from *Star Trek* are, can't approach the grave. Ringo and Leonard can both make the priestly blessing, the V-shape with their fingers, which Leonard introduced to the world as the Vulcan sign and Ringo kidded his daughter when she was a teenager that he too was a Vulcan, though without the big ears. So Paula, Shelley and Zoë (the swan-delayed pair having arrived in a taxi straight from the station) must stand by themselves with no menfolk to comfort them.

Shelley's second husband Mike is chairing a tribunal in Nottingham he can't get out of but will come later, in the evening, and Zoë's boyfriend Angus wanted to come, but Zoë suspected it was just an anthropological interest. He's always pushing her to explore her heritage, whatever that is. His previous girlfriend was from Cameroon, and she wonders if he sometimes looks at her and thinks she's a little vanilla for his taste so she supposes she should play up to the Schwartz side of the family, and play down the Fletchers, generations of Northamptonshire yeoman farmers turned bootmakers in the early twentieth century. How dull is that?

She had met her great-grandmother but only in extreme old age. She has been a distant fixture in family life, swaddled in crocheted blankets in a chair in an institution that smelled of disinfectant and gravy. She cannot say that she *liked* her, let alone loved her, because the old woman was just that, an unpredictable presence who talked on and off about a forest, and Zoë, of course, has heard the old story but assumes it's just a kind of fairy tale, not something that actually happened because no one on her mother's side of the family has ever really gone in for Nature. Her dad used to laugh at the Jews walking on Hampstead Heath in Gucci loafers and cashmere scarves and a few in state-of-the-art hiking boots to rustle through dead leaves for ten minutes, then retire for cake at the café at Kenwood.

Harry has successfully rounded up the men for the minyan on the phone and herded them down to the cemetery in their suits and ties lightly brushed with cigar ash. Prosperous old men in their seventies who come to funerals because it's a mitzvah, a good deed. They'll be next and some of them are already gone early. This is the thing about funerals, they remind the living that we're all in it together with the dead.

Looking across the grave they see the famous daughter, Shelley, in a well-cut black trouser suit. There's a story about how she nearly jumped off the garage roof when she was a teenager having taken LSD and thought she could fly. Nearly gave Paula a heart attack. With her is her daughter, whose name they can't remember, a young lady with light fine hair and long legs like spaghetti, looking round at everyone, whispering to her mother, 'And who is that?'

Yes, Zoë is trying to make sense of where she is and who all these people are, and what her grandmother is now – a used container for her being, spirit, soul, identity, she doesn't know what to call it.

When she was five years old she had asked her mother, 'Why are you a girl and daddy is a boy?' And, 'How do people become dead?' To which her mother replied, too quickly, 'Well, sometimes they get squished by a car when they're crossing the road because they don't hold a grown-up's hand like they're told.' And watched her daughter burst into hot terrified tears.

After the brief ceremonial of the Kaddish, Mina goes down into the earth next to her husband Louis. It's a pearl-coloured afternoon at the cemetery, they are out in a neighbourhood of the city they don't normally set foot in, apart from visiting deceased loved ones, and it occurs to Harry like a stone crushing his heart that there are more of the Liverpool Jewish dead now than the Liverpool Jewish living. His two sons have come from Manchester and Gateshead; the younger boy who has taken an orthodox turn, with peyas dangling in front of his ears and a black hat. He thinks his father is a hypocrite, the type of Jew who goes to shul in the morning and the football in the afternoon instead of observing the whole of the Sabbath day according to God's rigorous commandments.

Benny is in tears, Harry puts his arm round him, 'You're going to be okay, kid,' he says to his younger brother. 'We'll always remember her, she's not gone from our hearts.'

But Benny says, 'I never told her I loved her. Not in so many words.'

'She knew, of course she knew.'

'I stayed away too long. I could have caught a plane back every month, but I liked the beach too much.'

Some linger, some are keen to get out of there, the cemetery is depressing, and when the last Jew has left the city, who will look after the graves? A couple of times a year hooligans climb over the wall and deface the stones with swastikas. No one is ever arrested; it happens at night, with no witnesses, but they're out there, you could be sitting next to them on the bus.

Next stop is Paula and Ringo's house, the modernist mansion overlooking the Allerton allotments, there to drink tea or glasses of whisky and eat cake. Zoë can hardy believe her mother grew up in such opulent circumstances when at home it's all blond oak floor-boards, Farrow & Ball off-white walls and leaflets lying in bundles around the hall from the Labour Party waiting to be delivered by Shelley when she has a minute. The Prime Minister is talking about sending her to the House of Lords. 'My daughter the baroness,' says Ringo, 'the yiches in that.'

The house is full with friends, relatives, neighbours. The lapels of Harry and Benny's jackets have been cut, their faces will be unshaven for a week, the mirrors have been turned to the wall perhaps, Shelley suggests when her daughter asks, so the living can avoid the vanity of their own reflection. The rabbi has brought round wooden chairs with sawn-off stumps of legs for the chief mourners to sit on during the prayers. It all seems to Zoë so ritu-alised and theatrical, what are these traditions and what do they mean and what's their purpose?

In the middle of the eating and talking and reminiscing and telling jokes, her grandmother beckons her over to come and sit next to her on the mulberry leather Heal's sofa.

'Now, Zoë,' she says, 'I need you to do me a favour.'

'How can I help?' she replies politely, assuming that there is some task in the kitchen that needs doing, passing round cake, running out to the off-licence to buy more bottles of Johnnie Walker. Maybe she's going to get to drive her grandma's Jag.

'I've had one of these new things, an email. Ringo set me up with an account last year and I've been on the internet. What a place, eh? Everything is there, and more that you don't want to know about. I've printed it out. Can you go and see her and find out what she wants?'

'You didn't actually need to print it out, you could have for-warded it to me.'

'I know but I didn't know where to send it. There's no telephone book for emails, is there?'

'No, Grandma, there isn't.'

Postscript

The house was in Highgate. I rode the bus up the hill and London dropped away steeply behind me. I was ascending to a new kind of knowledge; I felt like someone on a quest into the deep past I had only recently become curious about and in which my mother had little interest. History isn't her thing. 'When I was a teenager I had the Beatles,' she once told me, 'why did I need old dead Jews?'

Grandma Paula hadn't even asked her what she thought about what she called 'this turn-up'. 'Shelley is always busy, busy, busy,' she said, 'with her crime and punishment. And there's something incurious about her. She has *no* imagination. You have, you must be a changeling child because you certainly don't get it from your father, that bore.'

I had taken over her email account and replied to the woman and suggested meeting up somewhere for coffee, but she said, no, I should come to the house, she had something I would want to see with my own eyes and she couldn't risk carrying it around. I felt slightly suspicious of what I might be walking into, but as Grandma Paula said, I can't resist a new experience, and this was one open to such speculation it was impossible to refuse. Even if Grandma Paula would have let me. She had grasped my wrist in her firm grip and said, 'Don't let me down. We need to get to the bottom of it after all this time.'

The woman who answered the door was in her mid-forties with reading glasses strung round her neck on a chain and dressed in pale, biscuit-coloured suede and cream cashmere. Her smooth blonde hair was pulled back into a tight ponytail, the whole monochrome arrangement setting off a porcelain complexion and expertly applied eyeliner and mascara. She looked at me as she stood on the doorstep as though she were a scanner inspecting every millimetre of my body, her eyes seeming to penetrate through my coat. I found it uncomfortable to be looked at so *hard* and she must have thought I was going to make a run for it down the garden path because the scrutinising façade cracked, she smiled, asked me to forgive her for what must have seemed like an examination, but she couldn't help it. It was an occupational hazard.

She welcomed me into the house, which was a blur of expensive silver wallpaper, and we passed into the kitchen with a pyramid-shaped atrium roof shedding the last of the December afternoon's murky light onto a table where she had laid cups and saucers and a plate of various shop-bought patisserie. At the other end of the table was a menorah which had not been cleaned out the night before. It seemed it had been the fourth night of Chanukah, and cold wax still dripped down from its silver candleholders. Later, when I got home, I looked up the dates. She was days early and I wondered if the menorah had been there for my benefit, as a prop to set the stage for the story she wanted to tell. Or if she thought the dates were notional, or the same every year like Christmas Day. Because the place seemed too good to be true, the woman who had answered the door quite the actress, as if she were performing for me. But as the afternoon went on, I realised she was just groping around the darkness, as we all are when it comes to the Mendel family.

Her name was Rosita Schifrin. She was a dermatologist with a practice at one of the private hospitals in St John's Wood, specialising in moles, psoriasis and adult acne. It was not, she assured me, cosmetic work, and she did not have anything to do with Botox or fillers. Her husband, Leon, who was in finance, worked at Canary

Wharf. 'He plays with numbers like they are the contents of a child's candy jar.' There was a framed photograph of the couple, him with pale eyes and gold-rimmed glasses, looking pinkly smooth-skinned as a baby, both standing smiling glassily with champagne flutes in their hands, next to Boris Yeltsin.

They had met in the last years of the old Soviet regime before the new era, at Novosibirsk State University, in the far cold east. It was hard for me to believe that I was sitting there at a Highgate kitchen table, while she matter-of-factly came out with a story of parallel lives in which the State was, she said, like a low roof over your head, forever coming down on you, threatening to smash in your brains.

'There were quotas for Jews at universities in Moscow and Leningrad so Novosibirsk was practically a Jewish university,' she said. 'To be Jewish in Soviet times was to have it as your nationality.'

'But that's not a nationality,' I said, 'not like French or British or ...'

A millimetre's worth of smile tried to crack her face, and though she had said she had nothing to do with Botox in her professional life, her private one seemed to tell another story.

'It was then. It was written on the fifth line of your identity document. And when your application was turned down, the saying was that you had been refused by the fifth.'

'Application for what?'

'Anything.'

Then she stood up and said, 'Now I have something special to show you,' and took from a cupboard an old, chipped coffee pot painted with a garden of garish flowers in unnatural colours.

'This is what was too precious to leave the house and bring to a café,' she said. 'We're not going to drink our coffee from it, I'll make a cafetière. It came here with me from Russia, to Chicago, to London – its wanderings have come to rest for a while. Isn't it something, that the most fragile things can survive?'

'Is it very old?'

'I think it's from the nineteenth century, if you can believe that.

For a long time I thought it was from Moldova, where my grandma was born – Kishinev, which is a famous Jewish place, have you heard of it?'

'No, I'm afraid I haven't.'

'It was the site of a massacre, but never mind that. I assumed it must be from her side of the family because it's women who like nice things not men, unless they are effeminate, which Solly never was – no, you could not accuse him of that, he was a great womaniser in his day.'

'Who was Solly?'

'He was my grandfather, the youngest brother of your great-grandmother, the little one. And according to my mother, with this coffee pot there was a story, I don't know how true it was, that my grandfather got it from his mother, your great-great-grandmother, and she brought it with her when they were driven out of Latvia.'

'Wow! Then it's really old.'

'Yes, but how true is that old tale? Because if you ever met my grandpa you wouldn't think he was the type to cherish a coffee pot, of all things, he really wasn't – let's say he was a loud, rambunctious character who had a lot of jobs in his life. At one point he was an actor in the Yiddish theatre, not Moscow, the provinces, Kharkov in the part of the country that is now Ukraine. So the idea that he inherited this from his own mother and managed to carry it round all those years – decades – and it never broke, he took care of it, like it was a baby – well, it seems implausible to me, but maybe miracles can happen.'

The coffee pot sat next to the menorah, a living fossil from a past that seemed to me as ancient as the Greek gods. It was quite ironic that this would be our family's only heirloom, a coffee pot of all things, when others had sewed diamonds into their skirt hems. It was just a chipped old coffee pot we were talking about and it was rubbish, you couldn't give it to a charity shop, yet there it was on the table and looking completely innocent of its history. I mean, a *coffee pot*, that's what I was in her house to hear about. Because she wanted to know if my great-grandma Mina had ever mentioned such a thing from her memories of her own mother's kitchen. I said I'd have to ask my Grandma Paula if she could recollect her saying anything.

'I can't decide if it's quite pretty or terribly ugly,' Rosita said, 'but it has been with us so long. My husband won't touch it, he says I'd kill him if it slipped through his fingers and smashed. He's wrong, he'd have to kill himself, I'm not going to prison to avenge his clumsy fingers. You see we have so little of the past except of course memories and fairy stories because we came from a regime where you couldn't trust what was inside your own head, your soul had been taken into public ownership, you doubted your own recollection, that was just the way it was, you accepted it, what could you do? So we had a coffee pot and we had a story and the story was *ours*. It didn't belong to the People, but to us. Was it true? At the time it didn't matter. But now I'm curious. My sons are quite interested too in this old history, and quite excited to learn we have relatives here.'

'What do you want to know about us?' I asked, having come prepared with notes to introduce her to the multi-branching families of Mina and Jossel, all the descendants, here and abroad.

'One of our family stories was about a girl, a sister, who had gone out into the forest and got into some kind of trouble, and had to be sent away across the seas to America with her brother. So from this I always knew we had relatives living in the West and that was both a good thing, because at least someone had got out, and also a bad thing because there was always the risk of letters. If you had those connections you could not be trusted, you might be a spy, or just someone who was being fed foreign propaganda about how much better life was abroad. By the way, is that a mole on your neck? Have you had it a long time? I can take a look, no charge for family.'

This abrupt change of tack made me jump. I had been taking in the flood of explanation, feeling quite meek and stupid, and now she had sprung me to a different type of attention. She took out an instrument like a jeweller's eyeglass and examined my skin. I could feel her breath on my neck and I tried to concentrate on a spot on the far wall where the wallpaper pattern was turning into viney green tendrils. The coffee pot stood like something that could be smashed and thrown into the dustbin or it could last another hundred years. It had got this far, endured this much alteration, but I didn't want to be the one whose elbow finished it off.

Rosita looked up. 'Don't worry, it's normal, but keep having it checked out, look for any changes. I'll give you a leaflet before you go.'

It seemed awkward to return to the Soviet past, because now Rosita was tackling a meringue tart with a pastry fork and recommending the chocolate brownie slices. 'My husband has no sweet tooth at all, so if you don't eat another one I might as well apply them directly to my hips,' she said. But I like the sight of women eating, I enjoy the sensual greed of it.

'My grandmother was very surprised to get your message,' I said, 'but not as surprised as she was to find out that my grandpa had got into genealogy on the internet.'

'Yes, my mother also heard about the internet and got curious, she asked me to try to track you down. And your grandpa was doing the same thing, and we all met up on that Jewish genealogy forum and look where we are now, the descendants of the Mendels of Riga.'

'Tell me the story of Solly,' I said.

But I could not even begin to follow her narrative. It made no sense when towns, cities, regions, countries kept changing their names and Solly fell in and out of favour with such and such a bureaucrat. As hard as I tried to keep up, I got hopelessly lost and it seemed to me that he was mostly in the wrong place at the wrong time and then suddenly his luck would change and now he was a famous actor and receiving bouquets of flowers in his dressing room and there were write-ups in the papers and then something went wrong, whether it was what he did or said, or just the times changing, because he would be off. But always, apparently, he had the coffee pot.

'Are you sure,' I said, 'that it was the same coffee pot? Maybe it did get broken and he found a replacement. It didn't have to be exactly the same.'

'You're not the first person to ask that. Leon is sure it's one of several iterations. Solly wasn't the most truthful person in the world, and he may have simply seen it as preserving the memory of his beloved mother, who was cracked in the head, like the coffee pot. How it survived, if it survived, no one knows the answer to, but to your first question, how *Solly* survived, the truth is he and his wife and his four children, including my mother, slithered through, like the snakes they called us.' She laughed. 'So we had good luck and we had bad luck. We lied, we paid people off, we probably slept with someone in authority. We did all the immoral things you have to do to stay alive. That is it, what can I tell you?'

'And in parallel,' I said, interrupting, 'the ones that got away were living in pebble-dash suburbia, the very epitome of bourgeois complacency!'

When I went on that swan-delayed journey to Liverpool for Mina's funeral last month the taxi took us past her house near Penny Lane and Mum pointed it out to me: terribly ordinary, terribly safe. It probably would have seemed like paradise to these Soviet-era wanderers.

Rosita, raising her hand to smooth down her blonde hair, said, 'Now it is your turn to talk. What I also want to know and why I got in touch is this: is it really true the old story that was our inheritance, that this Mina got tangled up with the Bolsheviks in a forest? In my childhood, my mother used to tell me this as a bedtime story. It was embroidered and watered down to suit a young innocent person, and maybe there were talking animals and birds with the gift of prophecy. We saw a film one time on TV, this was back in the mid-eighties, it was a really old British movie dubbed into Russian, about a girl who goes into the forest and she meets some boys then she turns into a bird then she's on a ship, silly childish nonsense, but my mother cried out, "So there was some truth in the story my father told me!"'

'My Grandma Paula was the continuity girl on that film. I can have her ring you if you like, I'm sure she'd be happy to tell you about how it came to be made. But I don't know the truth about what happened in the forest, I don't suppose anyone does. How could you? That whole world is a kind of fairy story, isn't it?'

'Not to us, who lived in it.'

'I suppose so.'

'I'm sorry our timing was so bad, I just missed Mina. We could have talked and settled things once and for all.'

'What things?'

'Who was who and what they did to each other. It is strange, isn't it, that you and I, sitting here over pastries, have the same DNA? But there is another person from the family tree we should discuss. Jossel, now what happened to him?'

And I embarked on the story of his daughter's wedding and all that happened afterwards, and Rosita said, 'One rogue after the other. What a family!'

When I got home I sat for a while, sitting with all the strangeness of it. The coffee pot, the stories, the woman with blonde hair and blonde clothes, that vaporous world of long-dead people and what their various fates were. Of Jossel who put his own happiness above all else. Of pretty Rivka who had no luck, and went into the forest with her children and never came out. Of Solly who kept the memory of his parents alive with a coffee pot, of all things. Of Itzik the turncoat, the selfish one, Rosita called him, who was only ever on his own side. I wondered what I would do in such circumstances, but I couldn't imagine it.

Then I called my grandmother and told her about Rosita Schifrin in her house in Highgate, with her coffee pot and matching stories about the forest.

'Could it have been true? That she hung out with Bolsheviks?'

'It may be true that that's who she *said* she met; what really went on is anybody's guess. Maybe she was sneaking out to meet a boy, an unsuitable boy.'

'She was only fourteen, surely she was too young.'

'What I remember about her was that she was discontented. Something happened to her in that forest, that is certain, something happened that made my uncle think he had to take her away, get her out of there as soon as he could. Maybe she was pregnant and miscarried, maybe she was . . . I don't know, anything is possible.'

'Why do you think she was discontented?'

'Why are all women discontented?'

'I'm not.'

'You wait.'

And I saw, not for the first time, why my mother felt it was such a curse to have been brought up by the indomitable Paula, whose secret history in London after the war was a time she had to spend the rest of her life making up for, who might have felt that the modernist house Ringo had built for her was no more than a gilded prison.

I thought, Yes, I should go to Riga and look for evidence of flour merchants' houses, forests within walkable distance, types of fungi, shipping routes. If I was that curious, it's just a plane ride away.

But would that really tell me anything about the story of the forest? What would real trees have to say about why Mina took her fairy-tale basket and went into the green canopy that hid the sky? The whole thing felt legendary, made up, yet Rosita, this post-Soviet dermatologist, had heard it. Was it a general folk memory, common in those times? Babes in the woods, wolves in sheep's clothing, Hansel and Gretel and gingerbread houses? Was it all a parable and the Bolshevik boys really monsters of the imagination?

Then I thought, Maybe Mina went into the forest simply because she wanted to, for the joy of being alone, away from that noisy family and their different fates. Yes, for joy and beauty amid all the absurdity and ugliness of life. And that's the story I'm going to tell if I ever do talk about it, though there seems to be no escape from telling our stories, true or not. Unless you stay silent and, as my mother says, that's not a Mendel trait, like my Great-Uncle Jossel

275

who I don't really remember, who talked my great-grandfather out of unconsciousness on a far-away battlefield.

These distant Jewish relations of more than a century ago have begun to reach out to me, specks of light artificially magnified, distorted, balls of fire and gas, remote and unknowable. No wonder the ancients saw fish and twins and ploughs in the constellations – the urge to impose human meaning on random patterns is overwhelming.

Mina went into the forest. The story begins. I am the inheritor of that girl, those boys, the rushing windy trees, the ship, the landing, the thwarted arrival in the New World, the settling for less while wanting the whole world.

Author's Note

I was born into a family with few written records, but stories and the art of storytelling were deeply valued: tell the authorities what they want to hear, whether it's an immigration officer or a bank manager. The ability to tell a plausible yarn was a requirement for survival and the honest, unvarnished truth was considered a liability that wouldn't always work to your advantage when you were fleeing from persecution or trying to avoid creditors. The story of Jossel saving Louis on the battlefield and promising him his sister has its origins in an apparently real event as related to me by one of my relatives. However, when I told it to another of my cousins, she scornfully dismissed it.

'Who told you that?'

'Your brother.'

Parts of the family were lost to each other for many years, and only rediscovered two generations later. Then there were those unknown, unnamed relatives left behind in Poland and Ukraine when my grandparents left their homes of centuries and arrived in Britain on their way to the New World, their ambitions thwarted by not having enough money to complete the voyage. Correspondence arrived until the outbreak of the Second World War, then an abrupt silence uninterrupted to this day.

My father who left Poland as a baby in 1904 never had a birth certificate and his real age was a matter of dispute. It was said that his parents knocked off a few years to help evade conscription in the First World War. One document we did have, carefully preserved, was the letter I have reproduced in full, signed 'Anti-Jew', which arrived through our suburban letterbox after the notice appeared in the *London Gazette* of my father's naturalisation, precipitating the change of name from Ginsberg to Grant, taken from the whisky bottle. My father always implied that the name was something else before: changed to aid their escape from pogrom-ridden Poland, or possibly Ginsberg was assumed when they took over the rent book of the house they moved into on Brownlow Hill. Either way, without that original name, any attempts at tracing my family tree peter out at the beginning of the twentieth century.

Among my mother's effects after we cleared her flat in 1996 was a typewritten manuscript, signed Jack Levy, a memorial to the shops and little businesses of Brownlow Hill where the Jewish community of Liverpool settled before lighting out for the suburbs of Childwall and later Allerton. My recreation of Jewish life on the Hill draws on Jack Levy's account, and I am grateful to Michael Swerdlow for identifying the author and giving me a fuller account of his life.

This novel was started in February 2020, most of its whole prepublication life was spent in the strange, lonely isolation of lockdown and my deepest thanks go to the friends and family who got me through it: writing comrades-in-arms Natasha Walter and Susie Boyt; my sister and brother-in-law Michele Grant and John Boughton; my nephew Ben Ari, his wife Farnaz and their daughter Talah, the repository of the DNA from Ashkenazi Eastern Europe, Persia and the Celtic lands. Some stories she will have to tell! Thanks too to Lennie Goodings, Susan de Soissons and Zoe Gullen at Virago, and Jonny Geller at Curtis Brown.

London, November 2022